50% OFF

50% OFF

A NOVEL

KAREN SALMANSOHN

ST. MARTIN'S PRESS

Note to Reader

This novel is a work of fiction. The names,
characters and events depicted in this
novel are fictitious or are used fictitiously.
 Some real products are depicted in
this novel. They are used fictitiously and
are included for literary effect. None of the
manufacturers of these products has in
any way endorsed, sponsored, authorized
or approved this book. Slogans attributed
to products in this book are not necessarily actual slogans, even where the product
is a real one.

50% OFF: A NOVEL. Copyright © 1993 by Karen Salmansohn. Printed in the United States of America.
No part of this book may be used or reproduced in
any manner whatsoever without written permission except in the case of brief quotations embod-
ied in critical articles or reviews. For information,
address St. Martin's Press, 175 Fifth Avenue, New
York, N.Y. 10010.

Design by Jaye Zimet

Library of Congress Cataloging-in-Publication Data

Salmansohn, Karen.
        50% off / Karen Salmansohn.
              p.   cm.
        ISBN 0-312-09465-5
        I. Title.   II. Title: Fifty percent off.
PS3569.A46216A614   1993
813'.54—dc20   93-685
                                           CIP

First Edition: July 1993

10   9   8   7   6   5   4   3   2   1

I'd like to dedicate this book to "The Girlfriend Board," who offered their encouragement and support during the many stages of writing this book. "Girlfriend Board" members include: Barbara Kanowitz, Jill Katz, Beth Klenosky, Lauren Lazin, Phyllis Leibowitz, Robin Liftman, Shelley Mazor, Emily Oberman, Vivian Paulson, Sharon Rapoport, Norene Rill, Dale Seiffer, Diana Serpe, Linda Shaefer, Susan Shapiro, Bonnie Siegler, and Sarah Tuft.

And, of course, I'd like to thank my beloved agent, Stephen Pevner.

ACKNOWLEDGMENTS

Grateful acknowledgment is made by the publisher for permission to reprint lyrics from the following songs:

"Ballad of a Thin Man" by Bob Dylan. Copyright © 1965 Warner Bros. Inc. All rights reserved. Used by permission.

"Like a Rolling Stone" by Bob Dylan. Copyright © 1965 Warner Bros. Inc. All rights reserved. Used by permission.

"Love For Sale" by Cole Porter. Copyright © 1930 Warner Bros. Inc. (renewed). All rights reserved. Used by permission.

"Nobody's Chasing Me" by Cole Porter. Copyright © 1949 Chappell & Co. (renewed). All rights reserved. Used by permission.

"Open the Door Homer" and "Blowin' in the Wind," both by Bob Dylan. Copyright © 1968, 1975 by Dwarf Music. All rights reserved. International copyright secured. Reprinted by permission.

"Love Is the Drug" by Bryan Ferry/Andrew McKay. Copyright © 1975 EG Music Limited. Administered by Careers-BMG Music Publishing Inc. Used by permission. All rights reserved.

1.

TAKE CARE
OF ALL YOUR
MEMORIES, FOR
YOU CANNOT
RELIVE
THEM.
—BOB DYLAN

**Shake before opening.
Contents settle when
not in use.
—Pepto Bismol**

Becoming involved in a relationship is a lot like being lured into a Hare Krishna cult. Slowly and subtly your defenses are weakened. In the beginning, both the Hare Krishna and the neophyte lover are kept awake till all hours, getting little to no sleep. Then comes the loss of rational thought due to missed meals. By now you're a little dizzy. Maybe you've drunk too much wine. Your sense of self begins to blur. Next thing you know you're wearing the same clothes. You borrow his shirts and sweaters. (We can only hope that he shies away from your dresses and high heels.) You start saying "we" instead of "I." "We" loved that movie. "We" loathed that restaurant. You share the same expressions: "That's basic." "I'm into it." Soon you're mesmerized beyond your will. A love cult is formed.

I know. For four years this is how it was with Bryce and me. We were one of those disgusting kissy-faced couples you see at restaurants, huddled together on the same side of the table. I was sure our love would last forever, but I suppose greater things have crumpled. Atlantis vanished. The *Titanic* sunk. Even "The Mary Tyler Moore Show" was canceled. I realize now it's easy to make someone hate you forever. But no matter how hard you try, you can never, ever, make them love you forever.

"It's not you, it's me," is how Bryce explained it. He looked at me with his deep brown eyes. His "Uri Geller" eyes, I call them. Geller claims he can melt metal with a stare. That's me with one look from Bryce. Such intensity.

"I know I should still love you," he said. "Believe me, I'm trying to love you."

"Thanks a lot," I commended him, "but it shouldn't be something you have to force yourself into."

"I know—what I really meant was . . . Oh, I don't know. I don't know why I say or do what I do. I guess I don't know myself. I don't. I don't know myself."

"Don't worry," I reassured him. "I know you, and you're not missing out on much."

I felt good about my comeback, like I got the upper hand in the end. Bryce came over my place to pack up his things. That's when it finally hit me: he's leaving me. I'm the loser. I'm the one being thrown away, erased, voided. *Hasta la vista*, baby!

Then I saw a sign of hope. On the day Bryce packed, a piece of my lingerie mysteriously left with him—a tattered piece Bryce had teased me about wearing.

"I think the rips make it sexier," I had explained.

"So, you think homeless people are sexier?" Bryce had laughed.

"The imperfections enhance it, the way a crooked nose makes someone more attractive, like your nose does."

Bryce has this large bent nose, a nose Picasso would appreciate. When Bryce used to kiss me, he'd tilt my head at an angle to compensate for it, grab me by the back of my hair, readjust my face. Very sexy.

"I think the most attractive people aren't perfect-looking ones," I had said, "but the ones with some sort of flaw, you know?"

"Does the same go for people's inner self?" he had asked. "Are you attracted to people with some sort of character flaw, or messed-up thing in them?"

"I'm attracted to people who, if they do have problems, are always trying to improve themselves, to change."

Bryce had laughed, a satanic Santa laugh. "People don't change, Sasha."

"You crazy? That's the whole point of life! To grow, to change. Look at the fashion industry. Fashions are always changing. That's to satisfy people's desire for change!"

"No, sweetheart. Fashions change to satisfy people's desire to make money. It's profitable to sell new styles. And man's greed is something that's been around since the beginning of time—proof that man does not change."

"You're so cynical."

"You're so naive. And you know what, Sasha? You'll never change."

The lingerie had been drying on my shower curtain rod. When Bryce left, the piece was gone. I pictured Bryce, in his apartment, listening to an old Bob Dylan album, puffing soulfully on a cigarette, my black tattered lingerie held tenderly to his unshaven cheek. He still loved me, wanted me. In time, he'd return.

Later that evening I pulled back the shower curtain to take a shower, and there it was: my tattered lingerie, lying crippled on the bottom of the tub.

Why do I torture myself with such memories—especially memories that never happened in the first place? Not having love at the present, I am nourishing myself on dead love. Necrophilia of the heart.

Never sleep with your psychic," says my art director, Jerry—or "Jerriatrics," as I jokingly refer to him with friends. Not that Jerry's old. He's only thirty-two. It's just that he's entirely prematurely gray (from a UFO encounter, he claims). Other than the gray hair, everything else about Jerry is youthful. He's got boyish good looks, an athletic physique, and a vibrancy he credits to B-complex vitamins.

Today Jerriatrics is wearing one of his purple T-shirts (he claims purple has spiritual powers), black jeans, black cowboy boots, and, of course, his Ray-Ban sunglasses, which he never removes, even while doing detailed layouts.

Right now we're supposed to be hard at work writing the Close-Up toothpaste ad campaign of the nineties, promising folks ideal love with a dab of toothpaste. In the background Ella Fitzgerald croons about the various weather conditions in which she enjoys Paris—one of the many songs Jerry and I have been listening to this

Monday morning, from the stalagmite stack of cassettes growing on my desk.

Out of all the offices at The Miller Agency, mine is by far the messiest. My office looks like it has a hangover: papers piled everywhere, crayons serving as paperweights, cans of Diet Pepsi in varying levels of completion, pens, pen caps, a corkboard loaded with memos—the lucky ones that aren't totally squished, torn, crumpled, or dangling from open drawers.

Who has time to clean? The life of an ad copywriter is a hectic one. It's only 10:30, and already Jerry and I have listened to over two dozen love songs, hoping to find just the one we can hone into a catchy jingle (i.e., "I love you just the way you are—but could you change your toothpaste?"). However, mostly Jerry and I keep getting sidetracked by conversations on love—and anti-love.

"I was involved with my psychic, Enza," Jerriatrics continues. "I broke up with her a few months ago, about the same time Bryce dumped you."

"Dumped?"

I stare him down—or rather, I try, but I am greeted by my own reflection in his sunglasses. My bush of black curly hair juts out like Mickey Mouse ears. My mother keeps bugging me to cut my hair. From her cozy home in Brooklyn she sends me photos of haircuts torn from glossy magazines. Attached to each is a little note: *Sweetie! This would look darling on you! Love, Mommy!*

I haven't had a cut since the Bryce breakup four months ago. There's nothing symbolic going on—just that my only trusted haircutter, Ramone, moved to Paris the same month. It was a traumatic month.

"Enza was a great gal, and a great psychic," continues Jerriatrics. "Problem was she was more than paranormal, she was *paranoid*. She kept predicting: 'I know you're going to leave me.' Or: 'I can see it, you're going to cheat on me.' When I finally did cheat on Enza, I wasn't sure if she'd driven me to it, or her predictions were correct. Then Enza got mean. She led me to do things she knew psychically were bad. Anyway, now I've got this new psychic, Bob. Hey—you'd like Bob. You should meet him, Sasha."

"No thanks." I straighten the cassette pile so it's less Tower of Pisa, more Empire State Building.

"I mean professionally." Jerry leans forward in his chair. "Bob could help you with this Bryce thing. Clue you in on what went wrong. It would be like going to a psychiatrist and a detective at the same time." Jerry smiles. If he had a tail, it would be wagging.

Jerry understands my determination (a.k.a. desperation) to piece the clues of the Bryce breakup together. Just last week I bribed Bryce's maid, Natasha, to look around Bryce's apartment for clues—signs of another woman, anything that might offer insight. Natasha agreed, saying: "I will do what I can. I am a woman before I am a maid." So now, for twenty bucks a session, Bryce's maid is going to get me all the dirt.

I want/need/must know the truth. What went wrong? I was Bryce's Pumpkin. Bryce would call me that. Now when I hear the word *pumpkin*, my stomach turns. Come Halloween I'm going to be a wreck.

"What's Bob's number?" I ask.

Jerriatrics raises his right hand high for me to high-five. I do.

"You're gonna love Bob, babe!" He pulls out his little black book, flattens it open on my desk, dials. Upside down, I see many of the names and numbers are whited out with correcto fluid.

"What's with the correcto fluid?" I ask.

"So I won't be tempted to call some of those people. Enza's number is whited out *and* crossed out."

Jerriatrics dials. I hold the book up to the light, curious; if he changes his mind, can he still read the numbers? Out falls a card, a little smaller than a baseball card, with a painting of St. Anthony on the front. On the back, where the RBIs would be, is a psalm.

"Hey Bob! How goes it!" says Jerriatrics enthusiastically into the phone. "Listen, man, I have a friend who wants to see you this week." He taps his fingers on the desk to get my attention. "Hey, Sasha, how's Thursday at noon?"

I shrug my shoulders.

"She says that would be fabulous. Her name is Sasha Schwartz. I'll give her your phone and address. Oh, and Bob, thanks. You were right about my Aunt Lillian's gall bladder. Blessed be."

Blessed be?

I flash Jerriatrics his St. Anthony card. "What's this?" I ask after he hangs up the phone.

"I carry that for protection."

"You are aware, of course, that most men carry condoms."

"St. Anthony protects me from muggers on the subway."

Before I can explain the benefits of mace over St. Anthony, the phone rings. Jerriatrics stares at me staring at the phone. He's accused me of being on the phone too much, even threatened to cut my phone cord off—which for me is like threatening castration.

"Make it a quickie," says Jerriatrics. "I'll get us more coffee."

I lunge for the receiver.

"Quelle nouvelle, ma belle?"

It's Frannie, my ex-art director, now working at a competing agency. I recognize her voice immediately. I have a thing for voices. Bryce has a beautiful voice: deep and manly. He sounds older than his thirty years. As a stockbroker he benefits from his voice, since he mostly deals with clients by phone. I used to wonder how his clients felt when they finally met him, when they realized they'd handed over their life savings to such a young face. They probably trusted him less because of it. For me, as a lover, it made me trust him more.

"Guess what? I'm going to a psychic," I tell Frannie. "Jerriatrics suggested it. He thought a psychic could help me figure out this Bryce thing."

"Arthur went to a psychic once."

Arthur is Frannie's man. They're always having marital problems. Arthur's married—she's not. I'm not a big believer in affairs. "Unfairs" I call them. Frannie's two years' worth of whining has supported my theory—and has inspired me to write a song dedicated to her:

THE BOYS WITH THE BAND
by Sasha Schwartz

I finally found him
The man to end my search
He filled my heart
Then he made it burst
I finally found him
But someone else found him first

No use falling for a married man
You'll keep falling but you'll never land
Keep away from the boys with the band
That wedding band
I've banned all men with wedding bands

There's one catch to my catch
He's already been caught
He's out there selling
What's already been bought
You'd think I'd have learned
What I should have been taught

No use falling for a married man
You'll keep falling but you'll never land
Keep away from the boys with the band
Not a single, single reason why
You should love a single married guy

You'd never guess Frannie to be a mistress. She dresses very non-sexually, in baggy, androgynous clothes. She's a no-bullshit, no-makeup, straightforward person. Her whole appearance is straight: straight black hair, straight long nose, straight slim physique. Very Modigliani. She's the type that looks taller than she is. Everyone's surprised when Frannie admits to being only five foot three.

"Arthur's psychic told him the weirdest story," says Frannie. "She saw all this stuff about his wife, how she's this petite brunette dancer, who danced in Broadway shows, went across country dancing in shows. This psychic described in detail the woman Arthur was dating *before* he decided to marry Barbara. Arthur told me he had this terrible feeling he had married the *wrong* woman, like it was *proof*. I told him I didn't know if it meant anything, but I had taken some dance classes at the Joy of Movement. Remember those dance classes?"

Frannie's always trying to convince everyone she and Arthur are meant to be, pointing out how much they have in common—stuff like how they both hail taxis by yelling "Taxirooni!"

"I think Arthur's going to move out very soon," says Frannie, "but he has to sell his house first. He needs the money for child-care support for his daughter. He really cares about his daughter, you know. He says the real estate market's improving. In the next few months, he should be able to sell his home, and then we'll be home free—that is, home free and *home-free*."

Frannie laughs. I don't join her in the festivities. I don't trust Arthur. Actually it's not that I don't trust Arthur. I don't trust words. Arthur just happens to use them as his main source of communication. I'm a writer. I work with words. I know. Words are slimy devils. Words are two-timers. Words are thoughts vamped up in costume. The trick is to see underneath words, catch them with their makeup off.

"I wish you'd trust Arthur more," Frannie says.

"He lies to his wife, doesn't he?"

"That doesn't make him a liar—I mean, well, so he's married. Everyone has some character flaw. Bryce had his flaws, too, you know."

"Bryce had flaws? Hmmm, well," I joke, "I can't think of any offhand, but I suppose Bryce must have been flawed deeply in some way if he stopped loving me."

"I'll help you out," says Frannie. "Bryce is cold and completely heartless."

Frannie is never one to beat around the ol' honesty bush. Her favorite saying is: "A friend is someone who stabs you in the front." Sometimes her undaunted honesty has led to big fights, months of not speaking. In the end, though, we've always kissed, shopped, and made up. I know all Frannie's blunt stabs are motivated by love.

I sigh loudly to let her know her comment has made its impact. "Bryce is just a little repressed," I say, "that's all."

"Bryce never wanted to talk about anything. He was always so secretive. He seemed like a man with a big secret."

"He's vulnerable. Bryce keeps up those defenses to protect himself."

"You and your Disney vision."

Frannie is always accusing me of not being tuned in to reality. Frannie is a pessimist, though she claims to be a realist. She is a woman with a drawer full of warranties. Me, I throw those papers out with the box.

"It's not so unusual, Frannie, to see only the good in people you're in love with," I say. "You're like that with Arthur."

"You're not in love, Sash. You're obsessed."

"Okay, okay, so I'm obsessed. But I'm glad—proud even—to be obsessed. It substantiates the staying power of love. When I stop being obsessed, it will defile the sacredness, the eternality of love."

"Have you considered therapy?"

Jerry sits across from me doodling on a storyboard pad with a fuchsia crayon. I stare at my typewriter, at the stark white paper twirled within until little fuzzy spots appear before my eyes. So much to do, so little desire to do it all. Before the Bryce breakup I was doing great at the agency. I had written a toilet bowl cleaner jingle, which Mike, my creative director, called "brilliant."

In advertising you hear words like *brilliant* and *genius* used all the time to describe ditties about things like acne cream. You also hear intelligent people say things like: "I don't sense the toothpaste is happy. I want this to be happy toothpaste." Hours are spent positioning a Brillo pad in a model's rouged hand to be sure it looks "most natural." You start living, breathing, and knowing more about underarm deodorant than any average human being ever should. You wake up consumed by breakfast cereals, instead of the other way around.

My "brilliant" idea for Bully Toilet Bowl Cleaner was to use the song "Wooly Bully" by Sam the Sham and the Pharaohs. With these few changes:

> *Had a dirty toilet*
> *Used to scrub and brush*
> *But now with Bully*
> *All you do is flush*

Bully. Bully. Bully. Bully.
Bully disinfects.
Crystal clear.
Yeah the sound of that flush.
Is music to my ears.
Bully. Bully. Bully. Bully.

Is it no wonder I am now "creative supervisor" of the Bully Toilet Bowl Cleaner account? It's quite a responsibility. If I do my job right, toilet bowls around the world will be cleaner and brighter. So, who has time for love anyway, right?

Wrong.

Beside the Close-Up and Bully accounts, Jerry and I also work on Bufferin, Mangia Frozen TV Dinners, East Coastal Airlines, Chromostix Crayons, and RC Cola. However, my lack of motivation has been particularly apparent on this Close-Up assignment. It's just not my idea of fun listening to love songs right now.

I know I could write an all-dialogue spot, or an announcer spot. But as a copywriter, I believe in the power of music spots. Look at music's résumé. Served the government doing national anthems. Brought in to help children with the alphabet, nursery rhymes, lullabies. Hired by the clergy to inspire congregations. Even feudal lords and barons had their bards. The masses, folk music. And "Gilligan's Island" had a great opening song that got me to tune in to these reruns every day after school.

Music—not language—is our oldest form of expression. Which makes being a musician, not a prostitute, the oldest profession— and we advertising jingle writers are the prostitutes of music. That's how I feel at least, like I've prostituted my music skills to make money in advertising—which I suppose I have.

As a teen, I had wanted to be a rock singer. I still fantasize about starting up an all-girl group called the Chicklets. We perform in dark, smoky, downtown clubs. The reviewers describe my voice thus: "as if a Renoir painting were to be sung."

My dad was a musician. The coolest. He played keyboards in a folk band called Bad Attitude. My dad let me drink red wine with my SpaghettiOs, and read me Bob Dylan lyrics at bedtime—whenever he was around. Problem was, my dad was always going on the road.

"If you leave again," my mom would tell him, "I'm going to be very depressed—because I'll have to kill you, and it will depress me very much to have to kill somebody."

My mom has this wacko sense of humor.

"It's only for a week, H.B.," my dad would say.

Years later, I found out H.B. was short for "Honey Bunch." A week later, I found out "a week" was short for "a month."

My mom was always threatening to kill my dad. You can imagine her guilt when he died in this horrific car accident, the summer I was seven. After his death, my mom became totally neurotic—or rather, her already natural neurotic talents were intensified. She rarely let me out of sight. She drew an invisible twenty-mile radius around our house, from which I was never to stray—even when I evolved to college age. I had wanted to study music at Berklee in Boston and be in a rock band. My mom convinced me studying law at Barnard would be a close compromise. So I—

"Are you okay?" a voice asks.

I look up. It's . . . Jerry . . . Kansas . . . Toto . . .

"You feeling all right, babe? Your aura's got some holes," Jerriatrics says.

"My aura *what*?"

"Your aura, around your head. Sasha, don't look at me like that. It's true. Everything has auras. People especially, because our brain activity is so high."

"Not in all cases. Remember Mike, our creative director?"

Jerry and I are always making fun of Mike. An almost too easy task, since Mike supplies us with fresh material daily. Mike loves to act tough with us creative people; then, when the time comes to defend our work to the client, he's spineless. We call him "That Worm." We've even come up with a series of expressions for him: "that's opening up a can of Mikes" or "the early bird catches the Mike."

"You know," says Jerriatrics, "in Christian portrait painting from the fifth century to the sixteenth century the aura was painted around the heads of people with great spiritual power. You've heard

it called 'the halo.' That's why priests and kings wear crowns—
they're symbolic of the halo."

"I've gotta pee," I say.

Jerriatrics hands me a storyboard pad. He knows I've come up
with my best ideas in the ladies' room, and takes advantage of these
bathroom flashes of genius. He's constantly feeding me coffee, bran
muffins, prunes.

I't's not that I miss
Bryce, the man
himself. I miss this vague shadowy
sense of him. I miss him for the oppo-
site reason men climb mountains: because he isn't there.

This is just the kind of wisdom that comes to me while sitting
on the toilet. Frightening, isn't it?

I flush, wash, then check myself out in the bathroom mirror,
looking for holes in my aura. All I find is the beginning of a pimple.
Other than that, I am looking pretty good. I don't look like a woman
without a man. I look like I could get one. A good one, too. Maybe.

Since the breakup, I've lost eleven pounds. I now have that Mia
Farrow gaunt look, like when she starred in *Rosemary's Baby*. It's
an effective combo, my black curly hair with all this pale skin
beneath. It heightens the drama of my blue eyes. My eyes are my
best feature. Bryce used to tell me that. He used to tell me I looked
like Elizabeth Taylor. At first I didn't know how to take this. I glanced
down at my thighs. Then, he explained. He meant *before*. When she
was thin. When she starred in *National Velvet*. He said I had her
eyes. Her lips, too. Sometimes Bryce would call me Liz. And I'd call
him Richard. Or Dick.

Yeah, I now think: *Dick*.

On my way out of the bathroom I bump into the one person I've been desperately avoiding. The Worm: Mike Miller.

"Sasha! Where the fuck are those goddamn crayon taglines?!"

Everyone in the agency stops talking. Typewriters stop a-typing. Phones stop a-ringing. Dogs stop a-barking. Babies stop a-wailing. Mike has spoken.

"You've had two fucking days to get me those taglines!"

Mike would make a fascinating psychological case study. With him, one moment you're "brilliant!" The next, a "scumbucket." I guess he's now in scumbucket mode. Mike named his agency The Miller Agency, after himself. I joke the agency should have been called The Miller and Miller Agency because of his drastic mood shifts.

It's disconcerting reporting to a schizoid. I've become like the person involved with an alcoholic who eventually takes on the traits of the alcoholic. But it's not just me Mike's affected. He has a way of bringing out the latent manic-depressive behavior lurking in all creative people.

"Where the hell are those taglines?"

"Uh . . . I just have to type those taglines up," I say.

In reality, I haven't written a single line. But I'm not lying. In theory, I do have to type them up.

"I want fifty fucking taglines on my desk by tomorrow noon. Discipline, Sasha! You need to learn discipline!"

I look up to see my peers peering. Quickly, I contemplate my shoes.

What's the big deal about this discipline stuff? Bryce used to brag to me about how disciplined he could be, the willpower he could have.

"So? But can you lose control?" I asked him. "How good are you at this?"

Me, I'm a master.

Though I'm starting to think maybe I've a knack for discipline after all—to be able every moment, of every hour, of every day . . . to not let go of suicidal thoughts.

Of course it helps that I'm expecting my period.

I should have gotten my period last week. I'm not worried. I am worried, however, about not having any reason to worry. I haven't had sex in four months. Not since Bryce. And let me tell you, they say sleeping around is unsafe. But not sleeping around also has its dangers. Take it from one who knows: celibacy can lead to an insanity that rivals that of syphilis sufferers.

Mmmmm, how I miss sex with Bryce! From the start, I was wildly attracted to him. So much so, I broke my "three date minimum" rule, and slept with him the first night.

I hadn't been expecting overnight visitors. The night before I'd had a torrid affair in bed with a box of Fig Newtons, stripping them of their caky crumbly outsides, devouring their chewy chunky insides. Little Fig Newton crumbs sprinkled my sheets.

Then at date's end, Bryce asked to use my bathroom. I innocently let him in. The next thing I knew he was sitting on my sofa breathing on my neck.

"You better go now," I meekly advised.

"I just want to kiss you—and stuff." Bryce looked at me with his Biafran eyes.

The next-to-next thing, we were onto "and stuff."

The next-to-next-to-next thing, we were in the bedroom, little Fig Newton crumbs scrunching beneath our naked bodies.

"I feel like we're fooling around on the beach," Bryce teased.

"I guess you could say I'm crummy in bed," I teased.

"Hardly." Bryce pulled me in close, whispered in my ear: "I want to pee in you, I want to pee in you."

I pulled away fast.

"What's the matter?" Bryce asked, worried.

"How's that done?" I asked, even more worried.

Then I found out he was saying "be." "I want to *be* in you."

We both got a good laugh out of that. I knew even then that Bryce was to be an important somebody. I joked with him not to throw out the tissue he used to wipe our tummies. I wanted to save it, press it between the pages of my diary.

God, how could things have ended? Everything felt so right. How could love just disappear—poof—like steam into air, hot, then nothingness?

I t's now 2:05, meaning 1:50. (I set my clock fifteen minutes fast to keep from being late.) I've missed lunch again. I can't believe how time just zips by. Why can't time ever take a rest, relax already? Time has a type-A personality.

"Hey, babe," says Jerry, placing two cups of coffee on top of a pile of papers on top of some newspapers on top of some magazines on top of my desk. He sits. He drinks his coffee. He shows signs of permanence.

"Jer, I can't work with you now. Got fifty crayon taglines due tomorrow, high noon." I stare in silence at the paper before me.

"How can you write about crayons without looking at them?" Jerry shoves a fuchsia crayon in my face. "Look! Do you see what you're selling?"

"Yeah, colored wax."

"No, the beauty of colors, the joy of sight, the appreciation of higher consciousness."

"Uh huh."

"It's a wonderful thing, a crayon. Did you know that man used to be color-blind, as color-blind as animals are today? Aristotle wrote about a tri-color rainbow. Democritus only wrote about four colors: black, white, red, and yellow. Life used to be so hard—survival was so hard—nobody bothered noticing the details. When man finally did, that was the beginning of evolution. That's, like, what separates man from dog. Not just that a dog is color-blind, but that man notices billions of details. A thousand years from now, who knows, we might be able to see even more colors and details. Then again, maybe not with the way people are. People today forget to look at things. The enemy of life is not death, it's forgetfulness."

"I'd like to forget about these tags," I say.

"Then, take a break," says Jerry.

"Fine. Wanna go shopping and become conscious of the new colors in vogue at Bergdorf's?"

"I meant how 'bout working on Close-Up. It's due Friday. We have nothing. This Close-Up spot means big-time exposure. Come on. Think Close-Up. Think love."

"Think pain, angst, disappointment, suicide."

"Sasha, Sasha, Sasha. Negative thoughts create negative energy."

"Maybe I should ask off Close-Up. After all, people ask off cigarette accounts if they're against smoking. I don't know if I'm pro-love."

"Come on, babe." He plunks a tape into my player. Cole Porter swirls through the air:

> *The breeze is chasing the zephyr*
> *The moon is chasing the sea*
> *The bull is chasing the heifer*
> *But nobody's chasing me*

I love Porter. I've always felt we've shared a kinship. Porter, like me, was raised as an only child in a fatherless house. And like me, he grew up using humor to deal with his pain and longing. One of my favorite Porter songs is "At Long Last Love."

He actually wrote this song in the midst of his tragic horse accident, lying on the dusty ground, legs tangled beneath him like a Gumby yogi. For me this song is proof the soul is separate from the body, for pain did not interfere with Porter's divine inspiration. Or perhaps it helps to write about love while in pain, since the two are so interrelated.

"How would your pal Porter sell love?" Jerry asks.

"Porter already did: 'Love for Sale':

> *appetizing young love for sale,*
> *love that's fresh and still unspoiled,*
> *love that's only slightly soiled,*
> *love for sale."*

"Cute," says Jerry.

"That was a Porter song about prostitution, banned from the radio for being too off-color. Obviously this was *waaay* before the time of 2 Live Crew."

I relate to this song—from the love angle, on feeling like a used-up love receptacle. I look down at my hands. Even my fingers look depressed. My nails are chewed to assorted lengths—all twenty of them. First, my ten natural chewed nails, then the ten fake plastic nails atop these, some still painted Barely Pink, the others barely not.

I was supposed to get my nails done with Frannie last Saturday. Turns out I missed an exciting manicure. Two guys came in with guns, tied everyone's hands behind their backs, robbed the place. Frannie said it was scary—and the first time her nails ever dried completely. She said it was the best manicure she ever had.

I was busy in my apartment being depressed about Bryce then. What a waste, all this thinking about Bryce, when I could be using my brain activity for something productive. For all the time spent, I could be fluent in Swahili.

Suddenly I hear my favorite music: a ringing phone.

I am greeted by loud crunching on the other end of the receiver. It's Viv. The girl can eat. Viv gets away with it. She has lots of inches to spread calories over, being five foot ten and all. Half of her height is accounted for in her legs, amazing limousine legs. People are always staring at Viv—even more so now that she got a part on "Beloved," an NBC soap.

Viv plays Kristen, a blond bombshell criminal lawyer with a criminal past, who's always having hunky guys fall wildly in love with her—which isn't too difficult a role for Viv, since it's basically her life, except that on the soap she occasionally gets dumped. In real life, it's Viv doing the dumping. Viv's a bedroom vigilante. A serial lover.

"How goes it?" Viv asks, crunching into the receiver, loud as a cartoon termite.

"Well . . . I'm going to a psychic on Thursday," I tell her.

"I went to a psychic once."

"They tell you anything revealing?"

"Yeah. The psychic told me I eat too fast. It's true. I do. I eat too fast. I'm surprised you're going. You hate that cosmic gunk, don't you?"

"Jerriatrics thought the psychic might have some insight into the Bryce disaster."

Viv stops chomping. "I should have known it had something to do with Bryce. I wish you'd stop thinking about him. It only gets you upset."

"It's good I'm upset. I'm in touch with my feelings. It's good I know how I feel."

"You know, Sash, Hegel believes feeling is the lowest form of intellectual thought, because it's confusing subjective with objective truth."

Viv was a philosophy minor at USC and always offers an interesting perspective on things.

"But don't they say a life unexamined is—" I begin.

"It's a happy one."

"But we are humans. This is our gift, to think. What about the old standby: 'I think therefore I am'?"

"It should be: 'I think therefore I am . . . depressed.' "

Yes, it's always difficult debating with a philosophy minor.

"Just forget the guy already," Viv advises—as if the idea hadn't occurred to me.

"I'm trying. It's not easy. If only I could find someone else, it would be a lot easier."

"You shouldn't need a man to get over a man, Sasha. Try being alone, learn to love yourself."

Why do I need another person to feel complete? I should be reveling in my solitude, proud to be independent, to have a monopoly on my life, but I don't. And I'm not. Without Bryce, I don't feel whole. I feel hole, like a song with the crucial beat missing, the Bryce beat missing. I've got to replace this beat to keep the syncopation going. It doesn't have to be the same beat in the same place. But there must be some compensation for this empty space. This is the basis of syncopation. Emotional syncopation.

Viv crunches loudly into the phone. "You don't hear me talking about Keith all the time, do you?"

Keith is Viv's latest love victim, a handsome, sensitive yet powerful TV executive—she met him at a Korean salad bar—she's been seeing for a record five months. Keith is twenty years older than Viv, a detail she hasn't mentioned to her parents—although in the beginning she hinted.

"This Keith you keep talking about," her mother had said, "is he someone new?"

"Actually, he's someone old," Viv had told her—then left things there.

"I keep men in perspective," says Viv. "I have other things of value in my life. My work. My friends. My pottery classes. Sasha, you've got so much going for you. You're a creative supervisor at the age of twenty-nine. You've got girlfriends who love you. If you let them, men—with their need to take over everything—will gladly take over your life. Like tonight for instance. Keith put up a fuss when I told him I was meeting up with you. You did remember, didn't you? We're getting together tonight: nine o'clock, the Acropolis Coffee Shop. It's the full report from Natasha."

H a, ha. Me forget about the Natasha report? How could I forget? I'm dying to learn the truth about what happened to Bryce's love for me. Bryce did love me. I mean, Bryce told me he loved me. Maybe I heard wrong. Maybe all along he was saying: "I leave you." *I leave you, Sasha, I leave you so much.*

Then again, I should know better than to listen to words. Me, I'm the worst abuser of them. I spend my days molding, shaping, tinting words to my clients' liking. It was my idea, when a cosmetic product at Frannie's agency tested poorly in the laboratory, to still report boldly on the label: "laboratory tested!" When working on my Bufferin account, I manipulated words to imply Bufferin worked better than other aspirins, when in fact all aspirin work exactly the same. I used words like "nothing works better," and "the strongest pain relief ever" to falsely imply a superiority.

The main problem with words is they're too easy to say—even a child can do it. Certain words should be made more difficult to pronounce, so the speaker might think twice before bothering to say them. Major i.e.: "I love you."

People should be forced to say: "I ishkabaturbinebolosuperlaifranglistiwintzagixboliboliboopiloxfonterickanmiltipcertize you."

People would say it a lot less and then other people would hurt a lot less.

Y ou should put 'mmm' and 'oh' sounds in your taglines," Jerriatrics says. "The mystics believed these sounds had great power. That's how 'Amen' got its success—and 'Mm-mm good, mm-mm good, that's what Campbell's soups are.' Also, *h* and *k* sounds. It's a physical thing. These sounds vibrate the pituitary area, which creates this, like, positive physical effect. That's why laughter's good for us. You've heard *that* I'm sure. In fact, Santa's constant 'Ho, ho, ho-ing' could be the secret to his generous gift-giving spirit."

"Jerry, really, you're too much."

I yank the paper from my typewriter. It makes a loud unzipping sound. I reread what I've typed. Jerriatrics grabs the paper from me.

"Let's see what you got," he says. Silently, he reads, his lips moving slightly, like a bad ventriloquist.

Chromostix. Makes writing exciting.
Chromostix. Fun for younger ~~ags~~ ages and ages.
Chromostix. All the colors found in a kid's nature.
Chromostix. Write without any wrongs.
Chromostix. Makes art child's play.
Chromostix. For the most exciting creations since Creation.
Chromostix. The most colorful word in the world.
Chromostix. Spoils your kids' imagination.
Chromostix. Draws out the artist in a kid.
Chromostix. Magic wands for kids.
Chromostix. Green is not the only color to say go.
Chromostix. A playground for kids' imaginations.
Chromostix. Crib notes for a kid.
Chromostix. Runs on creative energy.
Chromostix. Batteries not included.

23

"These are good," he finally says.

"Thanks." I fluff out the right side of my hair in his sunglass reflection. With Jerry around, I never need a mirror. Before presentations, I just position him against a wall, apply my lipstick.

"Only thirty-five more to go," I say.

Jerriatrics is quiet for a moment, then grins. "How about: Chromostix. Because the sky doesn't have to be blue."

"I like it. Very Zen." I scribble it on the bottom of the page.

"You know why the sky is blue?" Jerry asks.

"Because purple clashed with the grass?"

"Wilhelm Reich discovered why."

"Who?"

"Reich was a member of the Communist party—until 1933, when he was kicked out for saying that fascism came from sexual repression and not economic forces."

"Sounds like a fun guy."

"He was smart. He was the guy who discovered orgone energy—the blue aura around us. When we're healthy, it's, like, everywhere. They're these bions, right, and they work like this shield. It's what we see when we see the sky as blue—with those waves, you know, when we stare too long. It's orgone energy."

"Jerry? How do you know all these bizarre things?"

"I read."

I remember reading. I used to read. I don't have time anymore. Bryce was not a big reader, either. He only had three books on his bookshelf: *Webster's Dictionary*, *Winning Through Intimidation*, and *Solitude*. I was concerned about this last book, thinking it might be a sign of a man not interested in coupledom. When I asked Bryce about it, he said he never finished it. I interpreted this as a hopeful sign. Now it occurs to me it was still a bad sign—a sign of a man who doesn't finish what he starts.

"Jer, when do you find time to read?"

"Everyone can find time. Problem is everyone's rushing around, putting too much energy on *doing* versus *being*. They do, not be, when they should be, not do."

"Do be do be do . . ." I sing.

Jerry's not amused.

"You know, in Eastern religions it's the 'still man' that's looked up to," he says. "Calling someone a 'still man' is the ultimate compliment. It means he's this 'in touch' guy. Look at Buddha. All he did was sit around all day."

"Buddha was pretty wise, getting a job like that."

"But now life has speeded up and we're no longer in touch with our inner clocks. Now we have electricity during the day, heat during winter, any fruits, any vegetable, any season of the year—we barely notice time passing. Everyone's in such a rush to have things happen. What's the point of consciousness? To make big real estate deals? I like to think it's to enjoy life. I think man has it over on any animal when he notices a beautiful tree. A beautiful woman."

Jerriatrics gives me this smile—the kind mostly seen around cameras.

I t's now 5:05 (4:50). The hands on the clock have waved good-bye to another work day. These hands are not to be trusted. They move inconspicuously, stealing away the time we thought we'd spend later; these hands are the hands of a thief.

Basically, Jerry and I accomplished nothing on Close-Up today—just one lame idea, which I've tacked up on my corkboard, my "Wall of Shame":

> You've ~~get~~ got Close-Up on your brush,
> and now I Can't get you ~~aff~~ off my mind.

What a ridiculous promise, a toothpaste leading to love.

Though a good smile does have its charms.

Bryce has a very appealing smile. Not so surprising, with all the practice he's had using it. Bryce is always smiling. He's angry: he smiles. Disappointed: he smiles. Frustrated: he smiles. His smile is not a symbol of warmth but a defensive strategy, ensuring people never know what he's really thinking. Nuclear war could explode around him, and he'd remain smiling, cigarette dangling between his pouty upturned lips.

One time we did one of those photobooth things. In each of the four shots, my face was contorted like a cartoon character's. But Bryce always wore the same expression—his omnipotent and very potent smile. It looked like I was posing with one of those cardboard images. *Yes, step right up, girls, pose for a quarter and get a photo of yourself with the perfect happy boyfriend! Step right up!*

I tap my fingernails on my desktop. They make a clicking sound—which means I'm in luck. There's bitable nail surface left.

Outside in the hallway I hear Dave, another art director, chanting: "It's only advertising, it's only advertising." Everyone's gearing up for the second shift at The Miller Agency. This is a twenty-four-hour-seven-day-a-week shop. We have a saying: "If you don't come in on Saturday, don't bother coming in on Sunday." Mike's workaholic spirit inspired me to write a song:

WORKING EIGHT TO ELEVEN
by Sasha Schwartz

If you work eight to eleven
At your nine-to-five job
The odds are ten to one
You're not having any fun

Eight to eleven
are the hours I keep
Wake up
Go to work
Come home
Sleep
Life is so redundant
I wonder where the fun went

It's no fun being employed
Wake up
Go to work
Come home

Sleep
I'm an office android
Eight to eleven are the hours that I keep

Drinking coffee
is life's only stimulation
Winning Lucky Lotto
is my only salvation
A ten-minute lunch break is my only vacation
My life is being run by the corporation

Life is so redundant
Life is so redundant
Life is so redundant
I wonder where the fun went!

To Mike's horror, Jerriatrics doesn't share his work ethic.

"I'm outta here," he says now. "Got my Monday acupuncturist appointment. You should leave, too."

"Can't. Got taglines to write."

"Don't stay all night."

"Don't worry. I won't. I wouldn't want to be caught in the same outfit two days in a row."

Jerry salutes me good-bye. I stare at my messy desk, now covered with a fresh layer of snowball-sized crumpled papers. I shovel under, pull out a random cassette, a compilation tape Bryce made for me. I plunk it into my cassette player. Out comes "Don't Think Twice, It's Alright." Dylan. I love Dylan. I've been listening to him even before I was born—on a "Pregophone," a device that transmits sound to the unborn child. My dad had read somewhere that what a baby hears determines its first perception of the world. My dad wanted the world to make a good first impression, so he played me his mentor, Bob Dylan.

After birth, I continued to listen to Dylan. He was always blasting through our house, my dad singing along with him, his voice a little smoother than Dylan's, sweeter, like the voice of a man singing to a small child, that child being me.

From the moment he awoke until his bedtime, my dad would prance around the house with some song on the stereo, his hips subtly gyrating, like a lazy Elvis. Even when working—writing new songs—my dad would type by ratatatatting to the beat of music.

"You know what this is called, H.B.?" he'd say to my mom.

"No, what?"

"Stereo-typing."

My mom would laugh. My dad would attempt to explain to me the joke—while my mom teasingly punched him.

"Stop! You're a bad influence!" my mom would say. "You shouldn't be teaching her how to make bad jokes!"

When my dad died, his Dylan albums were the first thing my mom got rid of. Next was the stereo. It's customary for a Jewish family in mourning not to play music, maybe for a few months—in religious families, even a year. But after his death, there was never music in our house again. My mom didn't want to be reminded of anything related to my dad. But for me removing the stereo had the opposite effect, like cutting a stain from a soiled dress.

When I reached baby-sitting age, I regained access to a stereo. I saved the money paid me and bought Dylan albums—the first being *Highway 61 Revisited*. I'd play it over and over and over and over—to the point where the kids complained to their parents about me. But I was desperate to hear what my father had heard in Dylan's voice, Dylan's words, Dylan's pain. This black disc with its lines spiraling across its surface held a hidden message, like the inner rings of a tree trunk, signifying stresses, struggles, growth. These lines etched upon its surface were the only clue I had into my father's soul.

Bryce's compilation tape included five Dylan cuts. I was impressed he shared my dad's adoration. I saw this as a sign of a kindred spirit, one my dad's spirit would approve of. Yes, I thought Bryce was Mr. Right. I guess it was a case of mistaken identity.

What gets me is how hard Bryce tried to give up smoking, but never could, and me he just gave up and stopped seeing in one day. Kaput.

I t's now 6:17 (6:02) and I've written only one tagline since Jerry left:

Chromostix. The beginning of the endless

I'm just not inspired to work. Part of the problem is knowing how long it takes for ad work to get produced—longer than it takes to produce an entire human being. This is fact.

Ten months ago, I was assigned a Bufferin commercial. On the same day, my Aunt Rosalie called to say she was pregnant. She gave birth to a girl last month. My aspirin spot is still being tested.

Testing (or what I call "de-testing") is when a 2-D animated version of a commercial is created, that's totally lacking in charm and energy, and is then used to test the likability and effectiveness of the spot by showing it in shopping malls to housewives who resent Madison Avenue.

One of the secrets of testing well is to begin commercials with a loud noise. The commercial the client is testing (one of one hundred presented) began with a twanging electric guitar. It also used a spokesperson. Spokespeople are hot this decade—which just shows how hungry we are to be spoken to on a one-to-one basis.

Commercials can be very revealing. They're our twentieth-century portraits. This decade also shows a rise of commercials with people doing activities by themselves, and hardly any with all family members present.

In our Bufferin commercial, the camera cuts back and forth between a headsplitting rock band and a white-frocked spokesperson who urges viewers to turn up the volume on their TVs and test out Bufferin's power to relieve even the most excruciating headache.

29

At first the client worried the spot was corny. We convinced them it was "very British."

The phone rings, jolting me back to the present tense, my tense present. I pick up.

"How're those taglines coming?"

It's Mike.

"They're not due till noon tomorrow, right?" I say.

"Got anything now?"

Typical worm behavior, waiting with baited breath for work not yet due, further tormenting the already tormented artistic soul.

"Lemme hear what you got."

"You want to hear what I've got?" I repeat.

"Yeah, lemme hear."

I hold the phone up to the typewriter, type out a few taglines.

"Those are some of the tags," I say. "How do they sound so far?" I hang up.

It is twilight when I hit the streets, time for lovers to meet. I see them pairing up, walking, touching, kissing. Looks like Cupid is working overtime for everyone but me. That little pipsqueak. I'd love to replace his bow and arrows with a Made in the USA submachine gun. Next couple he aims at: *ratatatatatatatat!* It would save everyone involved a lot of pain. Love euthanasia. Fast relief from the slow misery that's sure to come. I know what I'm talking about. I used to be half of an embrace. I used to be a girl named Shnuggims.

Now here I am, yet another single girl, a sole soul, walking home, single file.

Luckily, it's a short walk. Only seven blocks from home to office. The rough part is passing by the bus billboard I created for East Coastal Airlines. I had written a series of fun headlines announcing East Coastal's nonstop flights to sunny Florida:

EAST COASTAL FLIES TO PLUTO*
*(as in Pluto from Disney World, with this as a visual)

EAST COASTAL FLIES TO THE STARS*
*(as in starfish on a beach, with this as a visual)

EAST COASTAL FLIES TO NOWHERE*
*(as in a deserted no-man's-land beach, with this as a visual)

The headline the client went with was:

EAST COASTAL FLIES TO FLORIDA*
*(as in a boring ad, with no visual)

Well, at least my name's not on it. That's one of the few pure things about advertising, the anonymity with which work is performed. Unusual in a world where art has become secondary to the artist, where the artist is not driven by the joy of self-discovery but by outer discovery: fame.

I cross the street, taking the scenic route, the one that allows me to peek inside the Soap 'n Suds Laundromat, check out the cute guys. Before the Bryce breakup, I did my laundry in my building's basement. Now I come here—even though these machines cost a quarter more. The extra money's a worthwhile investment. All I need is to meet one guy and have one date—dinner and a movie— and I profit in the long run. Not that I'm using the Soap 'n Suds as a free meal ticket. No, no. I go with loftier intentions. I go looking for love.

Tonight the Soap 'n Suds is particularly crowded with men. It's great to see so many men doing their laundry—particularly the attractive ones. More attractive men should do their own laundry. So many men, so many possibilities. Love carriers. One of them could be a love carrier.

I dash across the street, racing a dissolving yellow light. If I hurry, I can squeeze in a quickie load before the Natasha report.

H

i, honey, I'm home!" I yell out to my empty apartment, kicking my way past the stacks of newspapers, piles of clothes. I rationalize: at least the stuff strewn around—my black leather pumps, black lace brassieres, black-and-white newspapers—all color coordinates with my black decor. My black terry robe looks splendid upon my zebra-skin rug, as well as complementing the black-and-white Man Ray print hanging a little crookedly just above.

I've always erred on the side of sloppiness, however; since Bryce's departure, the simplest activity—washing a coffee cup—is beyond my control. I can see the coffee cup: black lacquer on the outside, a white porcelain interior. I can see the last remains of coffee floating on the bottom of the coffee cup: light, with skim milk and a half packet of Sweet'n Low. Yet the brain-to-hand message to wash the coffee cup—*Wash, wash, wash*—is quickly overridden by a staticky but stronger message: Bryce is gone—*gone, gone, gone*.

The only things remaining of Bryce are three ashtrays filled with his Marlboro cigarette butts. Two in the bedroom. One in the soapdish over the bathtub.

I rummage through a pile of clothes on the floor by my bed carefully selecting my laundry—aiming only for my newest, most alluring black lacy pieces—from La Petite Coquette, of course. After all, my underwear could be the first impression I make on a man at a Laundromat. I wouldn't want to be caught with some ripped old thing—even if I personally find an extra appeal in it that way.

Next I decide upon something appropriate to wear to the Soap 'n Suds. The look I go for is "available but not desperate." Men can smell a desperate woman a mile away—usually because she's splashed on too much perfume. I try to duplicate that same sexy yet casual air I had when I was with Bryce. When we were involved, I met men all the time. I've noticed this trend in past relationships, and have often wished I could take these men, put them in Tupperware, store them in my freezer, and defrost them when necessary.

Tonight it's my favorite black jeans, to complement my hair. And to bring out the blue in my eyes, I sport a turquoise tee. I check myself out in the mirror. My hair is a wild mass of mess. My skin, pasty pale, lurks shyly beneath. In the mirror, above my face, floats a headline, scribbled by Bryce in plaque-fighting mint gel: I LOVE YOU!

My face looks mismatched beneath, like that Magritte painting where there's a pipe and the word *chair*.

I roll out some toilet paper, smear the toothpaste off the mirror, flush these plaque-resistant words down my toilet.

Bully, Bully.

By the time I return to the Soap 'n Suds, there are only a few guys left— none of whom are Paul Newman material. More like Alfred E. Neuman. There's a cute dark-haired guy sitting on top of a washer reading a box of New Tide—but he was reading that box when I peered in the window fifteen minutes ago. Next to him is a redheaded guy. But I'm not into redheads. Ditto on the fat balding guy by the dryers.

I find a free washer, dump in my belongings. I am disappointed. The ideal situation is to locate a Prospective Cute Male (PCM) at the onset of rinse. Then I have sixty-three minutes to prove my relentless charm and desirability. I like to catch the PCM's attention as I'm unloading my basket, then tauntingly dangle my belongings— a lacy bra, a camisole—above the washer before throwing them in.

I take my usual seat atop my washer. An old Sinatra tune, "Witchcraft," plays in the background.

I think about the possibilities of using this song for Close-Up. One thing's for sure, the Soap 'n Suds always plays good music. The girls who run this place are hip, although they don't look it: two pudgy Spanish girls who sputter away at each other at 78 rpm, like Spanish Chipmunks, wearing clothes that look like they shrunk in their washers.

I wish my clothes would shrink. They've been hanging loose on me since I've lost all this weight. I keep missing meals. Like today. First lunch, now dinner. I'm just not hungry anymore. Even now, I'm not hungry.

In the past, about this time Bryce and I would be having dinner—or fighting about having it. Bryce would be trying to convince me to cook. I'm not one for cooking. My idea of a kitchen utensil is the telephone. With it, I order up Chinese food, pizza, whatever.

"Cooking can be a sensual experience," Bryce used to tell me, hoping to inspire me to whip him up a little something.

"Right, and I bet you think vacuuming is erotic, too!"

"Vacuums are known for sucking," he'd reply.

It was always difficult fighting with Bryce. He'd make jokes. I'm weak at the knees for funny men. Kidders, I call them. Bryce was a major Kidder. He knew how laughter worked on me. He used to tease me that the secret to getting me into bed was to crack five good jokes in a given night. He'd count them down as the evening progressed.

The song switches to "Love Is the Drug" by Roxy Music:

> *Oooo-ooo, catch that buzz,*
> *love is the drug I'm thinking of*
> *Oooo-ooo, can't you see,*
> *love is the drug for me.*

The music pulses through me. I love this strong beat, the repetition. This is music's main lure, the comfort of sensing patterns and shapes, setting us up for expectations:

> *boom, de, de boom, de, de, boom.*

Then exploiting our anticipation:

> *boom, de, de, boom, de, de, boom.*

And, occasionally, giving us an irregularity:

> *boom, boom, boom, de, de, boom, boom.*

A seductive rhythm sets up a feeling of ambiguity, suspends us between two solutions. It's this combination of knowing what will come—yet not knowing for sure—that excites me in music. In all things, really.

love is . . . love is . . . love is the drug

Yeah, love is the drug all right. And I need to get me into rehab for it.

I feel the washer beneath me switch cycles. I'm hoping in time all this vibration will lead to minor cellulite reduction, like the machines in the mail-away section of *Cosmo*.

The Laundromat door swings opens. In walks a PCM. Tall, blond, with a big laundry basket. He's a lanky sort. The kind that looks like he's been six feet tall since puberty and still hasn't gotten used to the idea. I find his awkward gangliness refreshing. This guy's body seems sincere. Now I'll just have to find out about the rest of him. He looks at me, heads in my direction. He wants me. Though, admittedly, I am cleverly hanging out by the only available washer in the place.

"Excuse me," Blondie says. "Is this machine free?"

"No, it costs a dollar twenty-five," I reply.

"What? Oh—I get it." He leaks a laugh.

This guy is obviously not big on the jokes. A definite minus. However, he does have great buns, another important quality in a man. Here comes the moment of truth. He's dumping his laundry into the washer. From my visits to the Soap 'n Suds, I have developed a skill for analyzing men by their laundry. I check for the following:

1. Does the man in question wear boxer shorts or briefs? Personally I prefer boxers—as long as they don't have loud patterns.

2. Does he have any unusual belongings? Smurf pillowcases? Silence = Death T-shirts? Boy Scout uniforms?

3. What kind of detergent does he use? I find generic detergent to be a real turnoff. (Cheer, New Era, Fresh Start, Yes, Dynamo. There's something very positive about laundry detergent names—with one exception: Solo.)

4. What kind of socks does he have? A lot of sweaty sweatsocks reveal a man with great promise. Not so with pairs of pink and lavender. Most revealing is catching men as they sort socks—and discover the dryer has swallowed up one of each pair. You can learn a lot about how a man handles frustration.

5. But mainly what I look for in men's laundry baskets are female belongings. I mean, why waste my valuable flirtation time?

To my joy, Blondie seems to be braless. I note a Harvard T-shirt. He's either very smart or very insecure. I note he's got matching Harvard sweatpants. A promising sign.

"Excuse me," Blondie says. He's talking to me again. Atta boy, Cupid! "Can I borrow some of your detergent?"

"Sure. Here you go. How 'bout some fabric softener, too?" I offer, hoping to soften him up along with his fine washables.

"Thanks."

Blondie smiles, rocks back and forth on his heels. He looks as if he wants to say something more. The man is obviously putty in my hands.

"I hate to do this," Blondie says, "but I only brought a dollar . . ."

"You want to borrow a quarter?"

"Could you?"

"No problem."

So, that's this guy's story. He's a user. Now I note he's using quite a hefty dose of my detergent.

"Better watch it with that detergent," I tease, "or you'll wind up like that 'Brady Bunch' episode."

"What?"

"You know the one where Cindy adds too much detergent and the washer overflows and there's all these suds everywhere!"

He looks at me like I am crazy. I suddenly have an urge to ask for my quarter back. Too late. He's already plunked his—or rather *our*—money into the machine. His washer starts up slowly, then picks up speed in time to the music, spinning to the beat, a kaleidoscopic effect of music, suds, and colors. Makeshift MTV. It's humiliating being single, putting oneself on the market, entering the auction, to see what price you might bring—that is, assuming there are any buyers. But what's this . . . he's shifting in my direction.

"That clock on the wall," says Blondie, "that can't be right. What time do you have?"

"Uh, eight thirty-five."

He looks down at my watch. According to Minnie, it's ten to nine.

"You know," he says, "your watch says ten of nine."

"Yeah. I know. I set it fifteen minutes fast to help keep me from being late."

"But you know it's fifteen minutes fast, right? So, if you always know it's fifteen minutes fast, who are you fooling?"

"I'm a master at self-deception." I flash him my devil-may-care aren't-I-just-adorable grin.

He laughs. Bingo! Could this be it? Could he be *him*? My man. The man for me? If only I had more specific information, a clue, like: look for a man with a butterfly-shaped scar on his left wrist. He smiles nervously. Yes, he is sweet. He's definitely a lanky one. He reminds me of this Pink Panther wire toy I had as a kid. I remember fondly bending its arms and legs to my liking. I wouldn't mind doing that to this guy. I bet legs as long and wiry as his could wrap around me at least three or four times.

"So—" we both say at the same time.

"It's okay, you go first," I offer.

"Uh, I was just gonna say thanks for the quarter," he says. "I gotta leave."

And he walks out.

I can't believe it. That's it. He leaves me. Another man who leaves me.

I hear a swoosh, look up to catch my dryer jolting to a stop. My stuff is dry, and so, it seems, is the man situation.

I gather together my belongings. Everything is warm and toasty. I love the smell. The smell of freshly powdered babies. I begin to fold. In the background Bob Marley happily reggaes it up. I sing along with him, and for the moment I am happy, folding my laundry, listening to music. For the moment my life feels rich and full. All I am missing is a man—and a yellow sweatsock. I can't seem to find one of my favorite yellow sweatsocks. It seems to have disappeared into that great Dryer Void.

Alas, love is like socks: one day existing as a pair, a team, silently promising to remain together forever, then out of nowhere, one of this twosome vanishes, leaving the other alone. Useless.

Of course I'm late to meet Viv. As quickly as I can, I run down Broadway. As quickly as anyone can who's lugging a laundry bag. I drag it by its string, like a stubborn dog on a leash—or better yet, Bryce on a rope. At Eleventh and University, I see Viv in front of the Acropolis Coffee Shop wearing her black leather coat, ripped jeans, and a big black hat with pom-poms dripping from its brow like black acid-rain drops. It takes a certain kind of woman to successfully wear this hat. I'm not that kind of woman. I am, however, the kind of woman who has friends who are the kind who successfully wear this hat.

I wave to Viv from across the street, trapped at a red light. I dodge a cab, then run across.

"Sorry I'm late." I breathe heavily, hoping to elicit sympathy.

"That's okay," says Viv, "but for penance, you're gonna have to stay at the coffee shop fifteen minutes"—she looks at her watch—"no, *twenty* minutes extra after I leave."

She smiles and gives me a big kiss on my cheek. "Whoops!" she says, and I know what she means is she's left one of her red lipstick marks. She rubs at it, kisses my other cheek, rubs that in, so both cheeks match. "There," she says. "*Now* you look great. Actually, you needed the color. You look a little pale."

Inside, the Acropolis is people-less as usual, except for the waiters, who are delighted to actually see customers. I used to come here all the time with Bryce. The booth by the window with the torn red plastic seat was where Bryce first told me he loved me.

We'd been building up to saying it for three months, beginning shyly, dangling the word *love* at each other: I love being with you, I love kissing you, I love that quality about you. Every variation on the infinitive "to love" but the definitive "I love you."

Finally Bryce said it. "I love you." He said it one morning over scrambled eggs and rye toast right here in the Acropolis. I wanted to second the emotion, but felt it would sound forced. I waited a few minutes, called the waiter over, asked for Sweet'n Low, then sprang it on Bryce:

"I love you," I said at last.

"Hey, that's *my* line, *mine*," he said. "I said it first. Geez, *every-one's* been taking my line. I've been in litigation with Hallmark for years for this."

Yes, Bryce was a Kidder. I was in love. *We* were in love. Both at the same time, even. *Both with each other, even.* Then Bryce started saying "Love you," chopping out his part in the deal. Then things got even worse. One morning he left a note:

> *We need O.J.*
> *Luv,*
> *Bryce*

L-U-V he spelled it. Luv. Not Love, but Luv, the Cheez Whiz of love. I should have known then and there we were doomed.

Viv plops herself into the booth by the window. I slide in across from her, dragging my laundry bag up on the seat beside me— where Bryce would otherwise have sat. This is what I'm now reduced to: sitting next to my laundry.

Within seconds, one of the Greek waiters approaches with a clatter of steaming coffee cups—and over a dozen Sweet'n Low packets. He knows Viv and I are coffee addicts.

"Hello, Chicken Lady," he greets me.

I always order their roast chicken, so he calls me "Chicken Lady."

"So, beautiful girls," he says, "you know what you like? Roast chicken, no?"

"No. No roast chicken tonight," I say.

"You want to split an order of french fries?" Viv suggests.

"Get whatever you want. I'm not hungry."

"You'll have some."

She states it like a fact.

"What will it be, beautiful girls?" our waiter asks, pencil propped to pad.

"We'll have an order of french fries," Viv says. She always does this, says "we'll" to the waiter, never wanting to admit that she alone will eat every last french fry, right down to the mutant brown crispy ones.

"So, what's up?" I ask. "How're things with Keith these days?"

Viv picks up a Sweet'n Low, rips it open, pours the whole thing into her coffee, stirs it with the empty packet. "He asked me to move in with him," she says.

"What? Really? Wow! That's great. What did you tell him?"

"I told him not yet. I need space."

"What?"

Personally, I think Viv's got the ideal man. Not only does Keith have a successful career, sexy good looks, great brain cells, but he's totally devoted. A biggie on my check-mate list.

"If it's space you want," I say, "you should definitely move in with Keith. That SoHo loft of his has tons more space than your studio."

Viv shakes her head in despair. The pom-poms on her hat jiggle. "Did I tell you what Keith did with the bust of Plato I have on my bedroom windowsill? He turned it to face *out* the window. He joked he didn't want another man watching me undress."

"I love that!" I say. "You see, Keith's great."

"He's too possessive. Sasha, you should enjoy being single, not having to report in to someone, having your freedom. All that freedom, not knowing what's going to happen next."

"Viv, not knowing what's going to happen next is scary and depressing."

"You shouldn't see it like that. You should see it as having this wide-open future. Take away someone's future, you kill a part of them. Part of me dies in a relationship."

"But knowing someone's there for you is comforting, that security is comforting."

"You know, Sash, Nietzsche said it all when he said: 'Man seeks play and danger, life gives him work and security.' "

"I thought man sought happiness and love. That's what I seek, at least. Isn't this what you want? Don't you love Keith?"

"Sure I love Keith, but you know there are many men I could love. Like, there's this producer at NBC. You should see this guy. He's totally my type."

"You have a type? Maybe that's my problem. I don't have a type."

"I know exactly what I look for in a man. I've narrowed it down to three things. The guy's got to have a keen mind, weigh more than me, and be very hairy."

"On second thought, I've narrowed it down to one thing," I say. "The guy must reject me. That really excites me in a guy."

"And it's not just this producer; there's a guy in my pottery class, a psychoanalyst who's also very appealing. It's exciting to me, the possibilities of men to fall in love with."

"You should date a schizophrenic, Viv. Then you could be faithful to one man, yet be with a different man every night of the week."

"Different men bring out different things in me. I hate limiting myself to just one."

"I'm not greedy. I'd take just one. One very good one."

In the background buzzes something approximately Beethoven. I've thought about using a classical piece for Close-Up. You know, touch the ol'-fashioned emotive chord in us all. Beethoven was quite effective back in Victorian times. Women would burst into tears listening to him. But back then, there were no aerobics classes, no Club Med vacations, no release for pent-up passion. Women weren't supposed to even talk about wanting release. So there was lots of fainting and crying at the drop of a hanky. Then Beethoven played. Anger, despair, horniness—everything repressed suddenly surfaced. Beethoven was the first music therapist. He doesn't have quite the same effect on me. Perhaps because I release my angst onto anyone who will listen. Breaking up might be hard to do, but talking about having broken up is a simple feat I have definitely mastered.

"So, did Natasha find anything of interest?" I ask.

"Oh, our french fries!" Viv announces, her blue eyes aglow. The waiter places the plate democratically in the middle of the table. Viv drowns the french fries in a pool of catsup. It looks like something out of a grade B horror film. *The Chainsaw French Fry Massacre.* She reaches for a particularly long, slinky, catsup-drenched fry, nibbles on it, slowly at first, then impatiently engulfs it.

"So, what did Natasha find?" I repeat.

"Great french fries. Want some?"

"Viv, did Natasha find something you think I'd be better off not knowing? You're stalling, aren't you?"

"Am I stalling?" repeats Viv.

Now I know for sure she is. Viv has this trademark behavior of repeating the question she wants to avoid answering. Unlike Frannie, Viv hates to be the bearer of unpleasantries.

"Viv . . ." I say.

"Sasha . . ." says Viv.

"Viv . . ."

"Sasha . . ."

"*Viv!*"

"Okay, okay! Does the name Glen mean anything to you?" Viv aims her fork at another fry, a bare one that has somehow escaped her catsup wrath.

"Glen?"

"Uhmm," she mumbles as she chews.

"As in Bryce's good friend from college?"

"Perhaps. How good a friend is he, this Glen?"

"They used to play basketball together—a lot. Why?"

From behind me, our waiter appears with a plate of steaming meatloaf and mashed potatoes that bring the word *savory* to mind. He delivers this plate to a Latin guy with a bad complexion sitting behind us.

"I should have gotten the mashed potatoes," Viv says.

Viv always does this. Viv suffers from post-order regret. The order at the next table always looks better. Viv stares shamelessly at the Latin guy's platter. He believes it's himself rather than his entrée Viv's admiring. He smiles hopefully back.

"Viv! What did Natasha find?"

"Flowers from Glen to Bryce, with a card that said 'Bryce. Thanks for a divine evening, I love you. Love, Glen.'"

"'Love, Glen'? 'Love, Glen'? Glen sent Bryce flowers?"

"According to Natasha."

"'Divine evening'? 'Love, Glen'?"

"Sasha, did you ever think Bryce could be gay—I mean bisexual? He does have a cat, right? You know what they say about men with cats?"

I always hated Bryce's cat. His cat made me look bad. I'd enter the room, the cat would hiss loudly. I tried earning the cat's love—bribing him with catnip and Fancy Feast. The cat was an ingrate. An hour later, he'd be hissing just the same.

"Fido's shy," Bryce would defend his damn cat. He loved animals. If his building had let him, he'd have filled his apartment with furry critters. In fact, the only time I saw Bryce cry in all the four years we were together was during the movie *Gorillas in the Mist*. However, not a lousy, stinking, fucking tear leaked out when we broke up.

I think back to the scene of our breakup: our favorite hangout, Cafe Lui—a place Bryce gauchely called "Cafe Loo-ey," like it was a truck driver stop. We'd been sitting in our usual spot, at our usual time, with our usual drinks, yet I'd never seen Bryce look so out of place. He played with his glass of Stoli, matching its wet bottom to the sweaty ring it left on the counter like an IQ test.

"Sasha, I want you to know I still care about you," Bryce began.

"You mean I'm more to you than just another pretty face, fabulous body, and brilliant personality?"

We both laughed, but I knew what was coming. Then Bryce finally said it, the sentence I'd been dreading, the sentence that would sentence me: "I think we should break up," Bryce said, then quickly continued: "I need time to think. I just don't know what it is I want right now." Those words hit me hard, like a Batman cartoon: *POW! KAZOOM! BOOM!*

Now I think back on what Bryce had said:

43

I just don't know what I want right now.
I just don't know what I want right now.
I JUST DON'T KNOW WHAT I WANT RIGHT NOW.

In the light of the information Natasha has shared, I wonder if this could have been Bryce's subtle way of admitting to being confused sexually.

Viv takes my hand again, squeezes gently. "Oh—it's probably very innocent," says Viv. "Bryce and Glen probably just had a really great basketball game that night. Just your good ol' all-American male bondage. Whooops—I meant 'bonding.'"

19

..., 20, 21, 22, 23, 24, 25, 26, 27, 28, 29, 30, 31, 32, 33, 34, 35, 36, 37, 38, 39, 40, 41, 42, 43, 44, 45, 46, 47, 48, 49, 50, 51, 52, 53, 54, 55, 56, 57 ...

It's now two A.M. I am wide awake. Perhaps I've gotten my bright yellow sheets too bright. But that's not it at all. I am up thinking about Bryce. Perhaps Bryce is bisexual, I am thinking.

... 62, 63, 64, 65, 66, 67, 68, 69, 70, 71, 72, 73, 74, 75, 76, 77, 78, 79, 80, 81, 82, 83, 84, 85, 86, 87, 88, 89, 90, 91, 92, 93, 94, 95, 96, 97, 98, 99, 100, 101, 102, 103, 104, 105, 106, 107, 108, 109 ...

I am counting sheep, fluffy white ones, jumping over a pretty white picket fence. Look at them leap, so light, so free, not a care in the world.

Ah, to be a sheep.

... 111, 112, 113, 114, 115, 116, 117, 118, 119, 120, 121, 122, 123, 124, 125, 126, 127, 128, 129, 130, 131, 132, 133, 134, 135, 136, 137, 138 ...

In a way, it's not so surprising. Bryce was almost too good a dresser to be entirely hetero.

. . . 141, 142, 143, 144, 145, 146, 147, 148, 149, 150, 151, 152, 153, 154, 155, 156, 157, 158, 159, 160, 161, 162, 163, 164, 165, 166, 167, 168, 169, 170, 171, 172, 173, 174, 175, 176, 177, 178, 179, 180, 181, 182, 183 . . .

And Bryce did read *GQ*.

. . . 185, 186, 187, 188, 189, 190, 191, 192, 193, 194, 195, 196, 197, 198, 199, 200, 201, 202, 203, 204, 205, 206, 207, 208, 209, 210, 211, 212, 213, 214, 215, 216, 217 . . .

He read *GQ* often while alone in the bathroom.

. . . 219, 220, 221, 222, 223, 224, 225, 226, 227, 228, 229, 230, 231, 232, 233, 234, 235, 236, 237, 238, 239, 240, 241, 242, 243, 244, 245, 246, 247, 248, 249, 250 . . .

He read *GQ a lot* alone in the bathroom.

. . . 253, 254, 255, 256, 257, 258, 259, 260, 261, 262, 263, 264, 265, 266, 267, 268, 269, 270, 271, 272, 273, 274, 275, 276, 277, 278, 279, 280, 281, 282, 283, 284, 285, 286, 287 . . .

He had three Bette Midler albums.

. . . 289, 290, 291, 292, 293, 294, 295, 296, 297, 298, 299, 300, 301, 302, 303, 304, 305, 306, 307, 308, 309, 310, 311, 312, 313, 314, 315, 316, 317, 318 . . .

Two pairs of pink socks . . .

. . . 321, 322, 323, 324, 325, 326, 327, 328, 329, 330, 331, 332, 333, 334, 335, 336, 337, 338, 339, 340, 341, 342, 343, 344, 345,

346, 347, 348, 349, 350, 351, 352, 353, 354, 355, 356, 357, 358 . . .

He made a great mustard-vinaigrette dressing.

. . . 361, 362, 363, 364, 365, 366, 367, 368, 369, 370, 371, 372, 373, 374, 375, 376, 377, 378, 379, 380, 381, 382, 383, 384, 385, 386, 387, 388, 389, 390 . . .

Plus, Frannie always said Bryce seemed like a man with a secret . . . perhaps this was his secret.

. . . 401, 402, 403, 404, 405, 406, 407, 408, 409, 410, 411, 412, 413, 414, 415, 416, 417, 418, 419, 420, 421, 422, 423, 424, 425, 426, 427, 428, 429, 430, 431, 432, 433, 434, 435, 436, 437, 438, 439, 440, 441, 442, 443, 444, 445, 446, 447, 448, 449, 450, 451, 452 . . .

It all makes sense. Bryce's bisexuality would explain why he'd be opposed to a lifetime filled to the brim with all the good times we'd already begun to share. For Bryce, it would only be half a life. Now it could be that for me, half a life, meaning bisexuality, meaning fear of AIDS, meaning fear of death, meaning oh my god . . .

. . . 461, 462, 463, 464, 465, 466, 467, 468, 469, 470, 471, 472, 473, 474, 475, 476, 477, 478, 479, 480, 481, 482, 483, 484, 485, 486, 487, 488, 489, 490 . . .

Oh, I'm probably overreacting. I'm sure this Glen thing is innocent. A joke. It was a joke, I bet, between the two. Some basketball humor. The real reason for the breakup is probably very boring: generic fear. I brought up marriage too often. A dangerous word if not handled correctly. It can have an almost physical impact on the recipient. It floats out of one's mouth, into the air, disturbing the dynamic of everything in a room. Suddenly a soft chair becomes like stone to sit on. (Someone should package a new kind of mace that when activated blasts out: "Marry me, marry me!" Rapists would run for the hills.) Bryce was simply afraid to marry me. But why?

    . . . 501, 502, 503—

    Oh, fuck it. I give up on counting sheep. I'm not getting tired; however, the sheep look piqued. I decide to give them a rest. Count sleeping pills instead.
    1, 2. I swallow.
    I pull my pillow into my side, envision it's Bryce beside me. I fondle its Do Not Remove Under Penalty of Law tag, pretending it's his earlobe. Outside cars zoom by, roaring like hydropowered ocean waves. Cars honk. Other cars honk back. New York City just doesn't shut up. Even an empty parked car is not without its need for self-expression. One—directly below my window—has an active alarm that goes off frequently (i.e., tonight). It sounds as if everything's in high gear tonight. Even the lulling *tickticktick* of my neon Coca-Cola clock sounds threatening, like any moment my apartment—or possibly my head—will explode.
    Relax, breathe, exhale. Relax, breathe, exhale.
    This was Jerry's instruction. He's offered many holistic cures for my insomnia, suggested I sleep facing north, turn all my shoes sole side up, place lettuce leaves beneath my pillow. In desperation, I tried them all—to no avail. However, I have come up with my own cure: I decide to call Bryce. I've found this not only calms me, it's only fair. If I can't sleep, why should Bryce? I've done this so many times by now, I've noted a pattern in the way Bryce answers his phone.
    First, his groggy voice: "Hello . . ."
    Then, his alert voice: "Hello?"
    Next, his angry voice: "Hello!"
    Then *click*, he hangs up.
    Very satisfying.
    In the dark I reach for the phone. I find the cord, trace it to a pile of black clothes, dig inside. It's a difficult search because the phone is black, my clothes are black, the room is black. I have to feel for textural differences. Finally, I strip my blanket off me, get

up from bed, turn on the light—first tripping across my quasi-emptied laundry bag, landing smack on a stack of *Vanity Fairs*.

I wait for my foot to stop throbbing, my eyes to adjust to the light, then trace the phone cord under a black leotard ensemble (Tuesday, low-impact aerobics), past a half-finished Pop-Tart (this morning's, blueberry), and a photo of Bryce. (A very, very taped up photo. I had ripped it up one night in a fit of passion. Then an hour later—in a fit of that *other* kind of passion—taped it back together.) I study Bryce's face. Even through the rips and tears, he remains a sexy man. Proof he could be in a tragic car accident and his beauty would survive.

I dial Bryce's number. The phone is ringing, ringing, ringing. Finally, it's picked up. I hear a click, then his answering machine message: *"Hello, this is 842-1903. . . . What's your number?"* Bryce says this last line with that sexy, seductive, and richly masculine voice of his. Bryce stole this message idea from Frannie's machine—with the one creative touch of putting his own number in the opening. Yes, the man has no backbone. But like the stolen message, I find him alluring nonetheless. I am contemplating dialing back to hear his voice again when the phone rings. Who could be calling so late . . . except maybe . . . Bryce?

I pick up.

"I've been thinking about you," says the voice on the other end—a deep, masculine voice, as rich as a radio deejay—it's the voice of Bryce. My Bryce. I knew it! I knew he'd come back.

Bryce breathes heavily into the phone. This is our Old Joke. Bryce used to call me up, breathing heavily into the phone. "I want to nibble on your nubile body," he'd tease. "Dad?" I'd joke back. Then Bryce would whisper all the stuff he wanted to do to me—except when he got to the nasty parts he'd press the phone's push-button so it would beep. "I want to *beep* you hard in your *beep*," Bryce would say. My Bryce. My Bryce is back.

"I've been thinking about you, too," I tell Bryce now.

"I'd love to caress you all over . . . with my tongue," says Bryce.

What a Kidder, that Bryce. But he sounds a little nervous. Of course he does. This must have been difficult, working up the nerve to call.

"Then I'd tie you to the bed," Bryce continues, "and come all over you with my long hard cock in a stream of hot semen."

Suddenly I'm suspicious this is not Bryce.

"I'd make you lick off the semen with your tongue . . . licking me all over, licking my balls . . ."

Yes, the contents are a bit graphic for my Bryce.

"Then I'd throw you up against the wall and fuck you from behind, fuck you hard, while pinching your nipples . . ."

Plus this guy's enunciating his *k*'s harder, stronger, than Bryce does. "Fukkke," he says.

". . . my throbbing cock would explode all over you . . ."

His *o*'s are a little fuller, too. "Exploahd," he says. Who could this be? A random pervert? Someone I know? Don't they say most obscene phone callers know their victims? Or is that only in the case of rape?

"Then I'd suck your big breasts . . ."

Obviously this is not someone who knows me well. Mine are medium sized, at best.

I hang up.

2.

X

MEN ARE SO
SIMPLE AND SO
READY TO OBEY
PRESENT
NECESSITIES
THAT ONE WHO
DECEIVES WILL
ALWAYS FIND
THOSE WHO ALLOW
THEMSELVES
TO BE DECEIVED.
—MACHIAVELLI

I can't believe it's not butter!
—Woman on margarine commercial

Tuesday at last. I've been looking forward to Tuesday. I have a dental appointment at noon and I can hardly wait. I realize I am one of the few people in the world who look forward to cavities. But my dentist is quite a cutie. Very nice, too.

"Please, call me Gregg," he has insisted.

Since I've started going to Gregg, I've stopped chewing sugarless gum.

I search through a pile of clean clothes (or are those dirty? I can't remember) for the ideal outfit to wear to a cute dentist (something sexy that will easily hide spittle). I find it (under my bed): my vintage gray cashmere mini sweater ensemble from the SoHo boutique Harriet Love. I team it with a black alligator-skin belt and black reptile pumps. Earrings are also a crucial accessory. After all, he'll be focusing on me from the neck up. I find a pair of black dangling fish earrings that suggest I'm a fun gal.

I study myself in the mirror. I look very toothsome—in an albino Rastafarian kind of way. I grab my black leather jacket, hit the street.

Outside, it's more than muggy; the sky looks mugged, its clouds stolen, the rest of it bruised up pretty badly, a combo of blues and pinks. Everywhere I turn is that dreaded two-headed, four-legged beast: *the couple*. One comes toward me, looking ever so content. I have an urge to push it in front of an oncoming truck, yell "Here— have a big Mac!"

Yes, solitude does not bring out the best in me.

I wonder if Bryce, too, is all by his lonesome now, as he said he'd be? Or if he's with Glen, as the flowers say he'd be? I must relax, wait, see if Natasha finds more incriminating evidence. She'll set things straight—I hope in every sense of that word.

Of course it's going to be hard for Natasha to find more clues. It would be easier if she were looking for signs of another woman—lingerie, barettes, lipstick marks on shirt collars. But Bryce's male lover could leave his boxer shorts lying boldly on the bed, and Natasha would just assume they were another of Bryce's.

So much to think about. In New York, space is rare even in one's own head.

"Hey, honey," someone calls to me.

I turn. It is a homeless man wearing a large, brown, batik-printed poncho. He looks at me with a burning hunger in his eyes. It used to be this man was called "a bum." Now he's been repositioned as "homeless." A reassuring sign of a growing empathy on society's part. I think about this homeless man's life: the struggle, the hunger, the ostracism. Who am I to be so wrapped up in my problems, my microdot part in this huge troubled world? I smile at this homeless man, give him a dollar, turn to go.

"Hey, lady!" he yells to me. "You need a haircut!"

I t's 10:44 (10:29) when the elevator doors to The Miller Agency open before me. The two Jeffs are playing Smurf basketball in the hallway, avoiding working on their account, Houston Cigarettes, an account I'll never have to work on because, when asked, I told Mike I was against promoting smoking. What's odd is one of the Jeffs—the short one, the one we call MuttJeff (the tall thin one is JeffJeff)—MuttJeff's mother died of lung cancer.

Farther down the hall, I hear Joy, as usual, shrieking on the phone at her boyfriend. "Neal!" she whines. "Neal!"

Joy might as well be yelling: "Kneel! Kneel!" She's got her boyfriend wrapped around her little finger. She's repeatedly told me how Neal repainted her entire kitchen a nice melon color. And just the other morning, Neal ironed her black linen suit before work.

Joy pretends to tell me these things girlfriend-to-girlfriend. But I know she's being competitive. She's always trying to one-up me, not just in love—and, needless to say, work—but even when it comes to our wardrobes. Joy's particularly spiteful on days I'm wearing a nicer outfit than hers. Women's wardrobes can be, to some women, what penises are to men. God forbid they should think yours is bigger.

Next to Joy sits Freddie, her ultraquiet art director, whom she also has whipped. Freddie rarely talks. He just draws what Joy tells him. Jerriatrics and I call him "The Wrist." That is, we did until a few months ago, when somehow Freddie quietly became a vice president. Now we refer to him as "The Big Wrist."

Next to him sits Tony, a very handsome jock copywriter with a thick Brooklyn accent and a Cro-Magnon attitude about women. Tony sees all women as tits. I see him as ass. Tony once told me he's so against committing to one woman that even when he masturbates to *Playboy* magazine, he never stays on one page. He keeps flipping.

In the next office down sits Tony's art director, Dave, a funny, cute, gay guy who leaves next week to go to another agency. (Another man I love who leaves me.) Dave's my favorite co-worker at the agency—other than Jerriatrics. I wrote a love song to Dave:

IF YOU EVER GO STRAIGHT
by Sasha Schwartz

Girl meets boy
Then boy meets boy
That's the story line these days
Oh, it's no joy
To love a gay

If you ever go straight
Go straight to me
We could live so happily
with one another
I'd love to bring you home to meet my mother
but chances are you'd rather meet my brother

There's no chance for romance
I can't fill the pants
So promise please
If you ever go straight
Go straight to me

You have all the qualities
I want in a man
And I wish I could better understand
But I still believe behind every man
should be a woman
Behind every man should be a woman

But if you ever go straight
Darling, do go straight to me!

When I first met Dave, I didn't know he was gay. I just thought he was very polite. Joy told me the dirt: Dave was married for eight years when he broke the news to his wife about his boyfriend, Kurt.

Hoo boy. Do any of us know any of us? Is Bryce who I thought he was? Was he really merely playing basketball with Glen all those nights? Come to think of it, Bryce spent a lot of time with Glen. They even went camping together a few weekends. And—oh, fuck— Bryce knew Glen from college. *Who knows how long Bryce could have been messing with men?*

I close my office door behind me, plop onto my chair. Something feels wrong. I reach beneath me, pull out a pile of papers: "The History of Toothpaste Advertising, 1970–1990." Then there's a machine gun rapid-fire knock at my door.

"Young lady. You're late!"

It sounds like Mike—a not very pleased version of him.

The door swings open. To my relief, it's Jerriatrics, doing his Mike imitation: one hand on his left hip, the other with pencil held cigarette style. His silvery locks are pulled back tight into a ponytail, so I can clearly see his face, his dimples pulsating in and out as he laughs.

"Jerry, please try to be nice. Remember, I am an abandoned woman with damn crayon taglines to write—and guess what— Bryce might be bisexual."

"Really?" Jerry makes himself at home in my guest chair, thrusting his feet up on my desk, soles staring at me, with what looks like either gum or tar on the bottom of the left heel.

"Do you think it's possible?"

"Didn't Bryce once borrow your lipstick?"

"Gee, you remember that story, huh?"

"I thought it was very strange."

"Bryce's lips were chapped. He was out of chapstick. We were at his place. No one but me saw."

"Uh huh . . ."

"Really. His lips were chapped. It was just that once—as a goof, you know?"

"Bisexuality's not so bizarre, Sasha. Bryce might have been female in his last life and has, like, carried over some of those preferences to this one. The guy might still have things to work through."

"You know I used to believe in reincarnation, but that was in a past life."

"Hey, I definitely believe. I totally remember this scene where I was King Henry the Third, and I was having marital problems with my second wife. I had on this velvet robe, and—"

"Jerry, no offense, but it's very difficult to take seriously a man who can't remember what he had for lunch three hours earlier but claims he can remember things from 300 B.C."

"Reincarnation is very sensible. Why should one person be rich and another poor? Another crippled, another strong?"

"Another produce a TV campaign? Another not."

"You got it. It's the way the soul learns, experiences all-ness. Reincarnation explains child prodigies, like Mozart coming up with concertos at age five. He was obviously carrying over knowledge from a past life. So what makes you think your buddy Bryce is bi?"

"Well, Natasha, Bryce's maid, found flowers in Bryce's apartment, with a love note from Glen to Bryce. Glen's the guy Bryce was always playing basketball with, remember? Glen gave Bryce flowers! I haven't gotten flowers from someone in God knows how long. The other day I was on the elevator with this messenger, right? He's carrying this beautiful basket of roses, so I joked: 'Those for me?' 'No,' he said. 'This lady on the thirty-seventh floor. She's been getting flowers like this for two weeks straight.' Next thing I know the elevator's going up, but my spirit's stuck on the lobby floor. I was jealous. 'Wow. That's love,' I said. 'No. A promotion,' the messenger said. 'The woman got a promotion.' Suddenly, the weirdest thing happened. Knowing the woman was *only* receiving flowers because of her career—not *love*—I was no longer jealous. I don't know what's happening to me. I'm becoming an old-fashioned gal, preferring love over a glamorous career in advertising. My needs are few. I just want someone to give me flowers."

This last line gets caught somewhere mid-trachea. My throat thickens, becomes a dam for stopped-up tears, tears that rise, never to fall. I never cry. I'm a Kidder, not a Cryer. My mom's always telling everyone the story about how when I first learned to walk, I'd fall down, and rather than cry I'd laugh. I'd pick myself up, walk a few steps, fall, laugh some more. I wipe the precipitation of tears from my eyes. I laugh now for Jerry.

"Ha, ha, ha," I say. "Sorry. I don't know why I'm reacting this emotionally. Ha, ha, ha."

"It's good to cry." Jerry smiles awkwardly. I see my hunched-over body in his sunglasses. I sit up straight.

"Ha, ha, ha. Don't worry," I say. "I'll be better once I get my period."

"Well, that's good for work that you're getting your period. A woman's more creative during her cycle, more interconnected with the moon and universe."

"Ha, ha, ha." This time I laugh sincerely.

"It's true, babe. That's why you feel so emotional right now. You're picking up vibrations from everywhere. Sensory overload, you know?"

"No, I'm feeling emotional because I have no outlet for my emotions."

"You just need to relax, get yourself centered."

"I am," I say. "*Self*-centered."

"How about if you take your mind off yourself, think about toothpaste?"

But the idea of working on toothpaste sends a new wave of depression cascading through my bloodstream. I don't want to write jingles. I want to be doing songs that make the world think, not brush. For

me, advertising isn't just selling things, it's selling out. As Bryce used
to say:

> *You said you'd never compromise,*
> *with the mystery tramp,*
> *but now you realize,*
> *he's not selling any alibis,*
> *as you stare into the vacuum of his eyes.*

Actually, Dylan said that. Bryce quoted him. Bryce knew a lot of
Dylan's work by heart. We'd be sitting around the apartment drinking coffee. Suddenly, Bryce would burst out with:

> *Something is happening here,*
> *but you don't know what it is,*
> *do you, Ms. Jones?*

Looking back, no I didn't. I definitely did not know what was happening.

Jerriatrics is jug-
gling my crum-
pled up papers, throwing them high with
his right, catching them with the left.
   "What about: 'I'm in the mood for love simply because you are
near me and you use Close-Up'?" he offers.
   "You're joking, right?" I ask.
   Jerry smiles. I'm not sure if I've insulted him or shared in his
joke. He continues juggling, let's see, it's one, two, three—they're
hard to count they're moving around so fast—six, I think it is—six
crumpled balls. *Six balls, sex, balls, Bryce.* Yes, all words lead to
Bryce. I think about sex with Bryce. He didn't seem gay—he seemed

to love sex—had to have it all the time. But maybe this was the desperate sign of a man who had something to prove. Perhaps he didn't think he could have sex with a woman. Perhaps I was his last hope.

"What about," says Jerriatrics, "a hook like: 'When your love life's down, try Close-Up'?"

I shake my head violently no in response. *Could Bryce be ... ? Could Bryce have ... ? Could I have ... ?*

"How about: 'Paste your relationship back together with Close-Up toothpaste,' " Jerry says.

"This is the nineties, Jer. We're selling gel, not paste." *Hmmm, I have been losing weight ... feeling nauseous ... suffering from insomnia ... all symptoms of ... Could it be ... ? First I lose Bryce, my reason for living, now life itself?*

"Are you all right, babe?" Jerriatrics asks.

"Except for the fact that I'm slowly dying, I'm fine."

"Cool out, Sash. Look, even if Bryce is bi, it doesn't mean you have AIDS."

"You're right."

"And even if Bryce is one hundred percent hetero, it doesn't mean you don't have AIDS. You could still have AIDS."

"Thanks for the reassurance, Jer."

"Why don't you get tested? I did."

"You? Really? Weren't you afraid? What if you tested positive? I mean you didn't, did you? I'm assuming you're OK."

"Chill. I'm fine, and if I weren't, I'd deal. I'm not afraid of death. I welcome it."

"Excuse me," I say. "Where I come from you avoid death like it's the plague."

"Death is just another phase of life, only without this prison of a body. It's all soul—the best part of life. When you're enjoying art, friendship, love, music, it's 'cause you're *outside* your body. Your soul has floated out, escaped, separated from the body. This is why I believe in reincarnation."

"How's it going with Close-Up?"

It's The Worm: Mike, standing, cigarette in hand, in the middle of my office. Seems he slithered in without either of us hearing him.

"Close-Up's going great," I say, trying to summon up as much enthusiasm as possible. "I'm so dedicated to the assignment I've arranged to get a cavity filled today."

Mike blows out a long feathery ring of smoke. It floats up, surrounding his face like a halo, a devil's halo, the halo of death. Mike once showed me an article against cigarette advertising that said one in eight smokers gets some form of lung disease. Yet Mike continues to sell the possibility of death not only to millions of strangers but to himself. Yes indeedie, we are a death-denying culture. Right now I can feel my blessed death-denial skills kicking in. For now, I'm convinced I'm overreacting about this flower stuff. *Go, death denial. Go!*

"I just got off the phone with the aspirin client," Mike says. "The scores were below norm. I've opened up the assignment to the agency."

"A gangbang," Jerry mutters.

A "gangbang" in advertising is when the same assignment is given to more than one creative team in hopes of creating a positive (ha, ha, ha, ha, ha, ha, ha, ha) competitive atmosphere. Gangbangs are aptly named because it's about getting fucked.

"It seems your spot didn't test well because of your use of humor," says Mike. "The research revealed humor doesn't work for this product base. Aspirin is serious medicine. People take their pain seriously." He puffs at his cigarette, which has developed a long ashy nose.

"So you want us to write a serious spot," says Jerry.

"And not mention pain," says Mike, tapping his ashes onto my carpet.

"Excuse me?" I say. "Not mention *pain* in an aspirin spot?"

"The research also revealed that if the spot reminds people of their pain, they tend to associate negative feelings with the product. People don't like to be reminded of their pain."

Really? People don't like to be reminded of their pain? *Who are these people?* Everyone I know loves talking about their pain. Ex-boyfriends, bad childhoods, dead pets—these are fodder for the best conversations.

"So to summarize," says Mike, "I want you to write a nonmusic

6 1

serious commercial for aspirin—without mentioning pain." He drops his cigarette butt into one of the cans of Diet Pepsi on my desk. It sizzles. "While I'm here, lemme see those taglines."

"But you said they're not due till noon," I remind him.

"Got anything you wanna bounce off me now?" he asks.

"Yeah." I take one of the crumpled paper balls Jerriatrics had been juggling, and throw it at him.

D amn," I say, "I wanted to produce that spot so bad. I'm tired of falling in love with things I can't have."

"Yeah, babe, I know," says Jerry. "I was hoping to play the drums in the rock band. I wanted you to see me play the drums."

"That's right, you used to be a drummer."

"Used to be? Still am one."

"Oh, it's like being an alcoholic. Once you're a drummer, even if you're not doing it, you'll always be one."

"Yeah, except rather than being in Drummers Anonymous, I'm just an anonymous drummer. Here. Feel this." He extends his arm to me across my desk, for me to feel. "Impressive."

"That's from jerking off. Relax, babe. Just toying. It's from drumming, hitting with the stick. You can also tell a drummer by his legs. Feel how much more muscular my right leg is? That's from my right foot getting twice the action as my left. You have no idea how hard sixteenth notes are on the high hat."

Jerry demonstrates the high hat for me, tapping his right hand high in the air. As if on cue, the phone rings. "Hello?" I say.

"Good-bye," Jerry says, and leaves, still drumming into the air.

"So, what's nouveau?"

It's Frannie. In a jumble of words, I spill out the story of Bryce's flowers, his *GQ* subscription, his mustard vinaigrette. Frannie doesn't think Bryce is sensitive enough, or complex enough, to be bi. But she does want his recipe for mustard vinaigrette. Then Frannie remembers: "Didn't Bryce have a thing about women's shoes?"

"What?"

"Wasn't Bryce always begging you to take him women's shoe shopping?" she asks.

"No, no, *no!* He only had a thing about *my* shoes."

"Oh, I see."

"What I mean is . . . Bryce liked me to wear certain kinds of shoes—*walkable* shoes. He liked to walk places. He cared about my feet, didn't want me to suffer in high heels. You see, Bryce could be sensitive."

"Cheap is more like it," says Frannie. "He'd make you walk rather than cab it to the restaurants he'd make you go dutch at. Some real sensitivity there."

"Anyway, you know me, I like high heels—anything to look tall and streamlined—even if it means suffering. I know by now: being beautiful is painful."

"Not as painful as being ugly," laughs Frannie.

"But Bryce was *not* into women's shoes," I repeat.

"He did have good style, though."

"Suspiciously too good, you think?"

"I don't know," says Frannie. "I always tease Arthur about being bi because he's got such style. Whenever he wears something that clashes, I tell him 'You look very heterosexual today,' which always gets him upset. But Arthur's straight as an arrow. You should see him today. He looks so cute because he got his hair cut. He did the sweetest thing. Last time he got his hair cut, he told his haircutter about me. His haircutter is this very moral Japanese guy who's dead set against extramarital affairs. He told Arthur unless he broke off with me he refused to cut his hair anymore. So yesterday Arthur went to another haircutter. Isn't that the most romantic?"

What I want to say is: "He should be giving up his wife, not his haircutter."

What I say instead is: "Sounds like you've got him right where he wants you."

"I wish you'd trust Arthur a bit more," says Frannie.

"Don't take it personally. I don't trust myself either."

"Arthur just wants to make sure his financial situation is together before he leaves his family."

"He's been saying that for over two years. When does he think that will be?"

"He's not sure."

"You should get him to pinpoint a time. A deadline."

"It's rough. He's going to need enough money to support two sets of wives and kids."

"Another set of kids? You guys talk about having kids?"

"I do. Arthur's not sure," says Frannie.

"Again, he's not sure."

"It's hard for him to think that far ahead right now."

"Funny how guys are," I say. "Bryce was the same. I'd ask him a question about our relationship, and he'd say he couldn't see that far ahead. Then later he'd call me up, telling me how he saw me naked except for red silk garters. Men have selective imaginations."

"Don't compare Arthur to Bryce. Arthur's much more sensitive. He's just trying to set things up so it will be as easy as possible for his wife and kid. He cares about their feelings."

"What about your feelings?"

"I'm okay."

"You know, you like to come off tough, but I don't think you're as tough as you pretend, Frannie. Underneath your tough exterior is a soft interior."

"Then underneath that is a tough interior."

"Then under that soft."

"Then tough."

"Then soft."

"Then tough."

"Then soft."

"What are you getting at, Sasha?" Frannie asks, her voice teetering on anger. "Are you saying you don't think Arthur will ever leave his wife?"

"The truth?" I ask.

"The truth."

I pause, weighing my words carefully—after all, these have to be special true words. Funny how we label truthful words separately. How in court we repeat the idea of truth three times to suggest "Hey, this is not only the truth, it's the whole truth, and nothing but the truth—*that* form of truth." And funny how Frannie prides herself on her blunt truthfulness, yet has chosen a man who lives by lies.

"No," I say. "I don't think he'll ever leave her."

"Well, I trust Arthur. He's totally devoted to me," says Frannie. I am silent.

"One thing I know," says Frannie. "Arthur would never cheat on me. Arthur's completely duogamous."

I hear a cough. I look up to see Mike in my doorway glaring at the phone receiver in my hand.

"What's that by your ear?"

"A very unusual earring?" I suggest.

Tagline time again. Lucky me! I type:

Chromostix. We raise kids' imaginations.
Chromostix. Brings out the kid in a kid.
Chromostix. They run on fun.
Chromostix. The write stuff.
Chromostix. They brighten up kids' lives.
Chromostic. The fountain pen of youth.
Chromostix. The art of expression.
Chromostix. What goes down is always an up.
Chromostx. A child's first language.
Chromostix. ~~Best~~ Better than color TV for a kid.
Chromostix. Every box is a million stories high.
Chromostix. The little one's medium.
Chromostix. Three inches long and ~~know~~ no end to them.
Chromostix. Helps a kid improve with age.
Chromostix. A million, zillion, trillion possibilities.
Chromostix. Teaches your kids to count to infinity.

I am doing as Jerry suggested: looking at the crayons, studying them, feeling them. I am becoming a crayon. I am Golden Rod, Sea Green, Ruby Red—my favorite color as a child, Ruby Red. When I was a child, my father told me he'd paint my room any color I wanted. I asked for Ruby Red. My father sweetly explained it wasn't a "right" color for a little girl's room. He said to pick *any other* color. I chose black, hoping Ruby Red would start sounding better in comparison. In the end my dad painted my room pink, telling me it was a shade of red.

This was my first education in lies. Me telling my dad I wanted black. My dad telling me red is pink. Lies come, I learned, in more colors than the standard black and white. There's a whole Ted Turner colorized world of lies. Many bright and playful. Others soft and romantic. Then there are those golden, glowing lies, the kind you want to bejewel yourself in, never remove, even while bathing.

For a long time after my father's death, I believed he was alive, just still on the road. In time he'd return. He was merely late getting back—as usual. He was always underestimating how long a road trip would be—and overestimating my mom's Understandingness Quotient. Once my mom was so upset at him she changed the locks.

"H.B., let me in!" my dad yelled, banging on our door like it was a bongo drum.

"You're three weeks late!" my mother yelled back, her voice tight as a librarian's knotted hairbun. "What took so long?"

"I stopped and got Mary Ellen doughnuts," he said.

To my amazement, my mother started laughing and let him in. My dad entered the house with the box of doughnuts outstretched toward her—now part food, part protective shield.

"Mary Ellen's!" my mom kept repeating.

These were her all-time favorite calories.

"You know," my dad said, "the guy who owns Mary Ellen Donuts named it after his two daughters. Guess what their names are."

"Mary and Ellen," my mom said.

"No. Do and Nuts."

My dad must have repeated this ritual joke over a hundred times, but that never lessened their laughter, nor the spray of powdery doughnut dust that billowed in the air with each new laugh.

Once in first grade, we had to talk about our parents' professions.

"My dad's a magician," I said by mistake. "Ooops, I mean magi-mu-musician," I corrected myself, to my class's amusement.

Musician/magician. I frequently confused the two. The words not only sounded alike, but felt the same. My mom and I would be upset with my dad for not being around. Then he'd arrive home, blast the stereo, sing, goof around, and suddenly the whole house would glow as brightly as a Mr. Clean commercial set. My dad had magical powers like that. My dad could not be dead, he was too alive. He was a magician/musician. He'd reappear. He must surely be on the road still, I thought.

On the road. I used to take that phrase literally. I'd be in the car, looking for my dad, his name on a road sign, DAD LANE, or a school-crossing-type sign, only with a silhouette of a man in a wide-brim hat.

Yes, it's amazing how potent our death-denial skills are, when all around us everything's dying. Over fifty million people die each year. Not to mention all the dog deaths, cat deaths, goldfish deaths, cockroach deaths, plant deaths, fish deaths, bird deaths, TV spot deaths. Even stars die! Stars! So close to heaven with all that mystical cosmic stuff, yet mortal just the same. One century a star's feeling great, then the next it's feeling a little dimmer than usual. Then poof, star death. Where do stars go when they die—is there a heaven for heaven?

We humans display our death denial particularly in the case of stars. It takes us

millions of years before we see a dead star as dead. I relate. Perhaps in another million or so years, I'll accept things are over with Bryce.

T
he fates are kind. When I drop off my tags to Mike, he's nowhere to be found. Better yet, I find a PCM waiting in the receptionist's area. A sexy Italian guy with eyes—two huge charcoal eyes with lashes that look like he's wearing mascara, but you can be sure he's not. This guy's all guy. If people had to come with their ingredients listed, this guy would be stamped 100% Beef. He's got a cowboy's muscular physique that indents his black T-shirt in all the right crevices. I am hoping this is Dave's replacement art director. I'd love to have him hanging around the ol' water cooler.

"Kurt!" Dave yells. He runs out, gives the guy a quick hug.

I recognize the name immediately: Dave's boyfriend. I'd never guess this guy to be gay—which makes me a tinge more worrisome about Bryce.

"Thanks for coming in to help," says Dave.

So, Kurt's come in to assist Dave's move. What a sweetie. From what Dave tells me, the two get along great. Who knows, maybe there's something to this homosexuality thing. Look how it was back in elementary school. Boys punching girls. Girls crying. The sexes didn't get along back then. I should have caught on sooner—maybe it was never meant to be between males and females.

"Whoaeee! Hot mama!"

It's Tony the Cro-Magnon.

"Don't you look hot today!" Tony shouts. "Big date tonight?"

"No, just a dentist appointment."

I smile mysteriously.

I know weight loss is a symptom of AIDS," I say, "but do you know, is it accompanied by nausea? Or loss of appetite?"

As a reward for finishing my tags, I've called Viv.

"I hope you're not still questioning Bryce's sexuality," she says.

"No. I've stopped *questioning*."

"Relax. Bryce has that bizarre sense of humor. I'm sure those flowers are just a gag."

"Still, I can't help worrying. . . . Do you think Bryce dressed . . . you know, effeminately?"

"Do I think Bryce dressed effeminately?"

Viv's repeating the question, meaning . . .

"Viv!" I yell into the receiver. "Tell me what you're thinking!"

"Well, didn't you once tell me you caught Bryce in one of your dresses?"

"Never!" I say.

"I seem to remember some story—"

"Oh, I know what you're talking about!" I say, laughing, relieved. "Bryce once told me he *dreamt* he was wearing one of my dresses. My purple Anna Sui."

"That's it!" says Viv. "How interesting. . . ."

"Do you think it's significant?" I ask. "You know, a Freudian thing?"

"A Freudian thing?"

"Viv!"

"No, no, I'm sure it was only an innocent dream."

But somehow her voice seems a separate entity than her words.

Wearing a DRESS? Should I have seen this as a clue? Who was this man I devoted four years of my life to anyway?

"Is there some guy you ever wonder about?" I ask Viv.

The telephone line goes silent while Viv reviews the men in her

69

past—which could take a while considering the amount of them. If we all have a one-in-a-million chance of meeting the right guy, Viv only has two or three guys left to go out with.

"Maybe Robbie," Viv finally says. "I do wonder about Robbie. Though we used condoms. Still, I like to call him once a year, just to make sure he's alive."

"I'm worried."

"Don't be. I'll be fine."

"I meant about myself, about Bryce."

Viv sighs loudly. I sense she's growing annoyed, which worries me, because she's always so patient, so even-tempered—unlike Frannie.

"Geez, I'm sorry if I'm getting on your nerves," I say.

"It's not you. It's something else."

"What's the matter?"

"I'm pregnant."

"What? Wow! That's great. Are you going to marry Keith?"

"It's Brad's baby. On the soap. *On the soap.*"

"Oh. Congratulations. That's great, too. I'm happy for you."

"No, it isn't great," says Viv, obviously irritated by the whole thing. "I don't want to be pregnant and have to get married. Not even on a soap! It's boring. The only exciting scenes I could hope for are maybe catching my husband in an affair, or my kid getting hit by a car. Marriage. I don't understand my character's motivation. I'll never be able to realistically portray a married woman. I'm trying to convince Gary, the head writer, to let my character have an abortion, but his personal politics are against it. He believes life begins at the moment of conception."

"Personally, I believe life begins after one's second cup of morning coffee."

"Sasha!"

"Sorry."

Viv exhales loudly. "Now I have to awaken Gary, educate him to his backwards thinking." She says this slowly, calmly—with the kind of calm that suggests she's not calm at all. "I asked Gary if he was for medical and social welfare programs. He said yes, so there's hope. I just have to convince him how much these low-income women need the freedom to get abortions. How can he be pro-life if he doesn't care about these women's lives? I'm hoping he'll come to his senses, rewrite the goddamn script. Unfortunately, the way I've been carrying on, I think Gary's ready to kill me off in a childbirth scene. Do you think I should drop it? What do you think?"

Her voice wavers and crackles like an old, dusty 45 record. I've never heard Viv get upset like this before. I am concerned. I am her friend. I offer her the best, most honest advice a friend can give:

"I don't know. Who knows, you know?" I say.

This does not appease her.

From behind me I hear a snipping sound. I spin around in my chair to see Jerriatrics coming toward me, scissors held *Psycho* style, ready to slice and dice my phone cord.

"Let's work on Close-Up," he says.

I might not be suffering from AIDS, but I'm definitely suffering from ADS.

It's almost noon. Jerriatrics and I still have nothing on Close-Up. Outside in the hallway Dave and Kurt are laughing hearty so-chunky-you'd-be-tempted-to-eat-it-with-a-fork laughter. Why must they sound so goddamn happy?

"Pipe down! People are working!"

It's Mike. For once I agree with his sentiments.

"You better not be packing any office supplies!"

From the sound of his voice, he's heading this way. Sure enough, seconds later Mike appears in my office, cigarette steaming in hand.

"Got your tags. One or two look usable. Meanwhile, I have another assignment for you guys," says Mike.

". . . . . ," I say.

"Mangia Frozen Dinners," says Mike. "You guys are perfect for it. Oh, Joy and Freddie are working on it, too," says Mike.

You don't get truth in advertising. I ask: "If we're so perfect, then why are Joy and Freddie *also* working on it?"

"The client suggested a stand-up spokesperson spot," says Mike.

My ad nightmare.

"Must we do a spokesperson spot?" I ask.

"The client suggested it, but you don't have to," says Mike.

Definition of "suggested": Achtung! Do or Die!

"I only need one spot," says Mike.

Suspicious. Mike's usually a believer in the wallpaper method of presentation.

"Just make sure it's breakthrough," Mike says.

"Breakthrough": something the client won't buy in a million years but supplies a masturbatory thrill for art director and writer.

"This could be a big opportunity," says Mike.

"Opportunity": torturous labor to come.

"It's due Monday," says Mike.

Hence, the torture.

"Before I go," says Mike, "are there any questions?"

"Yeah," I say. "Can you name all seven of the seven dwarfs?"

Mike raises a wormy eyebrow. Jerry laughs.

"I believe you can tell a lot about a person," I say, "by which dwarf they name first, and which ones they can't remember. Like if you say Grumpy but forget Happy, or you—"

"Can't you control her?" says Mike to Jerry, then sprints for the door.

Jerry laughs even harder.

For the last week, Mike's been turning to Jerry for shared responsibility for my little outbursts—ever since Jerry told Mike this agency feels like family to him.

What Mike doesn't know is Jerry's family is majorly dsyfunctional.

"Mike doesn't get to me," Jerry's told me. "I feel at home in this office, because I'm so familiar with his type. Mike's a lot like my father: manic-oppressant."

Mike, however, doesn't even scratch the surface of my paternal itch. Firstly and lastly, my dad was a Kidder Maximus. In fact, I completely blame my warped sense of humor on my dad. As a joke, he had taught me the wrong word for *pencil*. Up until I was three, I thought a pencil was called a "sledgehammer."

"Get me a sledgehammer, honey," he'd tell me.

He thought this was very funny.

And my dad would make up fake histories of words.

"Do you know why they call spinach 'spinach'?" he'd ask, serving bowl in hand. "Listen."

He'd take a big spoonful, plop it onto my plate.

"Did you hear that? The sound it makes when it lands? 'Spinach, spi-nach'? Listen again."

Down would go another spoonful.

My dad could make the worst meals fun. He renamed hamburgers "Wow, steak tartare, well done!" Fluorescent helpings of macaroni and cheese were "Mmmm, pasta à l'orange!" And chopped liver: "Oooh, Jewish pâté!"

Which reminds me: at last it's lunch time. Which means at last it's *dentist time*! I glance at the clock, then grab my black leather jacket, hurry out of the office, eager to get to the dentist. This is one of the few good things about advertising: it makes going to the dentist seem less painful.

Of course it helps if it's going to be Gregg doing the drilling; and of course it figures I'd fall for a man who causes me pain.

Gregg's place resembles a disco more than a dentist's office: airy, marbleized, with halogen lighting *and* Rogers speakers (an even better feature for a man than great buns). On the black marble table, by the water cooler (Evian, of course), are the latest trendy tabloids: *Interview, Zoom, Blitz, Town and Country, Spy, Vanity Fair*. I open the *Vanity Fair* and settle on an article about a Halston benefit to raise money for AIDS. There's this huge photo of the gay activists. I check to see if I spot Bryce in the crowd. I find someone who resembles him, but his nose is too small. I switch publications, seeking the safety of a *Highlights* magazine. I engross myself in a puzzle: find the hidden picnic foods. I am

73

locating an apple and half of a tuna fish sandwich when Gregg comes into the room.

"Good morning, Sasha."

He flashes a big, white, beautiful smile, befitting of his occupation. My man in white, just like the fairy tales promised. My Dr. Right. Yes, Gregg is a definite PCM. And the best kind: a PCM-DDS.

He takes me by the hand, leads me to our private dental workroom. A slight tingle breezes up my spine. I am glad to see I am still attracted to Gregg. I had some fear I had imagined the attraction thing due to the nitrous oxide.

"Have a seat," Gregg says.

He turns around to put on his plastic gloves. Nice to see Gregg practices "safe dentistry." Rather than plant myself on the foreboding S and M patient chair, I sit on Gregg's personal stool, so when he turns to sit, he lands cozily on my lap.

"What are you doing?" Gregg laughs—nervously.

"You told me to sit."

"I meant over *there*. Now, what do you want, stereo or TV?"

For Gregg's patients' listening pleasure, he provides a choice of high-fidelity stereo or color Trinitron TV. The latter he has hanging from the ceiling à la store detection style, at a position most comfortably viewed with head cocked back, saliva dribbling down chin. Gregg's told me for long sessions, like root canal, I could bring my own videos. "I don't suggest you bring *Marathon Man*," he had warned with a twinkle. Today I haven't brought any film. I've chosen instead to watch Gregg.

"Stereo today," I say. "And I brought my own music. That XTC cassette I told you about. Here. For you. For keeps."

He raises a bushy brow.

"No big deal," I say. "I'll write the thing off on my dental insurance."

Gregg hands the cassette to Theresa, his dental assistant, whom I'd conveniently forgotten was in the room with us. Theresa smiles at me. I wonder if she senses I have a crush on her boss. She doesn't speak much English—which means her sixth sense intuitive abilities are sharpened. I had been looking forward to an intimate chat with Gregg. I wonder if I talk fast and use advanced vocabulary, could I still ask the personal stuff: Are you presently cohabitating or involved in a connubial situation with the opposite gender?

"Okay, Theresa," says Gregg, "let's get the patient going with some gas."

Don't bother, Gregg, I am thinking, I'll just stare into your eyes.

Theresa places a little white plastic mask over my nose—not exactly the most attractive way I'd like Gregg to see me. The gas fills my lungs. The music is playing. It is my own one-woman Woodstock experience.

"I am going to try my best to save this tooth," Gregg says. "I think I can save it."

My hero!

"But I'll tell you, this tooth is just begging to be taken out."

No, no, that's me, you fool. Take *me* out!

"I'm going to drill a little deeper," says Gregg, "just to be sure."

That's right, Gregg, drill me deeper!

"Just raise your right hand if I'm hurting you."

But I'm enjoying this. They say adverse conditions are a stimulus for love. But if that were really true, everyone in New York would be in love.

"This might take a while," Gregg says.

That's okay, Gregg, fill my cavity! Fill my cavity!

Gregg's face hovers over me, like a shot from a Buñuel film. Such a warm handsome face. His eyes match his hair. He's got hazel hair. I try to smile up at Gregg, express to him my satisfaction at his being with me now, sharing in this experience, but it's difficult to smile with both his hands in my mouth.

"Burn up the old, bring in the new," Gregg sings along with the tape.

I raise my right hand. "Ow, ow," I groan.

Gregg stops. "That hurts?" he asks, concerned.

"No. It's your singing—you've got to stop!"

Gregg laughs. He pretends to come toward me with the drill. He is a Kidder, like me. We are at one. At last, a Kidder. I have found a Kidder. I love Kidders.

"Excuse me, Dr. Rosen," says a voice from the doorway.

Using the powers of peripheral vision I sense a pale blue blur that fits the basic size and shape of Gregg's squat receptionist, Margaret.

"Could you come out here for a minute? You too, Theresa," Margaret asks.

"Excuse me," Gregg says, and leaves. Theresa obediently follows.

Once alone, I take off the gas mask. My eyes are swollen. The whole back of my hair, flattened. I want to run to the ladies' room, spiff myself up. Then I see "It" on Gregg's tray of sharp spiky instruments, glaring up temptingly at me. "It" being that long metal dental tool with the little round mirror on the other end. I hold It at arm's length, view my face, one feature at a time: a nose, left eye, right eye.

"Don't tell me—you're continuing filling the cavity without me," says Gregg. He has returned.

"I . . . I . . . I," I say.

"You want to see how the tooth is coming along?"

"No—I mean yes. *Yes.*"

"Let me show you." Gregg takes the mirrored object from my hand—gently—and holds it at a new angle, one that offers a great view of my bicuspids.

"That tooth back there is your wisdom tooth," Gregg says. "We want to save the tooth next to it, this one. See? So if in a few years your wisdom tooth needs to be removed, you'll have this tooth for support. Understand?"

I've now earned extra points with Gregg. I'm sure he'd want a girl with an interest in dentistry.

"You know," Gregg says, "this is a very difficult tooth."

"It figures," I say. "I'm known for being difficult."

He begins drilling again. "You and my wife, both."

The drill is blaring. Perhaps I heard wrong.

"What was that you said?" I manage to garble.

"I said, you and my wife both." He enunciates the word *wife* sharply—like a knife.

"Wife"? Married? Gregg's married?

I feel like someone's slipped a Kick Me! sign on my heart.

I'm back," I say. Or try. It's difficult getting the words out. My mouth's numb from novocaine, like the feeling after eating too much Häagen-Dazs.

"I have a gift for you," says Jerry. "You said no one's given you flowers in the longest time. So, I got you flowers—or rather, a flower."

He creates a bald spot amidst the heap on my desk, on which he places a yellow plastic toy daisy bearing a little purple saxophone clutched in its leafy palms. He puts a cassette into my tape recorder. Out comes Stevie Nick's "Stop Draggin' My Heart Around!" The flower jolts to attention, then sways to the music, gyrating its leafy hips à la Elvis.

"How's it do that?" I ask.

"It responds to sound vibrations."

Jerriatrics coughs; the flower jiggles. I laugh; it jiggles. Jerriatrics does a bird call: jiggle, jiggle, jiggle.

"Your body is vibrating like this right now. Your chakras are getting revved up," says Jerriatrics. "That's the kick of listening to music. It's a physical response. The joy of penetration of the ol' electromagnetic field. That is, when it's positive sound. It's another story when it's negative. That's when you get headaches, feel whacked-out. But positive sound, good music, can get your endorphins going, the same ones that make you spunky from running. Music's vibrations can activate them without you even breaking a sweat."

"More stuff you've found time to read, huh?"

"I just want you to understand that the things I talk about aren't, like, bullshit, you know? There's a scientific explanation. Studies have been done for eons about the effects of vibrations . . . vibes. Back in the sixteenth century this Dutch scientist guy did a study on vibes where he hung two pendulum clocks side by side on one wall.

77

Turns out they swung together in the same beat—going against what was natural mechanically. He said he felt like the pendulums 'wanted' to keep the same time. He's since been proven right. This phenomenon's called 'entrainment.' It's a scientific term, not just some mumbo jumbo. Entrainment is when things naturally want to lock into the same rhythm. You see it when you fiddle with the horizontal and vertical doohickeys on your TV—they don't have to match perfectly for them to lock in. It's as if they want to pulse together. It's the same stuff when two people have a good conversation. Their brain waves are oscillating together. Or with a sermon, a movie—a vibrational power takes over the audience. It's like a physical reaction for an audience to come away feeling the same about a show. And jazz musicians—they're entraining when they're jamming, predicting each other's pitch and pattern. So are birds in flocks, fish in schools, investors in the stock market, mothers and kids, husbands and wives. There's been all sorts of studies that show entrainment going on, showing how we all want to connect, to be at one."

To be at one. Yes, that's what we all want, that's what I had wanted, to be at one with Bryce. I suddenly remember this dream I had last night. A dream about just this. Bryce was in it. (Surprise, surprise.) He was standing in my bedroom, by my antique Coca-Cola clock, wearing his jeans and red high-top Converse sneakers. Mmmm. I love the way Bryce looks in his red high-top Converse sneakers—they work on me the same way women's lingerie does for men.

"I am you," Bryce said to me—except when his lips moved, it was my voice I heard. "I am you, from another time," he said.

In my dream, it all was clear. That's what our love was: me coming from another time to help me. Of course. *Bryce and I are the same person.*

I repeat my dream to Jerriatrics, figuring he'll appreciate it for its spiritual value. Jerriatrics just stares at me, smirking.

"Isn't this what you've been talking about?" I ask. "What we seek from love? To merge, to be at one with another person?"

"We live, as we dream, alone," Jerriatrics says.

"Confucius?" I ask.

"No. Gang of Four, the rock group."

Jerry smiles, revealing a mouthful of teeth as white as his hair.

The phone rings. The flower dances with the joy I feel at hearing this sound, the winning buzzer on the Friendship Game Show of Life. Jerry groans.

"I'll be off in five," I say.

"Fine. But this is 'last call.' "

Then, still seated in my guest chair, Jerry wheels himself into the hallway by peddling the floor with his feet, like some Flintstone mobile.

"Hey, Sash."

It's Viv on the phone. She's in a good mood. Her syllables are ascending.

"I heard about a party tonight, down in TriBeCa. An artist's party. Should be an interesting crowd. It starts at eight. I thought we'd show up fashionably at nine, nine-thirty."

"You sound in better spirits," I say.

"I've decided not to let myself get upset about this pregnancy thing."

How can she do that? Like central heating, control her emotions to run hot, warm, cool, high, low, medium, at any level she chooses. Bryce was the same way. I remember this time we met after work at Cafe Lui.

"What's up?" I innocently asked.

"I can tell you what's down." He laughed. "Staley. This stock I bought about seven months ago. I finally sold it today. Lost eight thousand dollars."

I couldn't believe how casually he said it. I've been more upset over losing an earring.

"Aren't you upset?" I asked, upset.

"Sure I am. But getting upset isn't going to change things. The money's gone. I'm just not going to think about it. If I don't think anything, I won't feel anything."

That's probably what Bryce is doing right now: *not thinking or feeling a thing about me.*

"Viv, you should be ashamed!" I yell into the receiver. "You should let yourself be in touch with your feelings. It's good to let yourself feel—even the bad stuff! *It's good to feel!*"

I know I've gotten Viv's attention. She's stopped crunching for a moment.

"Sasha, what is the use of feeling bad? There's no benefit from dwelling on negative emotions. Like with you and Bryce. You should move forward already!"

"I'm trying, but for me it's not so simple. Love is powerful stuff. It's up there in the 'death' arena. You can't stop death. Love, like death, just can't be stopped."

"Not true. Some deaths can be prevented," says Viv.

"Well then, I guess that means love is more powerful than death," I say. "Death can be stopped. Love can't." Not bad for a Video minor, I think.

"Look," says Viv, "if you're going to waste time thinking about the past, then remember the past the way it was. You and Bryce had problems. You used to complain all the time how Bryce refused to talk about anything—remember how he said you talked too much? Remember how he was always trying to turn you off with the TV remote control?"

Yes, I thought, Bryce was not a big fan of dialogue. I remember the time we saw the Broadway show *Cat on a Hot Tin Roof*. He couldn't stop fidgeting.

"Don't you like the play?" I had whispered.

"There's so much dialogue," he had whispered back.

Too much dialogue in a play?

"Yeah, Bryce was fucked up," I say.

"*All* men are fucked up. The trick is to find one that's the least fucked up."

"And then go out with him and *really* fuck him up—right?"

"The address is twelve-twelve Varick Street, apartment four K. See you there at nine-thirty. . . ."

J erriatrics and I are in my office paging through old advertising award books from the sixties, hoping to get inspired on Close-Up. I am inspired. I'm getting inspired to find a new profession. The ads were so much better in the sixties. Everything was better in the sixties. It was a great time to grow up—or rather, stay young. My two favorite albums of all time came from the sixties: Dylan's *Highway 61 Revisited* and his *Blonde on Blonde*. Bryce also worshiped these albums. We both agreed that in the seventies Dylan seemed to lose his magic. Dylan's demise was sort of prophetic of the country's. You can tell where a culture's at by its music. In countries where there's a motley musical variety, there's also a smorgasbord of politics and morals. And where musical styles are limited—like China—there's a limited selection of traditions and lifestyles. An innovation in musical style in a country is almost always followed by a change in these traditions and lifestyles. Likewise, the decline of music usually means the doom of a civilization. It happened in ancient times to Egypt and Greece. It's scary to think what today's music, with all its electronics and high tech, is foreshadowing. A coldness . . .

"Yo, Sash? Mind if I interrupt with some work?"

"What?"

"How about 'Close-Up. The one that makes you two'?" suggests Jerriatrics.

"Cute," I say.

" 'Cute' means you hate it. You always say 'cute' when you hate my ideas."

"Okay, yes, I hate it—and I hate this assignment. I hate being constantly reminded of my single status."

Jerriatrics tugs at his white ponytail. "Do you want to take a break, work on something else? We could work on aspirin or Mangia—whichever you want."

"Wow, what a delightful choice. I am obviously being punished for some heinous crime I committed in a past life."

"I know you're making fun of me when you say things like that. It's okay. I believe you have a spiritual side. You couldn't be so into music if you didn't."

"Jer? Do you think it means something if people share the same taste in music, like there's a spiritual connection?"

"Definitely. It's a vibe thing. People like music that's in tune with their inner rhythm. So people who like the same music have the same inner rhythm. That's why sex is great for people in love—

you have the same inner rhythm, and the more you fuck, the more rhythmically in sync you get. There's a whole field called 'psychometry.' It's the belief you can sense the history of an object from its touch, because vibes get stored up, vibes that are a record of our past. Sex is like the ultimate psychometric thing. Holding a person close, you can sense their history, their being, who they are, where they've been. That's why you feel closer with someone after sex. All things have stored-up vibes. That's the power of crystals, the calming vibes they have. Maybe you should get a crystal. It would help you relax, find peace of mind."

"Jerry, dear, diamonds, rubies, emeralds—*those* bring peace of mind. Especially when receiving them from mysterious dark men with accents."

I t's now 9:18 (9:03) and the agency is abuzz like it's the A.M. variety, not P.M. Everyone's busy gangbanging—except Jerriatrics. He left at six for his Tuesday Float Tank session. I'm about to leave for my party. But first I head to the bathroom to primp, passing JeffJeff and MuttJeff in the hallway, playing Smurf basketball. *Basketball . . . Bryce . . . Glen . . . bisexuality . . . everything in life leads to my death.*

If I were to stereotype, Bryce's interest in sports could be viewed as support of heterosexuality—sports being a macho male thing. It's interesting how as children, little boys are given sports equipment to play with, while little girls are given dolls to love. And we girls do love our dolls, purely, unselfishly, knowing these inanimate dolls cannot return the emotion. In a way we're being trained for unrequited love. Meanwhile, little boys use their basketballs and baseballs to feed their egos, further defining their sense of self.

I enter the bathroom, dump my pocketbook on the counter, hunt in the Mary Poppinsesque clutter for my moisturizer, lipstick, eyeliner, mascara, blush, undereye cream. Jeez, we women invest a lot of money into trying to please men. For all the money I've spent on cosmetics, I could have just gotten plastic surgery. Or taken all that money and paid some guy to go out with me.

I hear a flush, then a "Oh, hi, Sasha." It's Joy, smiling over at me. I don't trust her. She's a wolf in designer clothes. She joins me at the mirror, pulls out a huge pink traveler's cosmetics bag. Inside are the usual cosmetics, as well as some other bizarre tools reminiscent of those on Gregg's dentist tray.

"Women should command higher salaries than men, don't you think?" I say. "We've got much more expensive upkeep."

"We should all get higher salaries for what we put up with at this agency," says Joy, dabbing perfume behind her ears. "You poor thing. It must upset you Mike's opened up your aspirin assignment to the entire agency. You were working on that account for the last six months, weren't you?"

"Ten months."

"Ouch! I don't know why your spot didn't score better. I loved it. It's going to be tough coming up with anything better."

"Thanks. That's real sweet," I say, zipping up my pocketbook.

How nice Joy and I pretend to be to each other. Yes, children aren't the only ones to have imaginary friends.

"Joy, where are you?" a male voice calls from the hallway.

"Neal! I'm in here!" yells Joy.

"We're late for Lutèce!" Neal shouts. "Our reservation's at nine! Where are you?"

Joy looks at me, rolls her eyes—as if we were sharing a conspiratorial moment against men, although her man is generously taking her out for an expensive meal and I'm without a dinner date. Joy has repeatedly bragged to me how wealthy Neal is, how he's always taking her to the trendiest restaurants—never, *ever* letting her pay. All this has always stood out in direct contrast to Bryce, who, when he wasn't suggesting I cook, was suggesting we go dutch.

"Dutch?" I'd reply. "I was thinking Italian."

Yes, Bryce was far from ideal. I should do as Viv suggested, remember his bad points. Frannie told me she's actually renamed guys who do her wrong to help her get over them. For instance, she was dumped by this jerky short guy, Tim. Soon after, Tim was christened "The Midget." It's an old advertising technique—"repositioning"—reselling a product under a different label to change people's opinions of it. It's effective for recovering from bad love affairs—as is writing mean-spirited songs to the man, like the following:

HEX YOUR EX
by Sasha Schwartz

In the game of love
You've been put on reject
You ask yourself: Okay, what's next?
Don't just cross that man off your Rolodex
Hex your ex
Hex your ex
You'll be pleasantly surprised by the effects
When you discover the joy of hex
Suddenly he's the next account the IRS inspects
A wrongly accused mass murder suspect
You know what happens when he eats Tex Mex . . .
When you hex your ex
Hex your ex
To the mystery of his architects
The second floor collapses in his duplex
Lightning strikes
His phone disconnects
When you hex your ex
Hex your ex
You'll be pleasantly surprised by the effects
When you discover the joy of hex
You'll bounce back
He'll bounce his checks
When you discover the joy of hex
Make sure the next girl he selects
Gives him more than he expects
Like a stubborn case of herpes complex
When you hex your ex
Hex your ex

When you hex your ex
Hex your ex
Don't just cross that man off your Rolodex
Hex your ex
Hex your ex

Joy and I leave the bathroom together and walk to the elevator, where her boyfriend, Neal, is waiting. He might have lots of money but he's low on hair. Practically bald. If I had *my* choice, I'd take a man with more hair and less money.

"Neal! Here I am!" Joy yells. "Neal!"

For a moment it sounds like she's calling him "Meal."

"Ready?" he asks.

"Yes, love," says Joy.

Together, we board the elevator. As peripherally as I can I watch them. They look happy. Neal winds an arm tightly around Joy's waist. Joy responds, wrapping her arm around him. Suddenly my arms feel heavy, hanging so lonely and limply at my sides— arms as useless as toes.

I hope this party pans out. I want someone's arms around me. I want to hold someone, be held by someone, be beholden. I've gotta find someone new to love. I am in the green room of love: ready and waiting.

My heart is all dressed up with nowhere to go.

I feel very bright colored standing here in my gray dress. Everyone else at this party is wearing black. The women are in dresses so tight they'd make a mannequin look fat. Most of the men have ponytails. Fine Young Cannibals is blaring from the stereo: "Funny How Love Is." The music pounds through the room, penetrating my body, activating those chakras. I am looking for Viv.

One of the good things about Viv is that she's easy to find. In party pumps she towers in at six feet. Sure enough, almost immediately I locate her blonde head sticking up above the crowd. She's in the corner, by the tahini and pita bread, lightheartedly chattering away to some guy in a black striped shirt. Viv's a maven at making small talk. She doesn't just make it, she mass-produces it.

I make my way toward her, dodging lit cigarettes and plastic cups overflowing with a mysterious green liquid. The party punch is either spiked Gatorade or Midori something, I'm not sure which.

Viv pecks me hello on both cheeks, blends me in. "You look great," she says.

"I feel petrified."

"The secret of the greatest fruitfulness, the greatest enjoyment of existence, is to live dangerously."

"Excuse me?"

"Nietzsche," Viv says by way of explanation. "Go get yourself a drink."

She gently pushes me toward the bar, which is a sink in the kitchen. I make myself a drink: rum and Diet Pepsi. R.E.M.'s "Orange Crush" vibrates around me. I love this song. I feel hopeful, like this song is foreshadowing a good scene to come, the way a background song in a movie would. But there's logic at play here, too. This is my music; therefore these are my people.

To my left stands a tall, dark, bearded guy, a definite possibility—as long as he agrees to shave the beard. I don't like men with beards. I attribute to them all sorts of fallibilities, like insecurity, weak chins, and acne scars. This bearded guy, however, seems confident. He's talking to this frail, pasty blonde woman who's a mere hue away from albino.

"These latest studies are really incredible," says Albino. "The dolphin communicated its needs, and when the researcher responded, the dolphin thanked him. Why are you looking at me like that? You don't believe a man can understand a dolphin?"

"I don't know if I believe a man can even understand a woman."

By golly, Beard's not only attractive, he's a Kidder! The woman doesn't laugh. I do. He turns, looks at me. We share a conspiratorial moment.

"You're a cheeky one," says Albino.

Just my type: cheeky.

I study Beard up and down. And up again. Other than the beard, he's practically factory perfect. He's the only man at the party wearing a suit, yet he doesn't come off stuffy. Most probably it's the eyeball tiepin he's wearing. A teeny tiny lifelike blue eyeball. Immobile and pentrating. Yes he's a PCM, perhaps even the most attractive man in the room—maybe with the exception of this one guy in a red strapless sequined gown—who's very sensational look-ing, if you go for that sort of thing. It seems a gathering at this party does. He/she's surrounded by a group of people, mostly men, none of whom seem bothered by the cigarette smoke he/she keeps blow-ing in their faces. I try not to stare, but I can't help wondering how he/she got his/her cleavage to look like that.

"Do you work with dolphins for a living?" Beard asks Albino.

"No, I'm a reader."

"Of screenplays?"

"No, no, I read auras. And palms," she says. "I studied under Wittengauer. He just read George Bush's palm. He saw much suc-cess, so I believe America will be—"

"Zoe!" a woman with a gold hoop nose earring throws her arms around this pale wisp of a woman so strongly I expect to hear crackling.

"Zoe, it's been eons! Come over here, I want you to meet my new boyfriend, Takees."

Nose Ring forcefully leads Albino away. At last it's me and Beard. I need a good opening line. Like in a commercial. Everything in life is advertising. We position ourselves like products. Our dress is our packaging, our thoughts are our body copy. Problem is, most people don't bother reading the copy. We read the headline, stop there.

I wonder what my packaging is saying about me right now. My hair—so wild and untamed—is definitely giving false advertising messages. In truth my hair's daringness is a sign of the opposite: fear. I'm afraid to risk a bad haircut right now. A bad haircut could be the final thing to send me over the edge.

Talking Heads' "Wild, Wild Life" blasts throughout the room— meaning this is a good time to sell myself as a product. This is the perfect music for my advertising message, selling myself as a life-time supply of Love! It's not so odd, the power of music to induce love. Darwin believed we first learned music as a mating call. Then primitive man discovered when he sang about wanting something, his prayers were often answered. It was through music that primitive man first created the concept of God. Later still, we started creating gods of our musicians.

Enough, enough . . . he's walking away! Quick! Think of something. *Think!*

"Nice tiepin," I say.

Yes, aren't I the brilliant conversationalist?

Beard smiles. "Thanks," he says. "It's a third eye. The watchful eye, from the Kabalah, a Jewish form of mysticism."

Which means this eye in my mother's eyes could be a portentous omen. My mother's always pleading with me to date Jewish guys. Bryce was Unitarian. I have this saying:

ONCE YOU GO GOY, YOUR MOTHER NEVER
HAS JOY

Believe me, it's true. My two greatest failings in my mother's eyes are: (1) I date goyim; (2) I buy retail. I don't know which upsets her more.

"So, you're Jewish," I say. (Yes, Sasha, you're a regular Johnny Carson.)

"Who? Me?" he teases—pronouncing the "who" part "chhooo," like a Hasid with mucus buildup.

Yes, Beard's a Kidder! A definite Kidder! A Jewish Kidder! Happy days! Happier nights!

"Yeah, I'm Jewish," he says. "In fact, I'm an artist, and . . . well, I just did a piece my mother finally said she liked. It was a collage

of the Wailing Wall montaged together from photos of businessmen from newspaper articles. I call it *The Wailing Wall Street Broker.*"

What a Kidder!

"Sounds interesting," I say. "You exhibit anywhere?"

"Yeah, right now I have a show at the Arpege Gallery in SoHo. I've been getting some favorable reviews for breaking new ground in an area I call 'supersurrealism.' Collages of buildings and human body parts. One of my pieces incorporates famous churches and synagogues. I call it *Body as Temple.* Another was of the New York Health and Racquet Club, constructed entirely out of photos of Arnold Schwarzenegger's limbs. That one I call *Body Building.* Oh, by the way, my name is Phillip Goldberg."

Sasha Goldberg. Not bad.

"I'm Sasha Schwartz."

"Nice to meet you, Sasha." He smiles a smile so warm it could defrost a TV dinner. Meanwhile, on the stereo Tom Jones is singing his rendition of "Kiss": "I just want your extra time . . . and your kiss."

"So, Sasha, what's your story? Are you an actress? You look like an actress."

"I'm in advertising. A creative supervisor."

"Really? Wow. Have you done anything I know, like 'Where's the beef?' or 'I can't believe I ate the whole thing'?"

"I wrote the famous ad '50% Off.' That was mine. I know a lot of people take credit for it, but I wrote it."

Phillip laughs, a nice warm laugh. He begins asking me questions about copywriting. He appears to be fascinated. Although it's a despicable career, it does make good cocktail party conversation.

"Did you know," I say, "that most of the casting for dogs in dog food spots is done out in California, because they say the dogs are better looking out there?"

"Really? You mean here the dogs are really 'dogs'?" Phillip kids.

"Yeah, you could put it like that. But it evens out, 'cause on the West Coast, the bitches are really 'bitches.' "

We laugh, our voices rising and falling in unison.

Now that Phillip and I have discussed our careers, we're ready to move on to the next New York party topic: the size and location of our apartments.

"I live in a great apartment," Phillip tells me. "I have a garden in the back where I grow things. Zucchini, tomatoes. You name it. You ever grow anything?"

"An occasional onion in my vegetable drawer," I reply.

Phillip smiles. God is he handsome. Everything is going great. He likes me. I like him. My palms are sweating profusely. He talks. I talk. We talk. But it's not the talking. It's something more. Who knows what it is? What lures people in? Frannie believes it's animal smell. We're led by the nose to a man. When the chemistry is right, it doesn't matter what's wrong. You can't escape the vapors of love. She might have a point. Right now, I'm smelling trouble—wonderful, blessed trouble.

"So, where *is* your apartment?" Phillip asks.

"Tenth and Broadway."

"Really? I live on Twelfth and University. If you ever want to borrow a cup of sugar, feel free to drop by."

"Actually, I use Sweet'n Low."

Again, he smiles. I wonder if he's got dimples under that beard.

"You can borrow that, too. Really. You live so close, we ought to get together sometime. You should give me your number before you go."

"Sure."

The Cowboy Junkies are now blaring, the song "I'm So Lonesome I could Cry." I look Phillip in his eyes—his top two ones only. They seem bright, alert, sincere, happy, and best of all—not roving. *Could Phillip be the next man I will love? The next man I will talk to in pouty baby voices? Could tonight be a sentimental, momentous occasion, one we'll look back on in years to come?*

At this point, Viv and Mr. Stripes walk by. They're either on their way to get drink refills or they're leaving together, I'm not sure which. Viv sees me and winks. She's either winking because they're leaving or to let me know she thinks Phillip's cute. I watch Viv's head bob through the crowd. It stops sinkside. She and Mr. Stripes fill up on green punch. (I interpret the events accordingly.)

Now that Phillip and I have discussed our apartments, we're ready to move onto the third New York party topic: whether our apartments are rental or co-op.

"If my apartment ever goes co-op," Phillip tells me, "I'll turn my garden into a greenhouse."

I think of the advantages this will give our children, to grow up in the city, yet be so close to nature.

"I have a you-know-you've-lived-in-New-York-too-long story," I say. "Last summer I was out on Fire Island. I was playing Scrabble on the beach, and my friend put down the word *C-O-O-P*. My first instincts were "Oh, co-op," as in apartment, but no, what my friend really meant was *coop*, as in chickens!"

I hear a laugh from my right, and look to see this slightly cross-eyed girl standing beside me. I must admit I'd been sensing her nearby for the past few minutes, trying to eavesdrop on our conversation. I had been ignoring her. I look over at her now. She smiles. Although she's cross-eyed, there's something almost sexy about her. Rather than taint her, her crossed eyes enhance her, making her face distinctive. In fact, if her eyes were perfectly set, she'd probably be merely plain.

I can tell the cross-eyed girl wants to be included in our discussion. She seems sweet and nice. I figure, hmmm, why not? After all, shouldn't we women stick together—exist as "sisters"?

"Hello," I say.

"Hi, I'm Lori," says she.

"Nice to meet you. I'm Sasha, and this is Phillip."

"Oh, I know Phillip," my newfound sister Lori says. "He's my husband."

Phillip's married? Yet another one who's married? What's going on here? I know I've been asking the fates to find me a husband— *but not somebody else's.*

Lori leans in and strokes Phillip's beard. Yes, the same beard I was going to have him shave off if he were to be mine, she strokes appreciatively. It was probably she who urged him to grow that fungus. I look at her, then at Phillip, then at Phillip's eyeball tiepin, then back at her, and all I see are eyes. Lots of eyes staring, every which way. And it's eerie. All these eyes are eerie. The music is pounding, seeping into my blood. Lori moves in closer to Phillip, entwining her arm with his, and tenderly kisses his disgusting flea-infested beard. Phillip responds by grasping her arm a little tighter, a subtle motion I can tell he's hoping I wouldn't pick up on.

I guess those weren't wedding bells I had heard tingling before, but *warning* bells.

I'm numb.

I t is now 1:18 A.M. (1:03 A.M.). Another sleepless night. This cannot go on. I've seen better days—and God knows, I've seen better nights. I push the pile of clothes on my bed to the left side, to Bryce's side, pull the sheet up over my head.

I am alone, all alone, I am thinking.

I am doomed to be alone, I am knowing.

Alone, I toss.

Alone, I turn.

Of course I cannot sleep. How can I sleep on this bed? *The* bed. The bed where Bryce made love to me. Now so empty, yet so crowded, with all those memories of Bryce—possibly his last hetero moments.

I turn on the lights, search my apartment for an untainted place to rest my weary head.

The sofa? No, Bryce and I made love there, too.

The bathtub's also out of the question.

And I surely can't sleep on the floor. Definitely nowhere on the floor is safe from our interlocked image.

Not much is left. I can't even sleep on the kitchen table. I remember the time Bryce and I did it on the kitchen table. It collapsed.

"Are you okay?" Bryce had asked.

"I thought I felt myself falling," I had giggled. "I just thought it was because of you—the way you were kissing me."

"Are you okay?" he repeated.

"No, I hurt here."

I pointed. Bryce kissed the spot.

"And here," I said.

Kiss, kiss.

And here and here and here and here and here . . .

Kiss, kiss, kiss, kiss, kiss, kiss, kiss, kiss, kiss, kiss . . .

I hurt now just thinking about that time. I hurt in a place Bryce never was able to kiss. In a place no one seems to be able to kiss.

I hurt.

In total desperation, I call my mother.

"Hello, Mom. It's your daughter."

"Sasha?"

"Very good—you remember."

"Sasha, it's two in the morning. Are you okay? Did you get your hair cut?"

"Mom, it's two in the morning and you remember to ask if I cut my hair?"

"So . . . did you?"

Yes, my mother is responsible for nine out of ten chewed fingernails.

"No, not yet, Mom."

"If only you'd cut your hair, you'd meet a nice fella."

"Mo-o-o-o-m . . ."

"I have someone I want you to meet. Your Aunt Rosalie's friend's son. He's in the clothing business and supposedly very handsome."

"Mom, *supposedly* is the operative word here."

"Just promise me one thing," my mother says.

"What is it, Mom?"

"Do you promise?"

"What is it?"

"Next man you find, you'll make sure he's Jewish."

"Mom," I say, "love is rare enough. Who am I to start pestering the fates with all sorts of special requests?"

She releases a long, heavy sigh. "So what's the matter?" she finally asks. "Are you okay? Why are you calling?"

"I'm upset about Bryce."

"Oh no. Don't tell me. You're seeing him again?"

"Just in a dream. That was the last I saw him."

It was good to see him, even if it was only in a dream. I open my mouth to talk, tell my mother how I am feeling, but nothing comes out—at least nothing audible to human ears. Maybe some dogs out there are hearing my pain. Maybe some dog is howling for me. I want to howl like a dog. I want to scream, let loose, wail a whale of a wail. I never cry. I joke. But now I want to cry. And I finally do. I cry. I am crying. And it feels good, freeing, the dam of built-up tears released at last. My crying is loud, it sounds as if it's echoing all around me. I'm confused. I am hearing from the outside what my insides feel like, but it's not all coming from me. It's my mother. She's crying, too. She, too, is feeling my pain.

"This whole thing is my fault," my mother says, sobbing loudly. Not your delicate sob—silk embroidered handkerchief held poetically to nostril—but the robust sob of a 300-pound walrus—though my mom is a petite 110.

"I set up a situation for you to be stuck on a man like this because when your father died, I never looked to meet anyone new. And now, now—you—you're doing the same thing. Remaining in love with a nonexistent man and it's all my fault. All my fault."

She's crying. Buckets, as they say. I've only heard my mother cry twice in my life. Once during a "Star Trek" episode (something about a planet that sapped people of their capacity for love). The other during a school talent show. I sang "I Don't Know How to Love Him."

I've stopped crying myself, mesmerized by the sound of my mother crying. She takes a big breath in, breathes out again real hard, then in again, like she's going to sneeze, but out comes this huge sob.

"All my fault, all my fault," she sobs.

I'm about to comfort her, then realize: this isn't about her, but me. I've called her up with *my* pain. This is *my* pain—*mine*—my own personalized, monogrammed, one-of-a-kind pain. Yet here's my mother telling me *she's* the star of my misery. She's responsible for my feelings. I did not create them on my own. I've been brainwashed by her: inputted like some computer. She and me. We are in this love-pain thing together.

"Mom, my thing with Bryce is totally different!" I yell this at her—partly out of anger, partly in order to hear myself over her tears.

"We're a family of women without men," my mother continues. "My mother didn't have a husband. I didn't have a father. And then your father, he was always on the road, and then he was truly gone. We've each grown up in a manless house. We are victims of victims. And if you ever manage to love again—"

"Mom—"

"Which I hope to God you do—"

"Mom—"

"And you have children, as I hope you will—"

"Mom—"

"Then I hope for their sake you will break the cycle, if you can." Silence.

"Are you okay, Mom?"

"Now, I'm all alone, all alone."

Her voice is faint, like an echo on a mountaintop and not the call itself, like the recording of a recording of a recording and not the master.

I have reached a new low, a sub-low. I am in quite a state. I am in more than a state. I am in a country. Luckily I remember the mystical healing effects of junk food. I head immediately to the kitchen.

My refrigerator is empty except for . . . an unfinished bag of

Chee•tos. I attempt to fill the emptiness deep inside with Chee•tos, but I am still depressed—only now my fingers are stained orange. I am blue, and I am orange.

The phone rings.

I am startled, but not surprised. I'm sure it's my mother, now the recipient of guilt for a change. I pick up and am greeted by music, something choral and pretty.

"Are you alone?" the caller whispers.

The music I recognize as 10,000 Maniacs. The caller as one definite maniac.

"I want to suck your breasts," he whispers.

I note he's now removed the adjective *big*. I wonder if it's because he's changed his mind.

"Who is this?" I ask.

"I want to feel your nipples grow hard in my mouth," the caller whispers.

It's freaky how much he sounds like Bryce. I remember the way Bryce softly whispered to me when making love: "You're as sweet as candy," he'd say. "Who's Candy?" I'd joke back.

"I want to taste you," the caller says.

His requests sound rather amicable tonight. I'm not sure if it's the softness of his voice or if it's the lilting music in the background, but tonight there's a soothing dimension to his words.

"Do you want me to taste you? Tell me you want me to taste you," the caller whispers.

He really does sound similar to Bryce. I am a bit entranced, in the way I'm sure that the Hitchcock character was by the sight of his wife's lookalike in that movie *Rebecca*.

"Yes, I want you to taste me," I say.

What am I saying? What am I doing? But it's too late. Next thing I know the caller's describing how he's unzippering his jeans, envisioning me as the unzipperer.

"What are *you* wearing?" he asks.

"Nothing," I say, "well, except my black lace panties—do those count?"

A repressed giggle slips out, but it goes unnoticed. It seems a repressed giggle resembles a breathy expression of arousal. The caller breathes back.

"I want to lick you all over," he says. "Starting with your toes. I want to suck your toes."

I envision it's Bryce wanting me, I envision it's his wanting. Ah, the comfort of another's wanting, the evocative power of the voice. Of all the senses, hearing is just what the imagination ordered.

"I'd lick you up the leg, till I got to your pussy, then I'd take a quick darting taste, taste your sweet, flowery juices."

I find myself relaxing, comforted, for the first time in a long time. It's nice to be paid so much attention.

"I'd lick you while my finger was deep inside you, so I could feel you getting hot, licking and thrusting my finger deep inside you."

And he's not only prolific but generous. He's spending a lot of time describing what *he'd* do to *me*, rather than the other way around. He's kind, gentle, imaginative—everything I'd want in a lover, except real.

3.

BUT EVERY LIAR SAYS THE OPPOSITE
OF WHAT HE THINKS IN HIS HEART,
WITH PURPOSE TO DECEIVE. NOW IT IS
EVIDENT THAT SPEECH WAS GIVEN TO
MAN, NOT THAT MEN MIGHT THEREWITH
DECEIVE ONE ANOTHER, BUT THAT ONE
MAN MIGHT MAKE KNOWN HIS
THOUGHTS TO ANOTHER. TO USE
SPEECH, THEN, FOR THE PURPOSE OF
DECEPTION, AND NOT FOR ITS
APPOINTED END, IS A SIN.
—ST. AUGUSTINE

**Please don't squeeze the
Charmin.
—Charmin toilet paper man**

Gotta get you outta my life!" I sing as I stroll down the street. The sun is shining, the opening titles of my day rolling. *Gotta get you outta my life!* This song nags at me like an itch. I suppose because it's the first thing I heard when I awoke. It was playing on my radio alarm clock. A good omen. That's what I should do: get Bryce outta my life. That's what I'm gonna do. *Gotta get you outta my life!* In part this courage is inspired by my talk with the obscene caller last night. Beneath his words of lust and longing lay the possibility of finding new love. Although it all was imaginary, I awoke feeling newly loved just the same. *Gotta get you outta my life! Gotta get you outta my life! Gotta get you outta my life!* I can't seem to shake this song. Good thing I didn't set my alarm on buzzer. I'd be going around singing "Beep-beep-beep." Or if the phone woke me: "Brr-brrr-brrr-ing." *Gotta get you outta my life! Gotta get you outta my life! Gotta get you outta my life!* Who needs Walkmans? So much music in my head, not just this tune; there's a veritable jukebox of thoughts up here. Things Bryce said, promised, moaned. Hits from the past, no longer transmittable on the dial of reality, yet playing loudly just the same. A veritable battling banjos of thoughts up there—but no more. I'm closing down the Bryce station, turning away sponsors to my bad emotions, firing the staff of neuroses. It's over and out, outta my life. . . . *Gotta get Bryce outta my life.*

I am singing it out loud when I enter my office.

"Into," shouts Jerriatrics from next door. "Into!"

I dump my leather coat on my chair, head over to Jerriatrics's. He's sitting reading the paper, drinking coffee. I hope he's drinking coffee. Either that or his shirt's on fire, because from behind his newspaper floats a swirl of steam. He lowers the newspaper. Sure enough he's clutching his favorite coffee mug, the one that reads:

LIVE NOW, PROCRASTINATE TOMORROW

"What did you say?" I ask.

"The song goes 'into my life.' 'Gotta get you *into* my life.' "

"Sure?"

"Mmm. Very." He raises his newspaper back up. He's mesmerized by whatever he's reading. I do admire his reading discipline.

"What's the article about?" I ask.

"I'm reading the horoscopes."

"Look up Gemini, would you?" I say.

He lowers the paper. "You were born in April, Sasha. You're an *Aries.*"

"I know. Gemini is Bryce's sign. I'm curious what's going on in his life without me. Not that I believe in astrology, but it would make me happy to hear bad things are in the making for Gemini. You know, financial ruin, back-stabbing co-workers."

Jerriatrics reads: " 'Gemini, the dual personality sign, will at last resolve an ongoing conflict between the two inner selves. The self that longs for change will win out; you will give up a long-held life pattern in trade for a new beginning.' "

" 'Dual personality'? 'Long-held life pattern' now gone?" I repeat. "Call me neurotic, but it sounds like they're talking about giving up heterosexuality for . . ."

"You're neurotic."

"Oh, Jerry, it's hard to stay positive in this world of ours."

"I'm gonna get a coffee refill," he says. "Be right back."

I pick up Jerriatrics's paper from his desk, decide to use this time to relax, forget my problems, catch up on the world, practice "being."

Hmmm, seems the world's not doing too well today, either. The world is low on money, can't get a job, and is having a hard time finding people to treat it with respect. Plus, the world's health looks pretty poor; it's coughing up smoke, running high temperatures. Yes, the world might even be in worse shape than I am. What's this? A big article on AIDS . . . something about AIDS spreading faster than ever. "AIDS from heterosexual sex is now the biggest cause of death amongst young women in New York," says the paper. *"This year the city health department predicts a 50 percent increase in AIDS for women,"* says the paper. *"By 1994 THERE COULD BE OVER 10,000 CASES OF WOMEN WITH AIDS IN THE CITY, A GREATER THAN 400 PERCENT INCREASE,"* says the paper.

Yes, those Korean chicks really do quite a job of gluing down these fake nails. But I too show my share of determination. It's a rough struggle. I tug. The pain tugs back. It's as if these surrogate nails have undergone an identity crisis. They've come to believe they truly are my real fingernails. They've taken up residence, refuse to be removed. I hope the rest of me is as resistant at being removed.

"You look deep in thought."

It's Tony the Cro-Magnon, standing in my doorway.

"What you thinking about?" he asks.

"Death," I say.

"You got a birthday coming up or something? You girls are all alike with those birthdays. How old are you, anyway?"

"Twenty-nine."

"You look older," he says. "Just teasing, don't get bent all out of shape. How old were you when you lost your virginity?"

"Beg your pardon?"

"I believe that's how old a person really is. When you lose your virginity, that's the beginning of life."

"I have a different theory," I say. "That your maturity freezes at the age you first get laid. Like if you lost your virginity really early, like at twelve, you remain eternally twelve. You never get past that maturity level."

Tony looks a little perplexed. "I lost my virginity at thirteen, but I don't feel young," he says. "I'll admit something to you. I've been feeling old lately, too. You know when it hit me? I was looking at this *Playboy* centerfold. All my life I've been looking at *Playboy* centerfolds. And all my life they've been these older women to me, you know? Now, this year they look like these younger women to me. A thing like that can make a guy feel old."

To summon up our alpha waves, Jerry has suggested we sit still, with eyes closed, and clear our heads of all thought. But I've got a clutter of thoughts up there. It would take Natasha weeks to clear them away. Thoughts about love, death, shopping, sesame noodles; should I cut my hair, quit my job, take taxis less often, see a therapist, see a mortician, see a video dating service?

"I've got it!" I yell.

"Lay it on me, babe."

"We'll write a Close-Up spot warning people that maybe they shouldn't use the product because it could be dangerous for their mental health. It could lead to love, which could lead to heartbreak. We'll put a warning label on the tube saying the Close-Up company cannot take responsibility for any dangerous side effects of love."

"The way you talk, babe, it's as clear as my crystal, you don't want to be in love."

"Jerry, I'm just joking."

"You joke, but you're serious about the stuff. You joke to avoid facing up to your serious feelings. You're never serious."

"I'm always serious—except when I'm joking."

"I think you're afraid of love."

"Bullshit. I'm afraid of *not* falling in love."

"Same bad deal."

"What are you talking about?"

"The big aphrodisiac: fear of being alone. Too many people do things out of fear, not pleasure. People don't do enough things for pleasure anymore."

"Aren't we all supposedly hedonists these days?"

"Because we drink, eat, take drugs and shop to the point of excess? None of that has to do with indulging in life—that's about escaping it. Sure, people tell themselves they do that stuff for the good times. Even getting involved in relationships can be passed off as looking for the good times, but all too often people fall in love like alcoholics, looking to lose themselves, hide themselves, save themselves, and it's a fucking waste, a fucking waste of love. It's just one of the symptoms of how people are searching *outside* themselves, rather than *inside*, for answers—turning to TV, organizations—their possessions. Look how we rely on atomic power! We expect atomic weapons to be our strength. Shit. Meanwhile we've stopped developing our inner potential, listening to our inner self."

"Not me. I listen to my inner self, and it's blabbering away about finding love for all the right reasons. Shhh. Hear that?"

"What?"

"Shhhhh. Listen closely, you'll hear it babble."

Jerry leans in. The phone rings. Needless to say, I pick up.

"Goddamn dog food assholes."

Frannie.

Jerry waves his arms at me like a runway controller. "Yo, Sash. We've got work."

"Give me five," I whisper.

"I think *you're* the reason my hair's this color." He flails his grayish-white ponytail at me, then, still seated, Flintstone-mobiles his way into the hallway.

"Are you listening?" Frannie asks.

"Go on."

"Legal just told us we're not allowed to use a veterinarian as a spokesperson for dog food. *Now* they tell us, after fucking six months of writing stupid vet spots."

"Isn't there any way around it?"

"How?"

"Like . . . how about getting a guy in a wheelchair who rolls himself into the frame, says he's a 'vet,' then goes into the dog food sales pitch."

"Sasha—"

"Or how about someone who mumbles? They say really fast, 'I'm a vegetarian.' Maybe no one will notice."

"Oh, shut up, Sasha. Must you always joke? You know, it's annoying when a person's upset about something."

"Look, Frannie, you told me you hated those vet spots. Right?

So why do you choose to see this as a negative? This could be a positive. You can write something better."

"You and your Disney vision *again*. Look, Sasha, I haven't produced shit in over a year. I take that back. I've produced a lot of shit. Meanwhile, you're producing Bully spots, and cool aspirin spots right and left."

"My aspirin spot died in testing."

"Really? Oh, I'm sorry."

We share a quiet, solemn moment, mourning the ad world's loss.

"Arthur's going to be so disappointed," Frannie sighs.

"Arthur what? You told him about my aspirin spot?"

"And showed him your songs. Arthur thinks you're brilliant."

"Brilliant? I know what you're up to, Frannie. You're trying to make me vulnerable to approving of Arthur." I laugh. "So . . . 'brilliant,' huh?"

"You *are*."

"Thanks. You know the biggest compliment Bryce ever gave my writing was to call it 'neat.' "

"I think I'm going to start fining you five bucks every time you bring up Bryce's name. It would be good for you—and better for me. I could be retired and out of this stupid ad business in a week."

"You know, Bryce never wanted to talk about my writing."

"Sasha, he couldn't. He wasn't creative. He couldn't even come up with his own answering machine message. How could you ever have loved a man who couldn't come up with his own answering machine message?"

"Bryce never appreciated my creative side."

"There are so many sides of you he never appreciated, layers to you he never got near to reaching. It's like you're this VCR, right? With all these buttons and amazing programming options, right? But Bryce only knew how to press your Play button. You need to find a man who knows how to tap into all your capabilities."

I need to find a man like Frannie. She knows how to tap into all my programming options, create new ones. She's a very challenging friend—which is the euphemistic way of saying "confrontational."

The good news is Frannie sees every side of a person. The bad news is she says everything she sees *out loud*. Eventually Frannie gets into big fights with everyone in her life. She's even fought with Viv, who never gets upset. This, in fact, is what got Frannie unruffled.

"How is it possible for you to always be so happy!" Frannie yelled at Viv. "Come on, admit it, you must be secretly miserable."

"I like being happy!" Viv yelled back. "Almost as much as you like being miserable."

"Excuse me!" Frannie yelled.

"Look at the way you dress," said Viv. "It's like you don't want to let joy into your life. You're so beautiful, yet you hide it all under baggy clothes and straggly hair. It's as if you want to keep yourself from feeling total happiness."

Those philosophy classes paid off. Viv was right. Frannie does have a tendency to be attracted to things that distance gratification. Not just when it comes to wardrobe selection, but men: i.e., choosing a married man. And before Arthur there was Tim: a man who lived in L.A.

Even I've told her: "Frannie, your thing is to either go for guys who are emotionally distant but physically close, or emotionally close but physically distant. And never the twain shall meet."

"The world sucks, doesn't it?" Frannie replied.

"Don't blame the world," I told her. "You're the one who sets up these situations that get you upset! Sometimes I think you even enjoy being upset. It's as if you take pleasure in saying: 'You see, I'm right about the world!' even more than you would take pleasure in *feeling right* about being in the world."

"Oh, shut up, Sasha!" Frannie screamed. "I don't *want* to be involved with a married man! I want Arthur to divorce his wife! And he loves me and will! This is *fact*!"

But it's obvious to me Frannie's setting herself up for heartbreak.

I wonder if it was as obvious about me and Bryce? Was I, with my Disney vision, seeing things as half full, my heart as half full?

Then again, who's to say Frannie's wrong for enjoying her hope? At least she's happy. I suppose we all need a little fantasy to live on, to sustain us. Like for me, if I just knew someday I'd find a great guy who'd love me, then I'd relax. Like if I had a husband in prison who I knew would be released in ten years, I'd be a happy woman.

W hat about the image of Balinese women carrying heavy bundles on their heads?" asks Jerry. "Then we say something like: 'If this is how your head feels after a day at the office, try Bufferin."

"But we're not supposed to show pain."

"We're not showing pain, we're metaphorizing pain."

"Same problem."

Jerry is juggling three neon tennis balls as he talks. I am seated facing a strangely carved mask that has one big eyeball and a long pointy nose. We're now working in Jerry's office, hoping the new setting will stir up new brain waves. Except for this bizarre mask, and a tall thin suede-wrapped drum, and one of those shake-up snow-scene thingies—one from Toronto, with a little Canadian snowman inside—Jerry has no extraneous nonoffice matter.

"What about symbolizing a headache by showing two rams butting horns?" says Jerry. "Then we at least dehumanize the pain."

"Same problem."

"At least I'm trying, Sash. You're not trying."

"My brain's worn out. I've got a headache."

"Ironic. Working on this aspirin account's giving you a headache."

"And remember that time we worked on that spa account, I got all stressed out?"

"With this in mind, Sash, you should never work on a contraception account."

I watch the yellow balls float up and around Jerry like astronauts in a Tang commercial.

"How'd you learn to juggle like that?" I ask.

"I used to juggle to help me drum better, master time. That's what a drummer is, a master of time. Juggling lets you feel time physically, control it—depending on how high you throw the ball.

This is why drummers make great lovers, we're aware of rhythm. Plus it helps we're ambidextrous. We can split up our lobes. Get the left arm doing one thing while the right arm's doing another— which can come in handy."

He gives me this smile that's as big as when you put a quarter section of an orange in your mouth.

"Guess what, kids!"

It's Joy. To be more specific, it's Joy's hand. She is waving it in my face. It's hard not to see what she's here to talk about, the diamond's so huge. It's more than pear-shaped. Watermelon is more like it.

"I'm engaged," Joy says.

"Congratulations. That's great," I lie.

So Joy and Neal have tied the knot. It seems they tied it in my stomach. The prospect of lunch no longer appeals to me, but my left thumbnail is lookin' mighty tempting.

"Isn't it beautiful?" Joy says, her hand flying toward my face again.

"Lovely," I say.

"Nice," says Jerry, looking straight at me, trying to gauge my reaction, which is to gnaw at my entire left hand.

"It's three carats," says Joy. "I was willing to settle for two, but Neal insisted. Bryce never got around to giving you a ring, did he?"

"No."

"Bryce would have gotten you a nice one too, I bet."

Yes, Joy has what I have coined "anti-charisma."

"Neal is so great," says Joy, "so generous. I'm really lucky to have found Neal. He's near perfect. He satisfies nine out of ten of my needs."

I smile. "Oh, you have only ten needs?" I say. "Maybe that's my problem. I have hundreds."

A re you okay?" asks Jerry. "You look so . . ."

"Depressed? I am. I'll never meet anyone."

"You've got to think positively, babe. Be positive."

"I am. I am very positive. I'll never meet anyone."

I switch to my right hand's index finger to chew on. It's a lot more stubborn than the left. I better be careful. It's not worth chipping a tooth now that I know Gregg is married.

"Why do you bite your nails?" Jerriatrics asks.

"Because I have nothing better to nibble on right now," I say. For extra measure, I sneer.

"Let me help you," says Jerriatrics. "I could do a candle-lighting ceremony for you, help you find love."

"Thanks, Jer, but I'm already burning a candle—at both ends."

"Relax, Sash. It's nothing freaky. You've already done candle ceremonies. In the Jewish religion, you guys do Sabbath and Hanukkah and memorial candles. And I'm sure you've done birthday cake candles. So come on, what's the big deal about doing one more candle ritual?"

Jerriatrics smiles big as a rock star. He's sweet. . . . Cute, too. . . . Smart . . . . Creative. . . . Open. . . . Am I actually considering . . . No way. He's too deranged. No, I shouldn't even think about Jerriatrics in a romantic way. How could I ever take seriously a man who insists he saw a UFO? Plus, my mom would kill me. Not that she'd mind Jerriatrics's stories of his UFO buddies. She'd be glad to invite them all to our wedding—if Jerriatrics were Jewish. Which he isn't. At least I don't think so. I don't know what religion he is.

"Are you a Buddhist?" I ask. "What religion are you?"

"I'm Wiccan."

"What's that?"

"Well, it means . . . to be honest . . . it means . . . I'm into the study of witchcraft."

"Witchcraft? You're a witch? A *witch*!"

I can't believe this never came up in conversation before. I thought I knew Jerry so well. Do any of us know any of us?

"Witchcraft is not what you think," says Jerry. "You know, witchcraft's our first religion. It goes back twenty-five thousand years, even before Christianity. Christianity felt the competition from witchcraft, so it ran a smear campaign to lure in customers to the Church. They spread rumors of Satan worshiping. False rumors. Witches aren't into Satan. The witches' god of hunting has horns. That's all the figure with horns represents: hunting. In some way he represents death, but only in the way hunting's associated with death. But he's not Satan. The Church was jealous that witchcraft was so respected. Rumors began to fly. Oh, and that stuff about witches flying on broomsticks—more bad PR. Brooms were used in ceremonies for spiritual cleanliness, and as fertility charms to bring good crops. Folks rode on a broom or a pole to represent the penis—you know, fertility. Some of these brooms even had penis-shaped ends. People saw that, rumors got spread. Accusations were fun for the mobs—and paid well. A pound a head for all convictions. And a nice opportunity to get rid of unwanted neighborhood folk, all the old, ugly spinsters men didn't much care for hanging around. Men were angry that women were living longer than them. It was part misogyny, witch killing, a way to kill off a lot of ugly old ladies. There's been estimates that nine million people were hung, burned, or tortured to death on charges of being witches. Like a holocaust. And with the same ugly motivations—jealousy and lack of understanding."

"Do you cast spells?" I ask.

"I'm in advertising. I cast TV spots."

"I've gotta pee," I say.

My art director's a witch. My ex-fiancée might be bisexual. Who am I? What has become of my life?

This is what I am thinking as I sit on the toilet. I reach for the toilet paper. Above the dispenser someone has scribbled:

> God is dead.
> —Nietzsche

Is this a sign?

I look closer. Beneath it, the same person has scribbled in tinier letters:

> Nietzsche is dead.
> —God

I laugh. I wonder if Viv wrote this the last time she came to the office. It's her style. Though I don't remember Viv ever coming to my office. It's funny, my friends and I talk on the phone, but it's a rare occasion when we get together eyeball to eyeball. I haven't seen Frannie in two months. My mother in four. If it weren't for the phone, I'd have no friendships. The phone is my friendship resuscitator. I breathe words into the receiver and magically friendships are kept alive.

No wonder I feel so alone. It's so cold relating to people mostly by phone, to rely so solely on words, on hearing, a mere one of our God-given senses. What about smell, touch, sight, taste? I want to sniff, squeeze, bite a friend. Perferably a male one. Man oh man, I want a man. I gotta meet someone real soon—someone just plain *real*, not just a voice on the phone; someone three-dimensional, though I'd settle for two-dimensional right now. Perhaps I should be satisfied with my obscene caller. After all, my other relationships are being sustained by phone. Why not one more? Perhaps it's the natural evolution to keep a man by phone. I can tell my mom: "I'm not seeing someone, but I am hearing someone."

I flush the toilet, head out of the bathroom, down the hall to my witch art director.

"Hey, Sash, want to see my new girlfriend?"

It's Tony the Cro-Magnon. He motions me into his office, lays open a *Playboy* magazine on his desk.

"Her name's Patti," Tony says, referring to this luscious red-head. "Read her interview. When they ask what her favorite hobby is, she says hanging out with her boyfriend—Tony Larusso—that's me. Isn't that sweet?"

"What happened to Naomi?" I ask, referring to the attractive blond he brought to Mike's birthday party.

"Patti is what happened. I traded up for Patti. Look at those breasts. That's not retouching, let me tell you."

"You know, Tony, next life, you should be a woman and have men treat you only as a sex object!"

"Oh, wish it upon me! Wish it upon me!" screams Dave from his office next door.

And I did not know this man was gay? Then again, Dave's wife didn't either. Nor did his mother. Dave told me his mother ultimately handled it well. Dave even brought Kurt home to meet her. His mother gave her approval by telling Dave if she had had a daughter, Kurt would have been the type of guy she'd have wanted her daughter to bring home. I'm not handling the possibility of Bryce's bisexuality nearly so well. Then again, I have more to lose: i.e., my life.

Maybe I should get tested. After all, I am a seeker of truth. So seek I shall. Plus, it would be helpful to know if I should start living life for the moment, or continue, as usual, putting life off till a week from next Wednesday.

Damn. I don't want to die a spinster! An old maid! Funny how our language doesn't have the male equivalent of these words—a word for *bachelor* with negative connotations. *Mistress* is another female word missing its male equivalent. Hell knows, there are plenty of them in the nineties, these male mistresses, these "misters," these "mis-takes." Plus, *hag* and *dog* are around to label females. What of ugly men? We gals need to verbally play a little "cock for tat." With a little wo-manipulation our vocabulary already offers some delightful possibilities:

MALE-VOLENT
MAN-IAC
MAN-GY
MAN-URE
MALE-STROM
DICK-TATORSHIP

I'm sounding angry. Why? There are good men out there. Men who aren't married, bi, or witches.

My dad was a good man. Whenever he was home, his good-natured spirit would fill our house with Dolby affect. His joking, laughing, singing, echoing in every room, loudly declaring love, silently promising protection.

I remember this one windy night. I was convinced a monster was out to get me. My dad held my sweaty little hand tight and searched with me throughout my pink room: under my pink bed . . . behind my pink beanbag chair . . . in the cluttered pink corners of my closet . . .

No monster.

But I understood the monster's psyche. It would wait until I was asleep, climb up the side of our house, enter through my window, and get me.

My dad didn't argue with my Monster Modus Operandi Theory. He nodded solemnly, went to the bathroom, returned with a jar of Vaseline.

"Not to worry," he reassured me.

He spread gobs of Vaseline all over my windowsill, explaining if a monster tried to climb through my window, it would slip on the slime and fall to a tragic death.

That night I slept soundly.

Yes, my dad was a good man. I want to believe there are others in this world. I've always been a hopeless romantic. Though I'm starting to feel romance is hopeless.

"Down?" a voice asks.

At first this voice seems prophetic. Then I emerge from my trance to see a neon-spandexed messenger holding the elevator door for me. I get in. Heck, why not? I could use some fresh air.

Outside, the street is speckled with people, many of them men, many of them PCMs, many of them PCMs not walking with women. Two PCMs approach from around the corner—both without wedding bands, those brass knuckles to a single gal's hopes.

Next thing I know I'm following these PCMs. I don't know what I expect to happen. Maybe I'll pretend to ask them directions, say I'm lost—which I am metaphysically, so I won't be lying entirely. I walk a few steps behind them, eavesdropping on their conversation.

"Admit it," says the blond one. "You've been sleeping with her for two years—admit it—she's your girlfriend."

Not to fret. I see another man, definite date bait, standing in front of my dreaded East Coastal bus billboard. I hurry in his direction. What's this? He is studying my billboard meticulously. He is admiring my work. I could approach him, tell him I'm the creator, impress the hell out of him. Then, on second glance I see: it is himself, not my billboard, he is studying. He's merely checking himself out in its glassy reflection. Egotist.

I continue my aimless single file march, in no hurry to get back to the office, in no hurry to go anywhere—one of the few out here who's not. Everyone else is quickly, quckly, qukly, qkly, qy, rushing past me. I feel like a wrongly placed eighth note, floating, not lightly, but heavily within this rhythm. Less like floating, more like being tossed about, like a note from a somber ballad lost in a song by the Sex Pistols.

Up ahead looms a big sign in the window of Don's Shoe Store:

50% OFF!

A sale. Maybe I'll do some quickie shopping. Shopping always cheers me up, all that yearning for an object, followed by its possession! It's a beautiful thing, shopping. I've even written an ode to shopping.

SHOPPING AND BOPPING
by Sasha Schwartz

Oh the excitement
taking off all my clothes
My whole body is tingling
right down to my toes
Yes, even the shoe department is having a sale
Spending a bundle at Bendel's
Then heading toward Bloomingdales

Shopping and bopping
Department store hopping
What a way to spend, spend, spend, the afternoon
and Thursday nights till nine, too

Don't wait for the dressing room
To start undressing
Could that be the price tag?
Oh how depressing
I might be broke
but I'm still gonna get it
If God didn't want us to shop
there wouldn't be credit

Shopping and bopping
Department store hopping
What a way to spend, spend, spend, the afternoon
and Thursday nights till nine, too

I've got my VISA
Going on a flight of fancy
Hello, can I help you?
I'm your salesgirl
my name is Nancy
Do you have this in fuchsia?
Do you have this in blue?
Do you have a size eight?
Good, I'll take two!

Every girl should know the joy of Saks
A hundred bucks can buy a lot of happiness—
not including sales tax

The scene inside Don's Shoe Store is wild: women grabbing, screaming, and lunging for the ultimate black pump, a Plato's Retreat for
shoppers. I know how these women feel. Such shoes at such a price!
This is the most excited I've been in a long time. This is what it's
come to for me, what I must do for excitement: buy something.
Buying has become my sexual substitute—which I guess makes me
"buy-sexual."

The system here is: one shoe of each pair is out; if you like it,
you request the other. I'm fondling a low-heeled black pump—the
kind of practical shoe Bryce liked me to wear, so we could walk all
those long distances together—and I remember: how lovely just to
walk, la de la de la, just being together.

I remember this one time, Bryce and I were walking and talking,
unaware of the world around us. When we finally looked around,
everyone was Chinese.

"Look, we walked all the way to China!" Bryce joked.

It was Chinatown. We had walked more than forty blocks to
Chinatown. That night had seemed proof to me of our love. To be
so lost in each other's words—lost in each other—that we could
walk forty blocks without noticing!

Then, to make the bliss of our night complete, we went to my
favorite Chinese joint.

The next week I returned to this Chinese joint with Viv, and had
the same waiter: Chang.

"That yo' boyfriend you come in here with last time?" Chang
asked me.

"Yes," I answered proudly. (After all, I was a woman with a man.)

"I not like him," said Chang.

"Why not?"

"He not let you get pork strips. You like pork strips. I not like
him."

Turns out Chang had overheard Bryce and me discussing our
meal plan. Chang knew I always order pork strips. (Add that to my

list of how I've betrayed both mother and motherland, Israel. But I don't eat the pork strips with milk, so it's not that bad.)

"No, no pork strips," Bryce had insisted. "We're getting egg rolls."

Then Bryce alone picked one from Column A and B, not caring that I wanted C, none of his above choices.

Chang had wisely keyed in on one of Bryce's character flaws: he always had to have his way.

I stare down at this low-heeled pump. Its pointy toe now looks sneaky and evil, like the head of a small rodent.

A pimply-faced salesboy approaches. "Who needs a mate?" he says. "You need a mate?" he asks me.

"What?"

"You need a mate?" he repeats, spitting this last word in my face.

Yes, there is no escape.

I t's not until 4:16 (4:01) that I return to the office.

"Where'd you go?" Jerriatrics asks.

"I needed some air."

"You're weirded out about my religion, aren't you?"

"You're a witch, Jerry. A *witch*."

"Look babe, I don't think you really understand what witchcraft is. There's a lot of bad PR out there on it. You should read about it, get some unbiased history books."

Jerriatrics reaches into his wallet and retrieves a card.

THE WICCAN BASKET
107 E. 9TH ST
OPEN TILL MIDNIGHT!

"You really ought to check this place out," says Jerry. "It's nearby, on Ninth Street. They've got lots of candles and love potions and interesting books about witchcraft. You could read up, see how witches have been respected through the ages. Witches were the village herbalists, midwives, psychologists, doctors—*all this, all in one.* There was a time people depended on witches for their lives."

"Yeah, and people only used to live to thirty years old, too."

"No fault to witches. Doctors were the ones recommending leeches and bleeding—all that stupid shit—when witches were already into real medicines."

"Yeah, like 'take two eyes of newt and call me in the morning.' "

"A lot of those potions you hear witches brew up are just fancy names for herbs. Like dragon's blood. When a recipe calls for dragon's blood, it's not really blood from a dragon. It's gum resin. Red-brown gum resin. Cat's foot is ground ivy. Swine snout is dandelion. Jew's ear is just fungus on elm. And hound's tongue is as innocent as vanilla leaf."

"Uh huh," I say.

"Look, just because you don't understand how witchcraft works doesn't mean it doesn't exist—like, if you can't describe how a TV set works, does that mean TV doesn't exist?"

"I wish TV didn't exist, so I wouldn't have to write these stupid commercials."

"Look at this flower I gave you. You see how when I raise my voice *to yell at you for your closed-mindedness, its leaves move?* It's being affected by a change in its energy field. We're all energy, right? Even Einstein believed all was made of energy. Witchcraft is just about controlling this energy. Let me do a candle ceremony for you. I could help you find—"

"Jerry, I—"

"Don't feel like I'm pushing Wiccan on you. I'm not. I'm not after you to join any organizations. We don't have one. And I don't want any money. When people want to give money to show appreciation for witchcraft, we say give it to ecological organizations. Witchcraft is about reverence for nature. Anything done for our earth, our water, our air, for our fellow creatures—this is the essence of witchcraft. And this is why I want to help you. What could it hurt? One candle. Isn't it worth a try? Nothing you're doing now is working, right?"

Because I value my friendship with Jerriatrics—and more important, because I am an ever-increasing desperate woman—I agree.

Jerriatrics raises his hand for me to high-five. I do.

He opens his desk drawer. Inside is a stack of candles. Some green, some purple, some red.

"Yours seems to be a difficult situation," says Jerry, "so we'll use a jumbo red candle."

"Thanks."

"Now—early evening—is the perfect time for candle burning. Also midnight, and when there's nothing good on television. Don't laugh. It's true. You need a time when the recipient will be vulnerable, like when the guy's asleep or daydreaming—like during bad TV. Another good time is rush hour. The guy's stuck on a subway—his mind is wandering—whammo!—his unconscious is yours."

Jerriatrics puts a cassette into his player. Out floats a musical montage of gushing waterfalls, sloshing oceans, harps, bells, and violins. The plastic flower turns willow. This is Jerry's famed *Water Tape*. It's supposed to have a soothing effect. But when I tried it, all it did was make me pee a lot.

"The music is to help you feel positive," says Jerry, "lift your consciousness to spiritual awareness. Okay, now, first we inscribe the candle with a special ceremonial knife—or, in my case, because I'm an art director, I use a ceremonial X-Acto knife—already blessed at home."

He carves into the candle my initals and a star—not the Jewish kind, the kind of star from second grade. At this point I get up, close the door. I don't want anyone nosying around (i.e., Joy).

"Venus oil," he says when I'm back in my seat. He holds up a cough-medicine-sized bottle filled with golden liquid. "To clean the candle. Some witches use plain ol' Lemon Pledge. It's a good scented mineral oil. But I prefer Venus oil, because it not only cleans, it charges the candle with extra energy."

"Like a product that cleans *and* deodorizes."

"Right. Only in this case, Venus oil cleans and charges the candle with love power."

He douses a small white cloth with Venus oil. The room fills with sweet scent. He hands the cloth to me, along with the candle.

"Rub from bottom to center, then top to center, as you think about meeting someone," says Jerry. "This brings good forces in. If you wanted to get rid of someone, you would rub from center to bottom, center to top."

I rub. I feel embarrassed by the sexual implications of rubbing a jumbo candle—like the candle's going to get even more jumbo.

Jerriatrics takes the candle back from me. He pulls from his knapsack a purple Bic lighter and a bronze candle holder. He gently jams the candle into the holder, lights it with the purple Bic.

"Stare into the flame," Jerry says. "Visualize meeting someone, being in love."

I stare at the flickering flame, trying to picture a man—trying to get Bryce's face out of my picture.

"Concentrate," says Jerry. "You've got to concentrate. If you think hard enough, your thoughts can become solid. Magic is not hocus-pocus—it is *focus*."

"Good tagline," I say.

"Concentrate," says Jerry. The music tinkles in the background, high and merry, lots of teeny bells. Jerriatrics calls out to the "gods and goddesses" (nice to know he's an equal-opportunity religious employer). He talks to them in fluent spiritualese about my situation, his voice cool and smooth as Noxzema. He sums things up with a "So mote it be," then turns to me.

"Now concentrate," he says. "We are the only creatures capable of changing our lives through imagination and will. Banish those feelings of I can't. Tell yourself I will, I will, I will find a man."

"I will, I will, I will, I have to write a will," I say. "I have to write a will."

"Concentrate on *positive* feelings. See yourself meeting someone. Stare into the flame. Fire is the element of transformation. Through it, change occurs. There is no end, no beginning, just change."

I stare into the flame, imagining the dark part in its middle as a man's silhouette, a flickering man, his arms outstretched toward me.

"You will meet someone. *You will*," Jerriatrics whispers, his voice soft as a Q-Tip.

I will, I will, I will, I
will, I will, I will, I
will, I will, I will, I will, I will, I will, I
will, I will, I will, I will, I will, I will, I
will, I will, I will, I will, I will, I will, I will, I will, I will, I will, I will,
I will, I will, I will, I will, I will, I will, I will, I will, I will, I will, I
will, I will, I will, I will, I will, I will, I will, I will, I will, I will, I will,
I will, I will, I will, I will, I will, I will, I will, I will, I will, I will, I
will, I will, I will, I will, I will, I will, I will, I will, I will, I will, I will,
I will, I will, I will, I will, I will, I will, I will, I will, I will, I will, I
will, I will, I will, I will, I will, I will, I will, I will, I will, I will, I will,
I will, I will, I will, I will, I will, I will, I will, I will, I will, I will, I
will, I will, I will, I will, I will, I will, I will, I will, I will, I will, I will,
I will, I will, I will, I will, I will, I will, I will, I will, I will, I will, I
will, I will, I will, I will, I will, I will, I will, I will, I will, I will, I will,
I will, I will, I will, I will, I will, I will, I will, I will, I will, I will, I
will, I will, I will, I will, I will, I will, I will, I will, I will, I will, I will,
I will, I will, I will, I will, I will, I will, I will, I will, I will, I will, I
will, I will, I will, I will, I will, I will, I will, I will, I will, I will, I will,
I will, I will, I will, I will, I will, I will, I will, I will, I will, I will, I
will, I will, I will, I will, I will, I will, I will, I will, I will, I will, I will,
I will, I will, I will, I will, I will, I will, I will, I will, I will, I will, I
will, I will, I will, I will, I will, I will, I will, I will, I will, I will, I will,
I will, I will, I will, I will, I will, I will, I will, I will, I will, I will, I
will, I will, I will, I will, I will, I will, I will, I will, I will, I will, I will,
I will, I will, I will, I will, I will, I will, I will, I will, I will, I will, I
will, I will, I will, I will, I will, I will, I will, I will, I will, I will, I will,
I will, I will, I will, I will, I will, I will, I will, I will, I will, I will, I
will, I will, I will, I will, I will, I will, I will, I will, I will, I will, I will,
I will, I will, I will, I will, I will, I will, I will, I will, I will, I will, I
will, I will, I will, I will, I will, I will, I will, I will, I will, I will, I will,
I will, I will, I will, I will, I will find love.
I am a woman with a mission.
Luckily I am also a woman with a health club membership.

I hail a cab, head over to my local health club, eager to do my part to give health clubs a bad name as pickup joints—which, joy of joys, they often can be. I know, it's "so seventies" meeting men at health clubs. But it is ever so practical. You get to check out the guy in shorts. It's like buying bacon—the kind packaged with see-through windows in the back. You get to peek—lean or fatty—so there's no surprises when you get home.

The health club's rather crowded for a Wednesday night, the Nautilus floor jam-packed with people pulling, pushing, pressing, compressing each with a look of determination that suggests they're here for a greater purpose, like energizing the bowels of some science fiction machine. Above me I hear the pounding of an aerobics class in progress. I think about joining in, but the last class I took was depressing. The instructor kept yelling: "Come on! Singles! Singles!" I thought she was referring to all us unmarried folk. Then when she yelled "Lunge! Lunge!" it sounded like "Lunch! Lunch!" so I left and got pizza.

I survey the place for PCMs. I note a rather yummy blond-haired, blue-eyed, pouty-lipped hunk with shoulders like the kind Norma Kamali outfits strive to imitate. He is a textbook example of love at first sight. And I definitely believe in love at first sight. It's love at ten thousand and first sight I'm no longer sure about.

I check myself out in the mirror. I am wearing my pink Danskin. Sometimes when I sweat my nipples show. No nipples yet. *I will, I will, I will, I will, I will, I will, I will, I will, I will, I will, I will meet him.*

I join him in line at an upper torso machine, pretend to do stretching exercises. One, two, three; up, two, three. I touch my toes, eager to impress him with my Gumby-like flexibility. Hunk-o senses my presence, looks down at me, smiles. My cue to speak.

"Now I know why they call this the weight room," I say. Hunk-o looks at me with sweaty furrowed brows. "Because all you do in here is wait." For emphasis, I motion to the line ahead.

Hunk-o finally gets it, laughs: a suppressed, asthmatic chuckle. I can tell he's not a Kidder. But he does have great biceps, another important quality in a man.

"Yeah, it's even worse on Mondays," Hunk-o says. "I usually come on Tuesdays."

I make a mental note: Tuesday, Nautilus room, wear black leotard.

Hunk-o continues: "I haven't worked out for a while—pulled my back out. This is the first I've lifted in, like, a month."

"Yeah, I pulled my back out a few months ago. It was awful. And a couple of weeks ago I twisted my knee. Every week, it's a different injury—sometimes I think it's healthier *not* to work out. Nobody ever hurt themselves opening a box of Entenmann's chocolate chip cookies. Although I must admit, there's a certain amount of joy you get out of the pain, you know, a kinda masochism involved—it feels good to hurt, you know?"

What I am saying? I now wonder.

"But I need these workouts," I say. "I have a lot of anxiety in me I need to get out of my system. If I didn't work out, I'd most likely be an ax murderer."

Hunk-o looks at me. He tries to read me—but I am like a subway map. Hunk-o smiles. Relief. I feel a trail of sweat trickling down my inner arm. *I will, I will, I will, I will, I will, I will, I will, I will, I will, I will, I will, I will get to know this guy.*

"So what's your name?" I ask.

"Mark Tivoli. And yours?"

"Sasha. Sasha Schwartz."

He puts his hand out for a handshake. "Nice to meet you," he says.

I pretend like the force of his hand is too much. I squinch my face in anguish.

"Wow," I say, "what a powerful grip."

Mark laughs. Although he's not a true Kidder, he does at least have Kidder appreciation skills. Finally it's his turn for the machine. He straps himself in. This is the machine where you flap your weighted arms up and down like a chicken. The Perdue Lean Machine.

"So, are you a dancer?" Mark asks.

Maybe I was wrong about this Mark guy. Maybe he *is* a Kidder.

"Me? A dancer?" I laugh.

"You look like you could be—you're in terrific shape."

"Oh, thanks, but, no . . ." I blush. I sweat. I am one big pink sweat droplet.

"So, what *do* you do?" Mark asks, struggling for a ninth chicken flap. His muscles bulge as he lifts. He's got voluptuous muscles. If Mark were a woman, he'd be a "chick."

"I'm in advertising," I say. "I write commercials."

"Oh yeah? Anything I know? No wait, let me guess. Soft drink, Coke? No . . ."

"Well, guess again. I wrote the Bully Toilet Bowl Cleaner jingle."

"The one to the tune of 'Wooly Bully'?"

"Yeah."

"Wow, you wrote that? That's great."

Mark smiles. I have impressed him. Not many women can claim to write toilet bowl cleaner jingles. He struggles for another chicken flap. His face alternates from grin to grimace, like the masks of Thesbus. Comedy. Tragedy. Comedy. Trage—

Trage—

Trage—

Mark seems to be stuck in Tragedy. He pushes harder. The veins in his neck grow junkie thick, plump and juicy, like a visual from a vampire instruction manual. Mark groans. Is this what he sounds like during sex? I wonder. Come on, Mark, get out of Tragedy. You can do it, boy.

—edy.

He makes it. Mark gets down from the machine, shakes himself out like a dog after a swim in a lake.

"Your turn," he says.

He's a tall one, this Mark. About six foot three. I'm only five foot two and suddenly feel like I've been amputated at the knees. I take my place in the Perdue torture chair. Mark gets on the next machine—the one that's like operating two extremely heavy stick shifts. We saddle ourselves in. That's when I notice the golden hair on his forearms—and his golden hairy legs, too. He's truly got a beautiful body. I begin fantasizing about what Mark must look like in clothes (since he's already practically naked). I envision how the folds of a shirt must fall over those sculpted muscles, how those muscles function at opening a cab door for me, or pulling out a chair for me at a restaurant—preferably a pricey French one, if that's his thing. I wonder what Mark's thing is. I wonder what he does for a living. At the health club it's difficult to figure. You're stripped of identity. Gone are all clues like jewelry, shoes, and taste in clothes. Basically, you stand naked before each other.

"So, what do *you* do?" I ask.

"Stock . . . bro . . . ker," he grunts . . . out . . . as . . . he . . . shifts.

Lovely. Just what I need. *Another* stockbroker. After Bryce, I swore I'd keep away from all stockbrokers—both romantically and professionally. Right before Bryce broke the engagement, he had sold me this one loser of a stock. It was bizarre. Both the relationship and the stock had started going downhill at the same time, as if the two were mystically intertwined. Within a month I went from being rich and loved to poor and alone.

But on the positive side, I am a good catch for a stockbroker. I'm already stock market inputted. Bryce used to talk with me for hours about the market. He'd get all excited discussing with me the latest bond deal or commodities trade. The *Wall Street Journal* was his *Playboy* magazine. Bryce had a philosophy for investing, typed and taped over his desk:

THE RISK AN INVESTOR TAKES
SHOULD BE BASED UPON WHAT HE'S WILLING TO LOSE,
AND NEVER BY WHAT HE SEEKS TO GAIN.

Not me. Me, I risk based on what I see to gain. And judging by the bulging contours of Mark's physique, I stand to gain a lot by the simple exchange of a piece of paper bearing my phone number.

I will, I will, I will, I will, I will, I will, I will, I will, I will, I will, I will, I will, I will get him to exchange phone numbers.

"So you're a stockbroker?" I say. "Got any hot tips?" I try to sound flirty and coy. A difficult task when you've got thirty-pound wings strapped to your arms. I see myself in the mirror. My hair's all stiff and spiky from sweat: nature's Dippity-Do.

"Actually I'm an institutional broker," he says, "not retail."

I nod as if I know what that means. I am afraid to reveal I'm not inputted for that subject matter. For a moment we're both silent, except for an occasional grunt and groan.

"So, you live around here?" I ask, trying to keep the conversation flowing with Johnny Carson ease.

"Hudson. Just a short walk over."

I finish up my tenth flap, climb down—to the obvious joy of this wannabe stud who's been impatiently waiting for the machine, arms crossed like a male genie, hoping I'd wimp out. He's wearing one of those ridiculous halfsie midriff shirts. A bright yellow one. "What's the matter?" I want to say. "Can't you afford a whole shirt?"

"And you?" Mark asks. "You live nearby?"

"About ten blocks away. I take a cab here. My yellow limousine. I feel guilty, lazy, you know, pulling up to the health club in a cab— and leaving in one—like the cab driver's looking at me, you know, thinking, like, 'Yeah, *sure* this girl's working out. . . .' "

"So, why don't you walk? It's good exercise," Mark says: the voice of reason.

"Yeah, I know, silly me."

What are these words coming out of my mouth? Sometimes I can do a great impression of a dizzy broad. I decide when I get home I'm going to yell at myself, and maybe not even talk to myself for a day or so.

"But it's good exercise hailing those cabs, too," I say. "Great for the upper arm and wrist."

I demonstrate: a woman hailing a cab.

Mark laughs. I'm not sure if he's just being polite. I can't figure out if he likes me yet. He keeps staring at my chest when I talk. I look down to make sure everything's in order: no nipples. My heart's pounding. My muscles feel tense. It's exhausting meeting men. Picking up a 180-pound barbell would be easier than picking up this 180-pound guy. I don't remember falling in love being this difficult. Isn't it supposed to happen in one swift motion, without all this concentration? Shouldn't one in theory be able to make a tuna fish sandwich and fall in love, both at the same time? With Bryce, it was that easy. *Bim-bam-boom:* LOVE. He was wearing turquoise socks. I saw the turquoise socks and knew. Silly, I know, but they matched his tie quite nicely. Yes, Bryce was a great dresser. Then I remember: *maybe too good a dresser to be hetero.*

"Are you okay?" Mark asks, wondering, I'm sure, why I'm standing motionless, staring into empty air.

"I'm beat from aerobics," I lie. But it feels like truth. I feel like I've just taken a high-impact aerobics class.

"I think I'm going to call it quits for today," I tell Mark.

He looks down at his sneakers: Reeboks, neatly tied. Frannie's done ads for Reeboks. The target audience is emulators. Nikes are for achievers. Emulators are those who imitate achievers, those a little on the insecure side.

"Hey, look, I'm pretty much done too," says Mark. "Would you like to grab a bite to eat?"

Bingo! Touchdown! Score! *Ding! Ding! Ding!*

"Maybe," I say, ever so calmly. "That would be very nice."

I can't believe it. From out of nowhere I have a date with an incredible hunk. Could he be it? The real thing? And could Jerry's candle ceremony be responsible? Could all this be due to the magic of a lit red candle? Or was it the magic of my plunging pink Danskin? Or could it be, as Frannie suggested, my smell that attracted Mark? An animal response to my primal sweat? To be on the safe side, I don't shower.

Mmm. That's for me!" I think.

I am looking at Mark, who's waiting for me in the health club lobby.

"Sasha!" Mark calls to me. "There you are. I was afraid I wasn't going to recognize you with your clothes on!" Mark says this loudly, for passersby to hear. He's trying to make Kidder status. I appreciate the effort, laugh to reward him.

Actually, Mark has a point. He looks different in his suit than he did in workout gear. I now empathize with Lois Lane's myopia. I never understood how she couldn't recognize Clark Kent as Superman in a blazer and tie. I mean, come on! But now here's Mark in a suit, looking totally different. The lines in his face have realigned with his suit's pinstripes, so his whole being appears straight and upward.

He takes my gym bag—so he's holding this, his gym bag, a briefcase, *and* a *Wall Street Journal*. With all this in tow, he still manages to open the door for me. Such a mensch!

We walk down the street together. I don't like Mark's walk. He's got that ride-'em-cowboy swagger that athletic men often have. But who am I to complain? At least he's not walking away from me.

"This restaurant okay?" Mark asks, referring to a place called Szechuan Palace. "You eat Chinese?"

"Oh, I eat everything. Even brussels sprouts."

Mark interprets this as a go-ahead. We enter the "Palace," and are immediately greeted by a young Oriental man.

"Good evening," he says, nodding at us both like we are a couple. We look like a couple, Mark and me. He leads us to a table near a young Oriental family, whose three-year-old daughter is discovering the artistic possibilities of sesame noodles, creating 3-D Kandinski effects over table and chair.

"Could we have a quieter table?" says Mark.

A man of action!

The Oriental guy nods, smiles, nods, laughs, nods, nods, smiles, nods, then leads us to the back.

Immediately upon sitting, Mark unfolds his napkin, places it on his lap. (A man of good breeding, too.) Now that Mark's sitting, not walking, he looks more attractive again. I definitely prefer Mark sitting to walking. And I can't wait to find out what other positions I enjoy him in. I study his fingers, so as to feel comfortable with them, in case they're going to be touching me later. I like them: thick, but not hairy; clean nails; no wedding bands.

"So," says Mark.

And nice thumbs. Not too wide.

"So," I cleverly counter. But I don't know what to say after that. Me, a woman who works with words, without any of these co-workers of mine to work for me now, when I need them. Chinese music tinkles in the background, reminiscent of Jerry's *Water Tape*. I can't wait to tell Jerry about this tomorrow. I can't wait for more tomorrows.

"So, tell me about yourself," Mark says. He clears his throat. "Do you come from a big family, small family?"

"Well, I'm five foot two, my mother's five foot three. . . ."

Mark looks perplexed, then laughs. Or he could just be clearing his throat again. It's hard to tell.

"I meant, any brothers and sisters?"

"No, just me. I'm an only child."

Yes, even in childhood I was cursed to be a "single."

"Really? I'm an only child, too," Mark says.

Way to go, Cupid! This shared trait will help us along in our relationship. We already understand a bit about each other. We grew up together being alone. *You don't have to be alone anymore, Mark,* I am thinking. *You can stay with me. I could use a little loving.*

"Mom almost never had me," says Mark. "She tried real hard to get pregnant. She loves kids. Before I came along she played with the neighborhood kids. We had a pool. All the kids came over to our house for the pool. One of them brought a Hula Hoop. Mom played with the Hula Hoop and soon after got pregnant. Dad was convinced it was the Hula Hoop, like it shook up something inside her. After her first pregnancy—me—Dad got Mom another Hula Hoop. But it didn't work again."

I wonder if Mark's going to make the moves tonight. He seems sweet and innocent, but those are the ones you have to watch out for—or so I'm hoping.

"I'm hungry," Mark says. "Let's order."

As Mark prepares to read his menu, I prepare to read Mark. Since my experience with Chang and Bryce, I believe you can tell a lot about a man by how he orders in Chinese restaurants. It's a matter of group dynamics. Is he assertive in his decision? To the point of aggression? Does he yield too quickly? Is he indecisive? Decisive? Willing to take chances?

To help family and friends analyze their family and friends, I've devised a list of categories Chinese food orderers can fall under:

> **The Wimp:** If your dinner date makes you do all the ordering, watch out. He's either unable to take charge or seeking an out, so later he can blame you for poorly made decisions. Either way, I wouldn't touch this guy with a ten-foot chopstick.

> **The Territorialist:** If your dinner date insists you keep your dinner orders separate, keep your lives separate. This guy is obviously not a generous spirit.

> **Mr. I'm Right:** If your dinner date insists: "Let's order what I say we'll order," order a cab home. This type's tyrannical demands will extend beyond beef and broccoli into beefs on politics and art.

> **Mr. Right:** If I'm lucky, Mark will fall under this fourth and forthright category. He will speak up, listen to my needs, and together, with a little spare ribbing, we'll both decide what to order. Rather than pooh-pooh pork strips, we'll order a Pu Pu Platter, so there's something for everyone.

And although Mark might not want soup, he'll ask me if I'd like some. Suddenly I'm a wonton woman. He's open to compromise.

"So, what do you like?" Mark asks.

"Pork strips."

I say it like the challenge it's meant to be.

"Sounds good to me. Okay, we'll start with pork strips. Then how about Moo Goo Gai Pan?" Mark asks.

"How about General Sao's Chicken?" I counter.

"What's that?"

"Same as Moo Goo Gai Pan, only spicier."

"Spicy? I can't eat spicy. I sweat. Really, I do. Just like I've been benching or something. When I eat spicy food, I need to wear a sweatband."

Wimp.

I feign a sympathetic smile. "We could ask them not to make it too spicy," I say.

"Okay then. As long as it's not too spicy. And let's see, how about beef and broccoli?"

Bad news. The less adventurous the dish, the less adventurous the man. But since Mark went along with my choice of General Sao, I agree.

Our waiter wanders over, takes our order, and to my horror leaves me alone with Mark to talk again. A silence spreads itself between us like an added table leaf. Mark clears his throat.

"How'd you get into advertising?" he asks.

So that's what it's going to be: the Sasha Schwartz 101 course. Good. I can handle this.

"It was my mom's idea. She was trying to convince me out of pursuing my own career goal, becoming a famous rock star."

"I wanted to be a rock star, too," says Mark. "I was a drummer back in high school."

If what Jerry has hinted about drummers having "ambidextrous skills" is true, I'm in luck—that is, if Mark's a talented drummer.

I throw Mark a pair of chopsticks. "Let's see your stuff."

Mark bangs out a little ditty on the table.

"Yeah," I say. "I think you have what it takes. You just have to let your hair grow long in back. Grow a ponytail."

"Yeah, right! Mom would kill me. Mom's always trying to get me to cut my hair."

"Mine, too."

More points in common. If this were a TV game show, we'd have won a refrigerator-freezer by now—or better yet, a bedroom set. Mark clears his throat again. That's his thing, I guess, when he's nervous, clearing his throat.

The waiter arrives with our pork strip appetizer.

"These look great," says Mark. "I love pork."

"Me too. I was twenty when I had my first pork," I say—then, realizing that sounds a bit provocative, quickly add: "My mom brought me up kosher. Pork isn't kosher."

"Are your parents very religious?"

"My mom became more so after my dad passed away."

"Oh . . . sorry about your dad. Was that recently?"

"When I was seven."

"It's rough having a parent die. I know. My dad passed away earlier this year."

In a sick, sick—very sick—way this is happy news. It's yet another thing to bring us closer in the years to come.

"It's been hard—not just on me, but on Mom," says Mark. "Mom's been in bad shape."

I note Mark's being democratic about sharing the pork strips. Waiting for me to take another before he does, like a game of checkers.

"Is your mom dating?" I ask. "Do you fix her up with your friends?"

"Yeah, right. I mean, no. Mom doesn't date. She's got a dog."

"I see."

"She believes my dad was reincarnated into this dog. She calls the dog Chooch—my dad's nickname, short for Choochee Face."

Good news: nicknames are a sign of a happy marriage. Mark is most likely bondable.

"It's interesting," says Mark. "The dog watches the same TV shows my dad liked—and leaves the room during the ones Dad hated. He even likes the same foods as Dad—and refuses to eat Mom's chicken croquettes, just like Dad, so Mom's convinced the dog is Dad."

More good news: when the guy's mother is like something out of a Tennessee Williams play, I know I'm the neurotic girl of his dreams. Though Jerriatrics would defend Mark's mom as not being nutty at all. Maybe Jerriatrics knows what he's talking about. His candle lighting seems to have helped me find a flame. Mark's great. Sexy. Sweet. A family man. And best of all, Mark's got no pinkie rings. I hate pinkie rings.

The waiter brings over two heaping plates of goopy food. Mark scoops out some on my plate first, then his, then reaches for his fork to eat. A bad sign. If Mark can't handle chopsticks, how will he ever be able to handle me?

"I'm worried about Mom," says Mark. "She spends way too much time with Chooch. She rarely leaves the house."

"Your mom will get over it in time," I say. "My mom freaked when my dad died. She didn't listen to music for years because it all reminded her of him—my dad was a musician. She threw out the stereo, all his albums, everything. She wanted to deny he was ever alive. We got into big fights about it 'cause I was the opposite. I wanted to deny he was dead. I always wanted to talk about him. I think to forget about a person is metaphysical murder. That's how you kill someone off. To forget the dinosaur, that's gonna be the dinosaur's real extinction."

Mark stares at me intently. What am I saying? My mouth just keeps going, and going, and going . . . like the Energizer bunny on those commercials.

"I lied to you before," Mark says.

I'm worried. He's married. He's one of quintuplets. I don't look like a dancer.

"About hurting my back lifting," he says. "I haven't lifted in months because—I can't believe I'm admitting this—my dad was the one who got me into lifting. I stopped lifting because I didn't want to be reminded of Dad. My girlfriend thought this was ridiculous."

A girlfriend who didn't understand him! A positioning point! I can appeal to my target audience by promising something the competition can't.

"I don't think it's ridiculous at all, Mark," I say.

Mark smiles. Little beads of sweat glisten above his brow. Mark's right. He does sweat from spicy food. It's kind of cute though, his sweating.

"But you shouldn't think it's bad that lifting reminds you of y dad," I say warmly. "That's his way of being in your life still. M(ory's a great power. Memory conquers death."

"Memory conquers death. I like that," says Mark.

"You know, it's good to be able to talk like this," says Mark. "That's why I finally broke up with my girlfriend. She never wanted to talk about things."

"Yeah, my boyfriend, Bryce, was like that, too," I say.

This time our eyes not only meet across the table, they do it on the table.

"So, what happened with you and your boyfriend? You still see him?" Mark asks.

"No, things weren't working out, so I shot him."

Mark almost chokes.

"Just kidding," I say.

When the waiter comes with the check, Mark refuses to let me pay—unlike the "Let's go dutch" settler Bryce.

"So what do you want to do now?" Mark asks, grabbing up our stuff to go.

"I don't know. You decide. I'm just the subservient female."

"Oh no, you're much more than that."

"You're right. I'm a very, *very* subservient female."

We leave the restaurant. I want so badly to hold Mark's hand, but he's busy holding my gym bag and assorted belongings. He clears his throat.

"I had a terrific evening," he says.

"Me too."

"You going to be around this weekend?"

"Sure."

"You should give me your number. Maybe we can get together."

Mark searches his suit jacket for paper and pen. My heart is pounding so hard I'm ready for Mark to ask what that noise is. Viv told me when men ask her for her number, she never writes it down. She makes them memorize it, as a test to see how much they really want to go out with her. I tell her she must go out with a lot of accountants this way.

I write down my number, aware of my handwriting, making sure it's especially feminine, pretty, and most of all legible. God forbid Mark won't be able to read it.

"Thanks," says Mark, holding my number as if it were a valuable autograph.

We continue to walk. It's a cold night; a slight chill wafts in the air.

"Cold, isn't it?" I say, trying to make conversation. "I wish God would turn the heat up just a bit. God makes a terrible landlord, don't you think?"

"Listen, if you're cold," says Mark, "I could get you a cab."

Before I can object, he raises his hand high. Immediately, a cab screeches toward us.

"You need money for cab fare?" asks Mark, opening the cab door for me.

"No, no, I'm fine."

"I'll definitely call you tomorrow," he says, smiling warmly. I sense the sexual tension between us, the two of us, magnetically being drawn together, the power of the planets overhead tugging at our mortal bodies. Mark gives me a peck on the cheek. That's all: a peck.

"Hurry up, buddy! I'm goin'!" the cabbie threatens.

I get in the cab.

"I really liked talking like this," Mark says to me before closing the door. "Nobody talks anymore. It was nice, just to talk."

Great. Out of all the sex fiends in New York, I wind up with a talker. Doesn't Mark realize actions are more fun than words? Not that I was asking for the whole sexual intercourse thing. Just something a little more passionate than a peck. He even made that sound my Aunt Rosalie makes when she kisses me hello at weddings and bar mitzvahs. "Mwah!" Just like Aunt Rosalie—except Mark pecked me on the cheek, and Aunt Rosalie pecks me on the lips; and it's kind of depressing to think I've gone further with my Aunt Rosalie than I have with Mark.

So far.

Bryce who? I am thinking as I head into the bathroom, strip off my sweaty Danskin. *Bryce who?* I am thinking as I turn on the bathtub water, watch it splash down in a panic, then calmly rise to the surface. I am rewarding myself for my strenuous night of picking up weights and men with an indulgent hot soak in the tub. I wait till the water's as steamy and frothy as cappuccino. I step in. Ah. *Mark,* I am thinking. My muscles melt into the water. My body transforms from solid to liquid. *Mark. Mark. Mark.* His name is my new mantra.

I've brought the paper into the tub with me. I've got all the comforts a girl could want right here in my tub: TV, phone, magazines, loofah pad—everything but a man. *Mark,* I think: *Mark, Mark, Mark.*

I randomly flip through the paper. The first thing I see is an article on AIDS. The word is starting to look different to me now: longer, taller, misspelled: *AIDS.*

According to the New York State Department of Health, "women and children are becoming a fast-growing group of people infected. New York City is the nation's AIDS capital, accounting for more than 20 percent of the total AIDS cases."

This is not good news. This is not good energy. I must think positive thoughts. *Mark,* I tell myself. *Relax, there's Mark, Mark, MARK.* Even if it's not love, a cheap tawdry affair—condomed, of course—could be nice.

Maybe it's my obscene caller who's got me all revved up about sex—but suddenly I'm thinking sex is all I've been missing. Not Bryce, but sex. Once I get some action, it will surely be: *Bryce who?* I wonder if I ask Mark nicely if he'll agree to have sex with me. If so, I hope I remember how. They say you never forget. It's like riding a bike. But in that case I must have forgotten, because I remember it more like windsurfing.

I try to creatively visualize as Jerry instructs: I envision Mark on top of me. Me on top of Mark. I'm having trouble getting a vivid picture. It's like TV without the cable hookup. I try for an easier picture: I envision Mark calling. Still no luck. I try for an even easier picture: I turn on my TV.

Lucky me. I'm just in time for Johnny Carson's monologue. I love Johnny. He is a High-Class Kidder. Joanna can have her alimony. I'd take the man over the loot any day. I sit in my tub, alone, laughing. My laughter sounds strange. The sound of one larynx clapping. Damn Bryce. He's even spoiled watching TV for me. An activity ripe for one now seems one man short. I feel stupid here alone laughing. Only insane people laugh in rooms all alone. Insane people, and single people.

Bryce and I used to love to watch TV together. We'd rent VCR films—and play VCR games. Our favorite was *Under the Volcano*, a film in which Albert Finney plays a swaggering drunk. Bryce and I rented the film one evening and sat watching Albert swig as we sipped at our bottle of Cabernet Sauvignon. Then Bryce suggested that every time Albert took a swig, we should join him. By the end of the film we had finished off two bottles of red—occasionally cheating by putting Albert on rewind so he'd drink, and drink, and drink, and so might we.

And then there were all those old musicals we rented, challenging each other on who knew more of the lyrics by heart. We'd sing along with *Hello Dolly, My Fair Lady, The Sound of Music.*

Hmmmmmm. . . . All stereotypical as *effeminately* loved films, and all loved by Bryce. Could Bryce have been . . . ? No, not my Bryce. And if he was, why oh why oh why do I still want to call/see/hear/fuck Bryce? *Mark,* I think: *Mark. Mark will watch TV with me.* Already my new mantra is losing its power. I concentrate harder: *MARK.*

I reach for the soap, find a sliver the width of a credit card.

Beside it rests a pile of Bryce's halfheartedly smoked cigarette butts, along with his bright yellow Bic lighter. With a flick from his Bic, I set Bryce's butt on fire. I inhale. It's a little stale, but tasty nonetheless. Then again, what do I know? I'm not a smoker. Though now seems an appropriate time to start, since I might be dying anyway.

I stand up in the tub, cigarette in mouth, feeling big and fiery: I am the Loch Ness monster emerging from the lake. I wrap the towel around me, stub out Bryce's butt on the newspaper, head to my bedroom, flip through my pile of cassettes for something inspirational . . . find a nonlabeled pirated cassette and plunk it into my player. "Rescue Me" comes wafting out. I love this song, its driving beat. The music blasts through my apartment, vibrating my walls, my nightstand, my hair.

Varro said flute pieces helped his gout pains. King David said harp music cured mental problems. Homer said a warrior's choral singing could prevent the plague. And my dad always said there's nothing like good rock 'n roll to stave off total depression.

I turn the volume up louder. "Rescue me!" I belt out. *"Rescue me, Mark! Yeah, Mark, rescue me!"*

Then the phone rings.

I turn down the music and listen closely to the ringing, wondering if it's Mark, trying to discern in it some Mark accent. I pick up.

"Hello," I say.

"It's me," says my obscene caller. "I have nothing on. What are you wearing?"

"This lovely, plush, terry robe I got on sale at La Petite Coquette last month. Twenty-nine ninety-five reduced from eighty-five. Quite a deal."

"Right now I'm envisioning you taking off that robe. Then I'd massage oil all over your luscious body, gently massaging it on your breasts."

I settle back on my bed, prop a pillow beneath my neck.

"I'd rub the oil near your pussy," he says, "never quite touching you, just a little out of reach, until you begged for me to touch you— or lick you . . ."

It's relaxing listening to him talk. Some people like to watch. I guess I like to listen.

"I'd rub oil on your toes," he says, "then lick the oil off, being sure to lick carefully in between each toe."

This guy could and should have his own radio talk show. He'd have definite followers. Of course, for me it helps that he sounds so much like Bryce. His voice works like music on me, reawakening in me, the way a song might, my memories of Bryce.

"Then I'd tickle your clit lightly with my tongue, quick and light, then slow, and hard."

I am starting to feel guilty—not about being part of this, but about not being *enough* of a part. I feel like I should be offering to do something back to him, hold up my end—so to speak.

"I'd want you to do more than lick me," I say. "I'd want your cock, your hard cock inside me."

"Oooh, baby."

"I'd love to feel how deep you could get inside me. I bet you could go real deep."

"I could, baby. And I want to, I want you sooo much."

For as much as I don't respect words, I admit they have power. Fairy tales advertise the power of *abracadabra*. Catholicism prescribes its dose of "take a few Hail Mary's and call in the morning." And me, I'm now a believer in the emotional restorative powers of phone sex.

4.

X

THERE IS ONLY ONE WORLD AND THAT
WORLD IS FALSE CRUEL
CONTRADICTORY MISLEADING
SENSELESS. . . . WE NEED LIES TO
VANQUISH THIS REALITY, THIS "TRUTH."
WE NEED LIES IN ORDER TO LIVE. . . .
THAT LYING IS A NECESSITY OF LIFE, IS
ITSELF A PART OF THE TERRIFYING AND
PROBLEMATIC CHARACTER OF
EXISTENCE.
—NIETZSCHE

**Sometimes you feel like a
nut, sometimes you don't.
—Mounds and Almond Joy**

H

ey, look at you!" Jerriatrics says.

"You look great!"

"It's the glow of death."

Jerriatrics hands me one of the two coffees he's carrying, then sits on my desk like a secretary in a B movie. Today he's wearing a black shirt buttoned up tight to the collar: a preppy priest. "You met someone last night, didn't you?" He sounds so confident that it crosses my mind he's paid Mark to meet me and go out.

I tell him about Mark. How we met. How cute Mark is. How Mark used to be a drummer.

"Ah, then Mark must be sexy." Jerry sips his coffee. He's smiling so wide I expect the coffee to leak out from his lips' edges. "Perhaps I'm going to make a spiritual believer out of you yet. I can't wait for you to meet Bob today. Bob's the best."

"Do you really believe the candle helped me meet Mark? It could have been a coincidence. I was due to meet someone. Believe me, I was due."

"I believe it was your believing. That's what witchcraft is: *wish*-craft. Even having a little faith in the candle helped. You know, years ago people lit candles all the time. They practiced all kinds of magic without thinking twice. They stirred cake batter clockwise for good luck, hung garlic over babies' cribs for protection. You still see some of this today. People throwing salt over their shoulder. Knocking on wood. But most magical practices are gone."

"Yeah, I guess we're getting more rational. As we get civilized, we get more rational."

"Rational? Sasha. Did you say we're getting rational?" He jumps up from my desk top. "Is it rational to destroy our earth, our water, our sky? And Vietnam? The Gulf War? Is that rational?"

"Well, I . . . uh . . ."

"Look what man's doing to nature," Jerry says, now standing behind my desk, talking at me from behind it, like it's a pulpit. "Man plays with minerals, gems, oil, as if he can pick up more at the 7-Eleven. Our forests, our big, huge forests, are disappearing. And mankind's not spending its time and money on studies to help its preservation, but to lead to its *destruction*. It's scary thinking what's in our atomic backyards—and knowing man has never created something he did not use."

"Not true. I never use half the gadgets on my VCR. I don't know anyone who uses all those gadgets."

Jerry gives me his don't-be-an-asshole grimace—the one usually reserved for Mike during meetings.

"Man hasn't been getting more rational, Sasha. Man has to *re-learn* to be rational, and not react to his needs of the moment." Jerry bangs his fist on my desk. "Man has to ask himself what the effects of his actions are! It's up to us, within the laws of karma, to use our will, our powers, to set things right again!"

I suppress an urge to yell "Hallelujah."

I suppress an urge to compliment Jerry on his diaphragm projection.

I suppress an urge to tell Jerry to give up advertising and become a preacher. What *is* a guy like Jerry doing in a job like this anyway?

What I finally do say is this:

"Jer, don't you ever feel guilty being in advertising? Don't you think it's spiritually wrong saying a toothpaste is going to help someone find love?"

Jerry smiles. He delicately sips at his coffee, like it's fine wine—or a Folgers taste test. "Hey, it couldn't hurt," he says.

"That's good, Jer, as a tag. An honest approach. 'Close-Up toothpaste. It couldn't hurt.' "

"If someone believes a toothpaste will help them," says Jerry, "who knows, who's to say, maybe it will."

The phone rings.

"Excuse me," I say. "I think that's my future calling."

I hear a crunch on the other end of the phone. Why can't Viv ever eat quiet foods? Oatmeal, bananas, cotton candy?

"How goes it?" Viv asks.

I tell her all about Mark—almost all. I leave out the part about Jerriatrics's candle-lighting ceremony, highlight the part about Mark's enticing pectorals—and not so enticing peck good-night. Viv thinks I shouldn't be discouraged by Mark's peck.

"It must mean he really likes you," Viv explains.

"Great, so if Mark throws up on me, that means he loves me, right?"

In response, Viv crunches. I switch ears. My left ear is starting to feel sore and flattened out like a dried apricot. I'm developing Phone Ear. This condition has struck before. I've considered getting a speakerphone at home to cut back on ear usage, only I like to move as I talk. For me, the length of the telephone call is in direct proportion to the length of the telephone cord. If the cord can stretch into kitchen, bathroom, living room, there need never be reason to remove the phone from one's ear.

"So, Viv," I say, "do you know what an institutional stockbroker is? That's Mark's job. Is it the kind where Mark could work from home once the kids are born?"

"Kids? So soon? Aren't you rushing things a bit?"

"Unlike you, I want to settle down."

"Do you hear that expression? The word *settle* in 'settle down'? Don't take the first decent guy that comes along. Continue shopping. You know what Plato says? Each of us is really half of a being, divided by a curse. Through love we pursue our other half."

"Yeah, that's how I feel since Bryce left: like I am fifty percent off. Like discounted merchandise. Like some marked-down dress

145

hanging wrinkled on some sales rack. Fifty percent off, that's me. Half my former self now that Bryce is gone."

Viv sighs loudly. "I say fuck Plato! I want a love that doubles my pleasure, doubles my fun. You should too, Sasha. You shouldn't feel like fifty percent off without a man. You shouldn't need a man to feel complete."

"Did you know that products that are consistently discounted are eventually seen by consumers as lower quality? Too much discounting can permanently ruin a product's value in the marketplace. No wonder no worthwhile man is running to pick me up, if I'm labeling myself at fifty percent off. If I'm going to find a valuable love—"

"Sasha?"

"Yes, Viv?"

"Why are you so stuck on this love theme? You know, there *are* other things in life. Love is just another emotion, like anger, fear, or hate."

I *have* been rather lovecentric.

"Maybe it's because I'm working on this love strategy," I offer. "You know, selling love for Close-Up."

"Bullshit. You've always been like this."

"I . . . I'm sorry. You're right."

"Of course I'm right."

"We'll talk about something else. How are you and Keith— ooops, that's still about love, isn't it?"

"Maybe not."

"What do you mean?"

"I don't know if I want to talk about it."

"Talk about what? *What?*"

"Keith and I had a big fight about this TV pregnancy. I'm very concerned about sending the wrong message to the TV public by not getting that abortion. Keith told me I'm not the chef, I'm the waitress, just serve the goddamn lines. Can you believe it?"

"Keith loves you. He doesn't want you to get fired—go on permanent pregnancy leave, you know?"

"I can't carry this child much longer. I'm making a statement I don't want to make. We women have a right to decide what to do with our bodies. It's not up to priests who don't even have sex or a uterus—or any man, for that matter. If white heterosexual men gave birth, you know abortion would be another story. It seems the only way to get someone to care about a cause is for it to personally concern them. Like I'm sure now that you think Bryce might be bi and you might be at risk, you're considering donating money to AIDS research."

"Good idea."

"What a selfish world we live in."

"Selfish? I just said I might donate money."

"Because it now concerns you. Don't you see? You should already be donating your time and money to AIDS research, just knowing so many are suffering. It's a good thing the media finally got white heterosexual men paranoid, or AIDS funding might never have gotten going. The media controls our fears. That's why I must talk Gary into giving me that abortion, so I can let the public know the dangers of losing our reproductive freedom."

"You're right."

"Of course I'm right."

"So what are you going to do?"

"I'm going to take Gary to dinner tonight, talk some sense into him."

"But, Viv, it's 'Girls Night Out' tonight."

"Ooops . . ."

Every few months we girls get together at an expensive restaurant to indulge in New York's finest cuisine and practice our eye-to-eye contact skills, which can get a little rusty from talking on the phone so much.

"Okay," says Viv, "I'll ask Gary for tomorrow night. But this is important. I don't want to put my selfish needs—my career, making money—before my personal beliefs—my values. I have integrity, you know? Integrity."

"Yeah, I know integrity," I say. "I remember integrity well. So, tell me, how's integrity doing?"

I

t was my mother who convinced me to go into advertising. She was constantly clipping articles from magazines that hyped how happy ad copywriters were; how they got to vent their creativity, write music, even sing in some commercials—and actually had money—and even better, *stability*. It was both of our second professional choices for me. My mom's first was me being a lawyer. My first was me being a performer like my dad. I had wanted to sing my lungs out about love and pain—make people feel, emote, question, laugh—in the tradition of a modern Cole Porter. I still fantasize about forming my all-girl band, The Chicklets. The reviewers will describe us as:

"A Rock 'n Cole Band!"

"Cole Porter with Cleavage and Soul!"

"The Past Mixed with a Promising Future!"

"Gutsy, Brazen, Thought and Laugh Provoking!"

"We've Got a Star in Sasha Schwartz!"

But I have sold my soul to the advertising devil. In exchange for fine Italian shoes, an enviable earring collection, and Chinese food delivery whenever I want, I now must convince the public that love, passion, and the lambada could be theirs with the dab of a toothpaste—and that no matter how good their lives are, they could be happier, more beautiful, more loved . . . this week only, at a special price not available elsewhere.

But alas, I am paying the price. Right now I am sitting here thinking the reason it's 10:20 (10:05) and Mark hasn't called is because he didn't find me attractive enough. If I were more attractive, Mark would have called by 10:20 (10:05).

It's ironic—some might even say *justice*—that I have become a victim of the very ads I write. Last year I had my chance for redemption. Mike put me on an ice cream account. I suggested to him we cast fat women in the spots, sell fat as chic. People would buy more product; millions of women would be a lot happier.

Admittedly I said this as a joke, but it's true. I do have power to change society's perception of perfection, and save a lot of women a lot of torment, when it's 10:30 (10:15) the next day and the guy hasn't called and they're wondering if it's because they're not attractive enough.

Though the movie industry is also to blame. What's unfair is the double standard for casting lead men. Look at Humphrey Bogart, Dustin Hoffman, Dudley Moore, Woody Allen, Danny DeVito, John Candy. None of them beauties, yet all have costarred in movies with beautiful women by their sides.

You'd never see a Roseanne type cast with Mel Gibson.

Not to stereotype—but then again, to go right ahead and stereotype—neither heterosexual men nor gay women—meaning, those appealing to a female target audience—neither of these groups torture themselves over their looks. But those of us appealing to a male target audience, like gay men and we heterosexual women—we all drive ourselves bonkers wondering when it's 10:40 (10:25) and the guy hasn't called if it's because we're not attractive enough.

Gay men share many of the problems that heterosexual women do. It's because we share the same oppressors. Chauvinistic hetero men who fear our feminine side, because they fear it in themselves. I'm sounding like a feminist—a word that unfortunately got itself caught up in a bad semantic crowd, hanging around with *bitch* and *angry bitch*. It's even worse for a man to admit to feminism. There's that dainty syllable "fem" for him to contend with. Feminism needs to be reintroduced, remarketed for the nineties. We need to find a new word. Like *equinist*. It's a *nice* word. There's no bitterness in it, no taking sides. If we found a way to imply that men who were equinists had large penises, you could be sure more hetero men would hop on the semantic bandwagon.

When we've accomplished that, if we could find a way to imply that men who call before noon had large penises, that would be something.

Why oh why oh why oh why is it 10:45 (10:30) and Mark hasn't called?

R eady to crank on Close-Up?" Jerriatrics asks. He is standing in my office doorway, shaking Toronto up and down.

"I'm already cranky from Close-Up," I say. "Dying is almost preferable to working on Close-Up. And if I do die, and there is such a thing as reincarnation, next life I don't want to come back as a human. I want to be something that doesn't feel, like a tree, or a rock—or *a man!*"

"Whoa! What is it with you, Sasha?"

"Why? What?"

"Even if Bryce is bi, it doesn't mean you're dying of AIDS."

"But—"

"And if Bryce is heterosexual, you're still at risk. So if you're going to be hypochondriacal, don't just limit it to AIDS. There's a whole selection of diseases brewing out there that the media has been less vocal about but are omnipresent just the same. Just think, you could have lung disease. With one in ten as the odds, you probably have a higher chance of having lung disease than AIDS."

"Thanks for cheering me up, Jer."

"It's just that I hate the way the media exploits advertising AIDS as this gay disease. Look at you. Suddenly you're so eager to think you're a dead woman because you might have kissed a bisexual."

"I don't think you understand, Jer."

"I understand, Sasha. It's a defense mechanism. You'd rather think about your own death than the death of your relationship. You've got to move on, get out of this negative mind-set. You're going to live. A long future awaits you."

"I'm trying. But it's hard to stay positive when you see nothing in this long future. It's now ten till eleven and Mark hasn't called."

Jerry chuckles softly. "That's the difference between you and me, Sash. I see it as only ten-fifty."

My turn to chuckle. "Tell you what," I say. "Can we at least not work on Close-Up for a bit? Let's take a break."

"Fine."

"Thanks."

"We'll work on Bufferin," says Jerry. He shakes up Toronto again. The snow begins drifting languidly toward the snowman's shoulders: snow dandruff. "Just until all the snow drifts to bottom on this."

:30 TV, Bufferin

THE VISUAL:

A man is diving in slow motion through a beatific blue sky. Very surreal. Or so it seems. Then we reveal below him a body of water. He is diving into the water. He goes in, and under. Beautiful fish abound. It is tranquil, peaceful. He is at peace.

THE COPY:

To attain a stronger control of the mind one must first set it free, release the clutter of the day's events, lighten it from stress, tension, pain. Bufferin helps the mind achieve this headache-free level. Within minutes it works, freeing the mind of headache pain, so you can get on to the important things in life.

THE TAGLINE:

BUFFERIN. FREES THE MIND OF HEADACHE PAIN.

We did it. Jerriatrics and I at last wrote a pain-free, humor-free aspirin spot. I count the words. Copywriters know they have room for only sixty-eight words in a thirty-second spot. Seventy words after a cup of coffee. Seventy-one after cappuccino. Mike always counts my words—so I make sure every word counts. The way Scrabble values some words more than others, so do I. When I pick a word, it's got to be worth at least one-seventieth of a national TV spot—and perhaps even more—or out it goes.

The word *actually* gets cast in a lot of my commercials. *Actually* definitely carries its one-seventieth value. For instance, if I say "Brand X removes catsup stains," that's good. But if I say "Brand X *actually* removes catsup stains," that's even better.

It's actually 11:26 (11:11), and Mark hasn't called. I hate time. What a tease, pretending to be there for you when you need it, then, when you do, time's never around. Time's a jerk.

"Why hasn't Mark called yet?" I say aloud to Jerry.

The phone rings.

Let it be Mark, let it be Mark, let it be Mark.

"Yeah," I say into the receiver.

"That's the way you answer your phone? 'Yeah'?"

It's Mike.

"At least it's positive, Mike. At least I'm not answering the phone by saying 'No.' "

"Bring in your Close-Up work today at four."

"But you said it was due tomorrow," I remind him.

"The finished spots are due tomorrow. I want to see your ideas—ten breakthrough ideas for love songs for Close-Up, in my office at four prompt! Got it?" He hangs up.

The good thing about having fake nails is that you get to bite them off twice. Now that I've partaken of my ten crunchy plastic layers, I'm ready for my ten soft, real nails—one for each breakthrough love song.

The tricky part of writing love songs is thinking up hooks without the word *love*. If you don't, you're stuck with only five mundane rhymes: *above, dove, glove, shove,* and *of*. French lyricists have it easier. They get to choose from over fifty rhymes, including quirky stuff like *suburb, deaf, work, drum,* and *tower*. And they get to rhyme singular with plural, because in French the *s* is silent. *And* they have the option of putting the adjective before or after the noun.

American lyricists are limited by *love*. That's why we wind up singing about "falling" for someone, or getting a "crush." All masochistic terms, when you think about it. "Fall," "crush," "landing head over heels." Even being "crazy" or "mad" for someone—and the concept of "commitment." "Being committed" is what happens to crazy people. Crazy people and lovers.

Since the beginning of time, there's been an intertwining between love's pleasure and pain. In Latin-based languages, the word *passion* also means "suffering." As a writer, I enjoy studying languages, gathering clues from them about a culture's psyche. For instance, in America we use the same word, *love*, to express our emotion for a car and for a spouse. French and Hebrew have separate verbs to differentiate between emotional and materialistic love. And the Japanese don't say "I love you," they say *"Aishiteru"*—translated: "Loving." They form a union even in words—the *I* is not separate from *you*. That's what I want. A love so strong you don't need an *I* and *you*. Instead, I keep getting loves with an IOU.

It's almost noon, and Mark still hasn't called. Ah, to be so close to love, so close to being close; but alas, as in horseshoes, close to close doesn't count.

"Hey," I say to Jerry, "what about a hook: 'There's close love. Then there's Close-Up love'?"

"Or: 'The difference between close and Close-Up is the difference between night and early morning'?"

I laugh. "Hey, we might have something. Maybe I should cancel Bob today, stay and work on Close-Up."

What I really mean is: stay and wait for Mark's call.

"No way. You gotta meet Bob. Priorities, babe. Plus, maybe Bob will have some insight on this Mark dude. Shouldn't you get going? It's almost noon."

"Yeah, you're right. I don't want to be late. Not out of respect for the psychic profession. I just don't want to give Bob freebie clues about my personality."

As I'm slipping into my black leather jacket, the phone rings. Jerry reaches for it. I bite his hand. The phone bounces to the floor. My call.

"Hello," I say in my best Marilyn Monroe voice.

"Are you okay? You sound like you have a cold."

It's my mother.

"Listen, Mom, I can't talk. I'm seeing a psychic and I don't want to be late."

"You're seeing a psychic?"

She's not pleased.

"Not romantically, Mom, don't worry."

"Are you seeing *anyone*—romantically, as you put it?"

I tell her about Mark. Already, she doesn't like the sound of him.

"Mark Tivoli? What kind of a name is *Tivoli*? Certainly not Jewish."

"Mom, Mark's handsome, he's smart, he's successful."

"So, there are a lot of handsome, smart, successful Jewish boys out there, too."

"Mark's great. You'd love him, Mom."

I can't believe I am defending somebody I don't even know. Somebody who hasn't even called yet. Though I know it's just a matter of time. Lousy, stinking time.

"I wish you'd meet Aunt Rosalie's friend's son. He's nice, handsome, Jewish, and works in the garment industry."

I know in my mother's eyes this guy's the ultimate catch. Not only is he Jewish, he could get her Dior suits wholesale. But I've already had one too many horrific blind dates.

My first two months after the breakup, I begged Frannie and Viv to fix me up with whomever, whatever. I went on a blind date rampage. The only good that came from it was a song:

I MIGHT BE LONELY, BUT I'M NEVER ALONE
by Sasha Schwartz

I might be lonely
But I'm never alone
Men are always calling on the telephone
But I'd rather sit and talk to the dial tone

I don't 'vant to be alone'
My life is on the rocks
but I'm a rolling stone.

My calendar is full
But my heart is oh so empty
I see lots of guys
but none of them tempt me
I see lots of guys
But I look right through them
They want to know my story
I ask what's it to them!

I don't 'vant to be alone'
(I might be lonely, but I'm never alone)
I'd rather date a homely guy
than stay at home

I get taken out to dinner
By men oh so rich
But I'd rather stay in
and eat a tuna fish
I date lots of guys
But they're all oh such wimps
Looking for Mr. Goodbar
Finding Goodyear Blimps

155

As hoped, I arrive at the psychic's on time. I check the address twice on the piece of paper Jerry gave me: The John Williams Hotel.

On paper it sounds great. In reality, the John Williams Hotel is a run-down downtown tenement building. The main door is held open by a crushed beer can—domestic beer, not even imported. I am beginning to doubt Bob's psychic abilities. If he's so good, why isn't he a Lucky Lotto millionaire?

I enter cautiously, find Suite 3B, knock. Paint comes off on my knuckles. I hear a rumble within. The sound of shuffling footsteps. A husky cough.

"Who's there?" a voice asks.

If he's so good, shouldn't he already know?

"Sasha. Sasha Schwartz."

He unlocks, unbolts, unchains the door.

"Hi, I'm Bob," he says, waving me inside. "Come on in. Come in. Want a Diet Pepsi?"

I suppose on some level Bob looks like a psychic. Though he's not wearing any flowing robes. No exotic ornaments. However, he does have a diamond stud earring in his left ear, and he does know I drink Diet Pepsi.

He is older than I thought he would be. About fifty, with a mass of white hair and puffy cheeks. A clean-shaven Santa Claus. Maybe this is Santa Claus, I chuckle to myself. Maybe Santa is a psychic in the off-season. That would explain how he always knows who is naughty and who is nice, and how when I was twelve he knew I wanted that game of Battling Tops.

"Sit, sit," he says, waving at a small table in the corner by a television set, on which a guy dressed like a caveman is waving a club over his head and screaming monosyllabically. Professional wrestling.

Bob opens the refrigerator. All the shelves are completely stacked with Diet Pepsis. He bends down, opens the crisper drawer, pulls out two Diet Pepsis.

"You don't mind if I keep the TV set on?" Bob asks, handing me my can. "I like to have it on while I work."

"No, no. I do the same thing." I laugh, nervously. Do I need to tell him? Mustn't he already know? "Only I don't usually watch wrestling," I add.

Bob pulls out a chair, joins me at the table. He stares at me, specifically my right cheek. He leans in, touches it.

"I sense a flutter in the upper right portion of your mouth. You have problems here, no?"

My cavity. Or rather: *Gregg's*-and-my cavity.

"I did have a cavity filled there," I say.

"Yes, I sensed a flutter."

I look at Bob suspiciously. Could he be in cahoots with Gregg? If not, maybe I should introduce them. They could work out a business arrangement. *To help reduce cavities, be sure to see your dentist and psychic twice a year.* Bob cracks open his can of Diet Pepsi. His eyes blink rapidly, like maybe some Diet Pepsi spurted into them.

"I see . . . I see the letter *I*," Bob says, his eyes still blinking. "The letter *I* is very important to you. Yes, yes, someone with a name that begins with the letter *I*. Do you know anyone?"

I flip through the Rolodex of my mind, come up blank.

"Just me. I mean 'I' am important to me. 'I' being me."

But Bob is not a Kidder.

"It could be an *L*," Bob corrects himself. "I mean, it's a little blurry."

But no, there are no *L*'s. There are no *I*'s. There is an *M*, however. It would have been nice if Bob had looked at me and seen an *M*. Or a *B*. At least a *B*. Bob should definitely be able to see a *B*. After all, I was with Bryce for four years. Could it be? After all we'd been through, could Bryce have faded out of my life so completely he didn't even leave a trace of his existence upon my aura? Not even a few fingerprints on my heart? Why can't Bob look at me and see a *B*? A giant *B* sitting on my lap. Or little *b*'s buzzing around my head. *B! B! B! B* as in bewildered. *B* as in baffled, bewitched,

betrothed, boggled, blundered, brutalized, broken, brushed aside!
B as in Bryce, damn it!

Bob takes out what seems to be an ordinary deck of playing cards. "Well, now, let's see what the cards have to say."

The crowd on TV cheers wildly. The Caveman wrestler is holding a Henry-the-Eighth-looking wrestler over his head like a surfboard. He is screaming something that sounds a lot like "Ooogagaooo-gaga!"

Bob asks me to shuffle (I do), then separate the cards into three piles (I do). He takes back the cards, then one by one lays them out. First, a three of clubs. Then, a five of diamonds. I wait nervously, like a patient for prognosis, each card prodding at me like a cold, steely stethoscope. The table jiggles as Bob lays down each card. I wonder if he uses this jiggle effect to his advantage during seances.

"I can see," he says, "you are very creative."

But I wonder if it's my dangling yellow smiley face earrings that Bob's responding to.

"You are a person who likes to help people."

Again, could my dangling yellow smiley face earrings be giving me away?

"You are entering a new period in your life right now. A difficult period."

He's got that right. My period's gonna be here any day now. And when it erupts . . . hoo boy.

"Aha," Bob announces, his voice full of great meaning.

I look down at the table: a jack of clubs.

"I see a man, slender, tall, dark hair, dark eyes," Bob says. "He's gone. He's far away. He's gone away. Am I right?"

"Well, there is a man that's left my life recently. Is that the same thing?"

"Could be. Is he a Gemini or a Scorpio?"

"Yes, that's him! Bryce is a Gemini."

"I can see him, this Bryce. I can see him very clearly."

Isn't he cute? I want to ask.

"I sense he loves you," says Bob, "but is confused. He is very confused."

I look down at the card. It looks like an ordinary jack of clubs:

a guy in a tacky Liberace blazer wearing an overly hairsprayed toupee. Could this card actually represent my Bryce?

Bob turns over the next card: a king of diamonds.

"Hmmmmm," says Bob. "I am sensing confusion coming from another man. A strong bond between Bryce and another man. Was there a brother, or father, who created a tension between you?"

No. No father or brother. Just—*oh, brother!*

"Is there any chance," I begin. "Could . . . How can I express this? Could that jack really be a queen?"

"Excuse me?"

I had forgotten: Bob is not a Kidder.

"Could my man be involved with another man? Could he be bisexual?"

Bob puts a hand over each card. "Your man is going through a process of change. He is being overpowered by this other man in some way. The king is stronger than the jack, you see."

Of course.

The Henry-the-Eighth-looking wrestler is now biting the Caveman wrestler's arm like it's a drumstick. The Caveman roars. Does Bob know what the hell he's talking about here, or is he improvising whatever sounds most dramatic as he goes along? Bob stares at the wall behind me. I look, expecting to see a roach or something. But nothing.

"I see a new man in your life," says Bob. "Someone with an *M*—a Mark, maybe."

"What? How did . . . ? I just met someone named Mark."

"He makes you very happy in bed, no?"

"Well, I don't know. He hasn't called yet," I say.

"He's shy, this Mark. He is afraid."

"You're right. He did seem shy. All he did was peck me on the cheek good-night. Not that I was going to do anything more with him . . . but I mean . . . you know."

"You need to help Mark over his shyness. Next time he gives you a peck, you squeeze him back."

"Squeeze him back?"

"Mark needs a sign from you that you like him. He's shy, but very sexual. He's . . . he's got a huge . . . well, *you know*."

"You can see that?"

"It's hard not to see it. Now, how about another Diet Pepsi? These readings take a lot out of me. I get real thirsty, you know?"

Without waiting for my reply, Bob heads to the refrigerator. He pops open yet another can. A light spritz sprays his face.

Could this man know? Could he really know?

The moment I open my office door, the phone rings.

Let it be Mark, let it be Mark, let it be Mark, let it be Mark, let it be Mark, let it be Mark.

"Hello," I purr.

"Hey, babe," says Jerriatrics.

"Jerry? Why are you calling? Where are you?"

"Next door. I figured since you're on the phone all the time, a good way to get work done is over the phone."

I slam down the phone. Jerry stumbles into my office, holding his left ear like an injured Van Gogh. "So, how was the psychic? Bob tell you anything interesting?"

I tell Jerriatrics what Bob said about Bryce: "He is going through a process, being influenced by a man in some way."

I tell Jerriatrics what Bob said about Mark: "Next time Mark gives me a peck, I'm supposed to give him a squeeze."

"A squeeze?"

"As a sign I want more to come."

"I like that for Close-Up," Jerry says. He pats my desk top (what little he finds), slowly at first, then builds to a frenetic beat. *It all starts with a squeeze, Close-Up toothpaste. It all starts with a squeeze, Close-Up toothpaste,* Jerry chants. The flower lambadas along with him.

"Very hypnotic beat," I say.

"It's a voodoo prayer dance beat. Cool, huh?"

"Jer, do you practice voodoo?"

"I'm into voodoo drumming. Don't look at me like that. It's not so bizarre. All drumming borrows from voodoo. Rock bands—even the American army. When soldiers use drums to get psyched for warfare, they're plagiarizing voodoo. If you need a celebrity endorsement for voodoo drumming, Newton will back me up: 'For every action there is a reaction.' If you beat a drum, you change the dynamic around you. Look at the flower when I beat the desk, shakin' like a bowl of Jell-O. What voodoo drumming does is slowly build up this energy, then release it."

"Do you practice any other voodoo rituals?" I ask.

"I dabble."

"Hoo boy."

"Chill out, Sash. I'm a vegetarian."

"So?"

"I don't sacrifice living things, like chickens—or creative supervisors. I sacrifice zucchinis."

"You sacrifice zucchinis?"

I*t all starts with a squeeze, Close-Up toothpaste*," Jerry chants as he pats his drum. He's rehearsing for our four o'clock presentation.

"Keep it down in there, guys!" shouts Joy from down the hall.

But in my ears the room is quiet; I hear beneath the sound of Jerry's drumming, to the sound of no phone ringing. It's 3:50 (3:35) and still no Mark. If Mark doesn't call, I'm going to be even more disappointed than before, now that Bob has promised there is to be something "big" in it for me.

Jerry continues patting the drum, only much softer, with the gentleness of little cat paws.

"You know, we have an eight-in-ten chance of getting a good vacation out of this account," says Jerry. "I've drawn palm trees and crashing ocean waves into eight of our ten storyboards."

I laugh. I could use a vacation. If you ask me, Jerriatrics doesn't need vacations. He's already on another planet.

Although we only want to sell our "Squeeze" spot, Jerry and I have managed to eke out nine other hack jingles to present. We know by now we could never sell a spot to The Worm otherwise. He's a believer in the quantity, not the quality, method of advertising, often requesting upwards of one hundred storyboards for one assignment.

In the back of the office is a huge room called "the morgue" where the hundreds of storyboards we don't sell go. Sometimes I'm relieved when a spot goes to the morgue, because during the process of presenting, the client mutates the original idea beyond recognition. That's the worst, giving birth to a deformed spot, being haunted by it on TV while trying to relax watching "Golden Girls."

"Oh—and when we present to Mike," says Jerry, "don't tell him our 'Squeeze' spot has a voodoo beat. He wouldn't understand, like you do."

"I understand?"

"Sasha, haven't I enlightened you at all?"

"Enfrightened is more like it."

"Bad news," says Mike. I look up to see him standing in my office doorway, wearing a gray overcoat, smoking a cigarette, looking very much like a gangster, an ad gangster. Shit. I don't know if I can take any more bad news. He blows out a blurry ring of smoke. I don't know if I've ever seen Mike not smoking. Maybe Mike feels safe from cancer because he works for a cigarette company, as if he's got special connections, like people high up at Phillip Morris, to protect him. It wouldn't surprise me if he did. These cigarette companies have bizarre amounts of power—*power* being another word for "money." They have enough of this powermoney to purchase thousands of consciences annually, keeping bad press suppressed.

"I've got an emergency meeting with the Houston cigarette client," says Mike. "I'm leaving the office for the rest of the day. We're gonna have to meet tomorrow on Close-Up."

This is bad news?

W hat do you say we go out and get a couple of beers?" says Jerry, his motorcycle helmet tucked under his left armpit.

The thought here is: if Mike's gone for the day, there's no reason for us to hang around. If you do work and Mike's not here to see you do it, it's sort of like that tree falling in the forest. . . .

"You go," I say. "I can't leave yet."

My thought here is: It's 4:17 (4:02). Any minute now Mark should be calling. It's just a matter of time. I'm a prisoner of time. I'm basically doing time.

"I hope Mark calls soon," I say. "Though I hope he just calls. Maybe he won't ever call. Maybe he didn't find me attractive enough. Maybe that's why he didn't give me a better kiss good-night."

"Maybe it was your toothpaste," chides Jerry.

"Maybe it was my hair. Maybe my mother's right, I should cut my hair."

"Don't. Definitely don't. Long hair is power, babe. That's why I keep mine long. That's why Samson had it good until Delilah castrated his hair. Every strand carries vibes—memories of your life experience. When you cut your hair, you lose that vibrational recall. That's why the military and prisons and religious cults shave everyone, to weaken their sense of identity, their libido. That's part of your power, babe. That mane of yours makes you look mega wild and sexy."

"It's false advertising."

"You've got to believe more in yourself," says Jerriatrics. "I believe in you."

That's sweet. And I know Jerriatrics does believe in me. But then, Jerriatrics believes in little green men from the planet Velcro.

"You're very sexy, Sash. Out of all the women I know, you're, like, one of the sexiest."

"Thanks, Jer. And out of all the guys I know, you're one of them."

Jerry laughs. "Look, chill out. This dude will call. Why wouldn't he? You're happening, babe."

I like the sound of this. I am happening. I am a verb. I breathe in deeply. I must relax. Jerry's right. Mark will call. I must give Mark time. There's that jerk Time again, controlling my life. I don't get it. We should have it all over Time. After all, we're the ones who invented it. Somewhere along the line, Time managed to surpass us. Now we are slaves to Time. We make idols to Time in the form of clocks. These clocks warrant an estranged belief in our ultimate control of Time. Yet the worshiper never successfully overpowers its idols. We don't have idle Time. We have idol Time.

"You really like this guy, huh?" says Jerry.

"I definitely don't *not* like him."

"I suppose you've got to start somewhere."

5:52

(5:37).

Still no Mark. Maybe he's having a busy day.

He's an institutional broker, whatever that means. It could be one of those jobs where horror of horrors you can't talk on the phone.

5:53 (5:38).

Another minute has dissolved into the cosmic wasteland, and still no Mark.

I look at the phone.

Then back at the clock.

Phone.

5:56 (5:41).

Phone.

5:59 (5:44).

Phone.

6:02 (5:47).

Maybe he'll call tonight at home.
Phone.
6:25 (6:10).
Phone.
6:28 (6:13).
Mark better call tonight at home.
Phone.
6:33 (6:18).
Phone.
6:35 (6:20).
Phone.
6:38 (6:23).

If he calls tomorrow for tomorrow night I'm going to have to say no. I'm in advertising. I know good sales technique. I never accept a date made that day for that night. It's better to say I'm busy, look popular—a subtle manipulation of emotions like I get paid to do in the ad biz. Romance and advertising are the same game. To lure a guy in to buy into me, I say and do things that imply what a great catch I am. Soon he's thinking the same. God willing.

Phone.
6:41 (6:26).
Phone.
6:44 (6:29).
Phone.
6:46 (6:31).

Still no Mark. Each moment that passes is another non-moment, a space of time labeled "Mark not calling."

Phone.
6:49 (6:34).
Phone.
6: 51 (6:36).
Phone.
7:01 (6:46).
Phone.
7:02 (6:47).

What's Cupid's problem?! He gets everything going just fine, then, when trouble's abrew, he's nowhere to be found. Cupid lacks follow-through.

7:09 (6:54).

Phone.

7:12 (6:57).

Phone.

7:22 (7:07).

Phone.

7:30 (7:15).

Phone.

7:34 (7:19).

Phone.

7:44 (7:29).

Cupid's obviously a sadist—hence, his sharp pointy arrows. Cupid's obviously suffering from a height complex, and taking it out on the rest of us.

Phone.

7:48 (7:33).

Phone.

7:51 (7:36).

Phone.

7:55 (7:40).

Phone.

7:57 (7:42).

"Look at this!" says Joy. She's come into my office with a *Bride's* magazine. She might as well be holding a dangerous chunk of Kryptonite.

"I'm busy," I say—though it's probably obvious I'm sitting staring at my phone.

"I just thought you'd get a kick out of this." Joy points to a photo in the magazine of a very Addams-Family-esque wedding scene where the bride is dressed in . . .

"A black wedding gown?" I say.

"She's gorgeous enough to come off cool," says Joy, "don't you think?"

I look at the photo. Not only is the bride blessed with stunning looks, so's her husband. I stare at the photo thinking: I hate myself.

"Don't you just hate her?" asks Joy.

This, in a nutshell, is what clarifies the difference between Joy and me. Joy turns her negativity *against others*. I, *against myself*.

I look at Joy, her watermelon ring, her arrogant glee, and feel the negativity seep into me, like sweat going backward.

Why hasn't Mark called?

Of course I'm late to the restaurant.

Outside Viv's waiting alone, petting a huge Doberman pinscher chained to a No Parking sign. Her blond hair's pulled back tight in a bun, held in place by a purple fishnet holder. She's wearing her long black leather coat, so I can't see her outfit, but I figure it must have green in it because her shoes are green.

"Whose dog?" I greet her.

"I don't know, but if it's true dogs take after their owners, I want to meet its owner. Just look at that."

Viv points to the dog's endowed genitalia.

"Viv!"

"I'm hungry. Let's wait for Frannie inside, get a table."

The restaurant is dimly lit, candles flicker on lacy tables. The breathy steam of Edith Piaf's voice fills the dining room like a warm summer day: *je t'ai dans le peau.* The maître d' approaches, a pinched-faced woman who looks like a fourth-grade schoolteacher.

"Do you have a reservation?" asks the maître d'—like this is a dare. She's a toughie, this one. *Matron d'Auschwitz* is more like it.

"Under Schwartz," I say, "for three."

"Are you all here?" the matron d' asks.

"I'm definitely not," I say.

"Yes. Our friend's in the ladies' room," Viv lies, knowing this is the only way to get seated immediately and thereby get her hands into the bread basket.

The matron d' neatly checks us off in her book, enhancing her fourth-grade teacher persona: teacher taking attendance.

"Schwartz party this way," she says.

"Did you hear that?" I say. "I'm having a party."

She leads us past a huge painting of a black horse—which I hope is not representational of the food here. I must be careful. The menu is in French. Hmmm, how do you say "horse" in French? I must remember. We pass a few scattered empty tables, all with little signs that read RESERVED. If you ask me, these signs should be labeling the *peopled tables*. RESERVED and VERY RESERVED is how I'd describe the clientele. It's a very uptight, uppity crowd—the kind of people you read about who literally die of politeness, preferring to choke on a piece of lamb rather than disturb friends and loved ones—or God forbid, strangers—by gagging for help.

The matron d' motions us to sit at a small table by a painting of a swan. "Bon appetit," she says.

"Merci beaucoup," Viv replies.

"Ooooh! I just love it when you speak Italian!" I say.

"That was French."

"And *that* was humor. I know French. I'm a classy broad, you know. I'm fluent in French shopping. In fact, I know how to say 'Do you have this in a size six?' in five different languages. Plus, I remember in French the word for 'arm' is *bras*, for silly reasons."

The busboy brings over a basket of anorexic French bread. Viv rips off a piece, dips it into the butter, a Freudian reminder of Bob's predictions of Mark.

I tell Viv what the psychic promised.

"You're suddenly believing psychics?" says Viv.

"He knew about my cavity."

"How about the one in your head?"

"Sorry I'm late," says Frannie, reaching for the empty chair. She's wearing a black smock dress that hangs loosely on her thin frame. Yes, you'd never guess this woman to be a mistress. She sits, pulling her chair in, and flipping her straight black hair behind her ears in one fluid motion.

"For penance," says Viv, "we've decided you have to pick up the check."

Frannie bursts into tears.

"Just kidding," says Viv. "Just kidding."

Frannie continues crying. I've never heard her cry before. It turns out Frannie is a loud crier—like Lucy, from "I Love Lucy."

This isn't a restaurant for crying. People here don't even like to cough or sneeze. Here, they deny the humanness of humans. I'm surprised they even have bathrooms.

"You okay?" I stupidly ask.

"Arthur's in the hospital," says Frannie, coming up for air from a sob.

"My God, is he okay?" Viv asks.

"Unfortunately *he's* fine," says Frannie. "It's his kid who's sick—she's got a hundred and five fever. Arthur's very upset. He told me he stayed there all night, making deals with God for the kid to be okay. I know I was part of his deal-making. I know Arthur auctioned me off to God in trade for his kid being all right."

Frannie lets loose a new series of bass wails. Viv slides a glass of water in front of her. The women at the next table blatantly stare over at us. We have now become their dinner theater.

"It's now clear he'll never get divorced," says Frannie. "I'm competing with another female and it's not his wife. It's his daughter." With this, a new batch of tears arrives. "He's told me his wife will make it impossible for him to see his kid if he ever divorced her. All this time he's been deciding: his kid or me. And his kid's part of him, he created her. It's part love, part egotism, the love of one's child."

The waitress, a long-legged gazelle-like creature, with an upturned nose and thin slivers for lips, approaches our table. I fear she's going to kick Frannie out for crying. She hands Frannie a fresh linen napkin.

"It's a man, isn't it?" the waitress says.

Frannie floppily nods her head.

"How about a drink? On the house," says the waitress. "What do you want?"

"A Bloody Mary," Frannie sobs.

The waitress heads off to the bar, forgetting to ask Viv and me if we want anything. Frannie blows her nose into the linen napkin. The table of women continue to stare over at us. There are three of them, each very attractive in her own right, each about ten years older than each of us. The first is a blonde, dripping in pearls—a very sexy look, like Aphrodite emerging from the sea as envisioned by Chanel. The second is a pretty brunette in a simple black dress whose major fashion accessory is her cleavage. The third is also a brunette, very pretty, wearing a maroon Romeo Gigli dress I lusted for in an expensive boutique but couldn't afford.

The waitress brings over Frannie's Bloody Mary. "Here you go. I'll be back in a bit for your dinner orders." She says all this to Frannie.

Frannie stirs and stares into her Bloody Mary, hypnotized by the black pepper spots circling 'round and 'round.

"Frannie," says Viv, "it's time you made a decision. For two years you've been letting Arthur decide what will happen. All he did was make excuses. It's time you decide what *you* want."

"It doesn't matter what I want," says Frannie, sipping her Bloody Mary through the stirrer—or trying. The black peppers clog the way. "Don't you see? Arthur auctioned me off. I don't think he ever had it in him to leave his daughter. He kept blaming things on having to sell the house, waiting for money to come in, but he's been lying to himself, or to me, or both of us."

"Then this is a good opportunity," I say—then stop, realizing, to my horror, that this is what Mike says when disaster strikes. He's ruined the word *opportunity* for me. I begin again. "This might hurt now, but if it allows you to see more clearly what the situation is, then all this is a good thing, a very good thing."

"Fuck you, Sasha!" says Frannie. "This isn't a good thing. This is horrible! I don't want to give Arthur up. I want him!" She bursts into a new wave of tears, a veritable downpour. Any moment, I expect to see lightning flash across her face. The women at the next table stare at me, curious as to what I will say next. I feel an added pressure to say the right friendship thing.

"Maybe you'll feel better if you eat something," I say.

Frannie nods weakly, blows her nose into her linen napkin. I open my menu, careful not to set it on fire. There are these small white candles on the table. Candles—witchcraft—Mark—shit. I now remember: I feel miserable, too. Suddenly, I want to break down and cry along with Frannie. I want the waitress to bring me a free drink too.

"Oh, I see they serve fast food here," I say.

"What?" Viv asks.

"On the menu, they have rabbit—fast food, get it? We can order it, then complain to our waitress there's a hare in our food."

"Don't upset our waitress," says Frannie.

"Or we can order slow food," I say. "Escargot."

Viv's blue eyes flash me a warning signal. I clear my throat.

"So, what are you all getting?" I ask.

"Something not too fattening but that tastes incredible," says Viv. "I'm dieting."

With this, Frannie bursts into tears. "It's so unfair. I gave Arthur the thinnest years of my life."

Viv and I each stroke a Frannie arm.

"Is she okay?"

It's the woman at the next table—the one with all the pearls. She's leaning in toward us, pearls dangling into her bread dish. I smell her perfume, Opium.

"Would you like a few Valium?" she offers.

"Oh, sorry if we're disturbing you," I say.

"It's quite all right. I know how she feels," says Pearls. "I hope you don't mind, but we couldn't help but overhear. Your friend has man problems."

Frannie looks up.

"I've been crying all day myself over a man," says Pearls.

"Boy, has she ever," says her friend to the left, the one with the cleavage.

"And how," says the other friend, the Romeo Gigli gal.

"Men!" Pearls reaches for her drink, a Bloody Mary like Frannie's, and lustily gulps it down.

I don't know if it's the shared choice of alcoholic beverage that encourages Frannie to respond, or the shared trauma, but suddenly Frannie pulls her arms away from me and Viv, leans in toward Pearls, and asks: "So, what did your asshole do to you?"

Pearls leans in to our table. Viv and I, too, now shift closer, toward Pearls.

"Three months ago I met this guy," Pearls begins. "He's been sending me flowers and love notes. He told me I was like a miracle to him. A miracle! Ha! Then today he tells me he's moving to San Francisco for business—*next week*. He says he just found out today. I can't believe that. I can't believe he had no idea before today."

"It's possible," says Cleavage. "He did just have wall-to-wall carpeting put in his apartment. You don't put in wall-to-wall carpeting if you think you're moving."

"Unless he knows that no matter what he does, his office will reimburse him," says Romeo Gigli. "I told you from the start this guy was trouble—ever since he showed you that photo of his daughter."

"This guy was fifty-five. I'm thirty-seven," says Pearls. "He had a daughter about my age. He showed me a photo. She looked just like me."

"There are always clues," says Romeo Gigli. "My last boyfriend, his first attempt at kissing me had been a hand signal. He motioned with his finger for *me* to come over to *his side* of the table. I had seen this as a clue of a man not willing to put himself out for me. Then I told myself I was overanalyzing. Turned out, this was exactly the problem in our relationship."

"You're right. James was very controlling," Pearls agrees.

"He asked me to lose weight," says Romeo Gigli. "Ten pounds. I bargained him down to eight."

"You don't need to lose weight!" Viv says.

Really. From what I see she has a beautiful figure.

"James was into control," says Cleavage.

"He was superficial, too," says Pearls. "A superficial asshole."

"I must have an anal fixation," says Romeo Gigli, "because all the guys I go out with seem to be assholes."

We all laugh. It's amazing how quickly women open up to each other. Already we're talking as if we're all long-lost childhood friends. No wonder so many women are dissatisfied with their men. Years could pass before a man even thinks about mentioning how he was abandoned at birth: "Oh, yeah, you mean I didn't tell you I was raised in an orphanage, where I was adopted at age two by a Latvian albino dwarf?"

"There's always clues warning you about men," says Romeo Gigli. "I stupidly ignore them. I center in on what I want to see. Like, when I first met James, he wore this beautiful antique watch that never worked right. He was always asking me for the correct time, then resetting it. I told him he should return the watch, but he said he didn't want to, because he loved it too much. At the time

I had seen this as a clue that when James fell in love with something, he fell deeply in love. He didn't care about flaws. I felt safe he'd love me, flaws and all. Then, when he started getting down on me about my weight and my looks, I realized this watch was a clue about James's superficiality. He cared more about how a thing looked than what was inside it. *That* was the clue I missed."

Silence dominoes around each of our tables and lands on Cleavage. For some reason we all look at Cleavage.

"Don't look at me for a bad relationship story," says Cleavage.

Of course, with a cleavage like that, men must be newborn puppies around her.

"Because I haven't been in a relationship for seven years," Cleavage says. Then she laughs a nervous laugh, which builds softly but steadily into an uncontrollable laugh, a loud hee-haw laugh, like the Penguin from *Batman*. It's an infectious laugh that seeps its way into my system, and soon I'm laughing, Viv's laughing, Cleavage's friends are laughing—and best of all, Frannie's laughing. *No relationship in seven years! Ha, ha, ha, ha, ha!*

"Good to see you laughing," says our waitress. "What's so funny?"

"We're talking about how hard it is to meet good men," says Pearls.

"You're telling me!" says the waitress. "I don't think there are any left in this city."

"I met a nice guy last night," I offer shyly.

"Really?" says the waitress. "He must be the last eligible guy in New York."

"Tell us about him," says Romeo Gigli.

"He has a huge penis," laughs Viv.

"Viv!" I say.

All the women laugh—including Frannie. For Frannie's sake, I continue.

"That's what my psychic told me," I say. "Actually, he's not *my* psychic."

The women stare. I know they're eager for me to get onto the penis stuff.

"Anyway," I say, "last night at the health club I met this adorable guy, Mark; then today, I went to a friend's psychic, who said he saw a man named Mark in my future, and he could see Mark was great in bed—that Mark has a huge penis."

"I'm having penis envy of you," says the waitress.

"You think penis size is all that important?" I ask.

"Definitely," says our waitress. *"Definitely."*

"Me, I have a foot fetish," says Cleavage quietly. "Anything a foot or longer!" She bursts into her Penguin laugh.

"I never really thought penis length mattered," says Viv.

"It doesn't," says Pearls. "It's *not* how long the guy's penis is. It's how long his *tongue* is."

Yes, more scientific evidence that it doesn't take women long to shed those barriers.

"Oh, you're making me think about James," sighs Romeo Gigli. "He might have been an asshole, but he was great in bed. Once, we went to this motel that had mirrors on the ceiling. What a night! James wanted me on top the whole time." She pauses. "Wait a minute. I just thought of something. James wasn't being generous. There were mirrors on the ceiling. He just wanted to see us going at it. Selfish bastard!"

"Remember Drew?" asks Cleavage. (Her friends chuckle in response.) "A nice, stable guy, but sooo boring in bed. Having him inside me was as exciting as putting in a tampon. Then there was all that rubber upon rubber. Drew in a condom. Me with my diaphragm. Together we sounded like new sneakers in a basketball game—one in which the players had trouble getting the ball into the basket." Again, she does her Penguin thing.

"I once went out with this doctor, right?" says our waitress. "So afterwards, we're lying in bed and he tells me that when he was touching my breasts, he was checking them for cancer. He was loony. He complimented me on my body—not by telling me I'm sexy but by telling me I was in great cardiovascular shape. He said I had both sets of stomach muscles. The upper and lower ones, I forget their names now. When I looked for myself, he said I could only see them when both my legs were up in the air. That's what he was thinking about when we were fooling around, my stomach muscles."

"Ugh!" says Pearls. "If you ask me, men can all be summed up into three categories: animals, vegetables, or fruits."

"God, it's been so long since I've had sex," sighs Cleavage.

"Me too," sighs the waitress.

"Yeah, me too," I sigh.

"I'd like to have sex again just to make sure my bodily parts still work," says Cleavage.

"Yeah, I hope I remember how," says the waitress.

"I'm not sure I remember why," laughs Cleavage.

All these women are attractive, smart, warm, funny, yet here they all are—we all are—speaking with one voice, united by pain, united by the enemy: men. Or at least bad men. Some men are good. Mark seems like a good man. Who knows, he might just be the last eligible man in New York. Please God—or Goddesses—or Cupid— whoever's in charge up there—the giant grandmother yenta in the sky—please, let Mark call!

"Excuse me, Cerilla," says the matron d' to our waitress, continuing her fourth-grade teacher imitation quite faithfully. "You're wanted at the next table."

Quickly we order: three broiled halibut and a round of Diet Pepsis.

"Be back soon," says the waitress.

"So, what's your psychic's number?" asks Pearls.

"The psychic isn't the one with the big penis," I remind her.

"Arthur has a beautiful penis," says Frannie.

We all turn to look at Frannie. This is her first complete sentence since we started talking.

"Sometimes when I picture Arthur, I picture just his penis with his wire-rim glasses sitting on it." Her eyes glisten with potential tears.

"What exactly was the problem with your guy again?" asks Cleavage.

"He was married," Pearls reminds her. Pearls obviously eavesdropped on every word of Frannie's story.

"Now that's a clue," says Romeo Gigli. "Talk about clues! Married!"

"I'd never go out with a married man," says Pearls. "My thing is to find a guy who seems normal and nice on the surface but who has latent psychosis that sneaks up on you just when you think everything's going great."

"All guys come with some kind of emotional baggage," says Viv. "The trick is to find one who's carrying something small, like an overnight bag."

"Men are emotional cripples," says Cleavage.

"They're afraid to let themselves feel anything," says Romeo Gigli.

"Except horny," says Pearls. "They're in touch with that feeling."

I think about Mark, how open he was about discussing his feelings. How he said he liked to talk. Nice to meet a guy who likes to talk. My caller likes to talk, but that's another story.

There's so much negativity from these three women. I feel like I'm having an out-of-body experience, watching the possibility of me and my friends in a few years. These women are about ten years older than us. I could be here in ten years. That's almost how long it's been since Cleavage has had a relationship. I, too, could go from four years of feasting with Bryce to seven years of total famine.

When our waitress arrives with our fish, it's one of those whole-fish things, with the little eyeball staring up at you pleadingly.

"Yikes," I say. "I'm glad I didn't order steak. You'd probably bring out the whole cow."

"So, what did I miss?" our waitress asks.

"We're talking about the demise of love," says Pearls.

"Whether love even exists," says Cleavage.

"I don't believe in love," says Viv.

I stare in horror at my friend.

"I don't," says Viv. "Love doesn't exist. *Compromise* exists. There's not love, just compromise."

"You're so negative! All of you! Love exists! It's out there!"

This from me.

Everyone gets real quiet. They stare at me with eyes that bug out as big and round as the one on my fish.

"There are too many songs about love for it not to exist," I say. "If it were all about compromise, everyone would be singing 'I compromise you, baby,' and they're not."

"Those songs are just fantasy," says Pearls. "Like the movies."

"Yeah, you saw one too many Doris Day films," says Frannie.

She laughs, an evil laugh. Oh no, she's becoming one of them. It's like *Invasion of the Body Snatchers*; some force is taking over our minds. Soon I'll be one of them: a negative, bitter, single woman.

"Another table's calling me," says our waitress, and she scurries off.

The mood has changed, like an ocean you swim in, all warm and cozy, then suddenly cold. In the background Edith Piaf sings: *ou sont tous mes copains?*

"I just don't think all men are so bad," I say.

"Come on," says Frannie. "You've been looking for four months for a good guy, and haven't found one. There's a reason."

"What about Mark?" I say.

"Mark? You just met him," says Frannie. "You don't even know him. Has he even called?"

"Not yet, but—"

"They say they'll call, then they don't," says Pearls.

"I hate that," says Cleavage. "When men say they'll call, and they don't."

Why hasn't Mark called? Perhaps my mother's responsible—perhaps she's sending out goy repellent vibrations.

A discussion ensues about broken promises and hearts and the overall rottenness of men as a species. I excuse myself to go to the rest room. I head in back to where the phone is and call myself up—call my answering machine, that is. At last—I've got one message. Thank goodness. It seems lately, if I didn't call myself, nobody would call me. I rewind. I've trained myself so I can tell by the tone and rhythm of the rewinding tape, even before I hear a voice in forward motion, I can tell whether it's a man or a woman who's called. I listen for high *blipblipblips* versus low *blipBLAPblips*. Invariably I'm right. Invariably it's a woman.

It's a woman: a recorded female saleswoman pitching a free trip to the Hawaiian tropics if I call her back immediately and buy a magazine subscription. Damn, an advertisement is calling me on the phone! This is not what I need! Advertisements calling me! I already have enough advertising in my life! It's men I need more of!

I am disappointed. No Mark. Not even my obscene caller. Another quarter thrown into the wishing well of pay telephone expectations. It's amazing the power Panasonic has over my life, that this stupid box of wires can make me miserable or ecstatic. It's not an answering machine. It's a demonic mood-altering device.

"Did Mark call?" Frannie asks when I return to the table.

Frannie knows me well.

"What makes you think I was checking my machine?"

"Don't worry," says Viv. "He might have called, gotten your machine, and hung up."

Viv knows me well—enough to know why I avoided Frannie's question.

At meal's end, when I open my wallet to pay, I see Jerry's Wiccan Basket card next to my American Express. On the bottom, near the address, I note it says:

OPEN TILL MIDNIGHT!

We girls all pay our respective bills, then, giggling, exchange phone numbers and promises to call.

"Let's not be like men," says Pearls. "Let's *really* call."

Everyone looks at me and laughs—then quickly apologizes for laughing.

I t's 11:09 P.M. (10:54 P.M.) and I am heading down Ninth Avenue, nervously—and more important, *quickly*. My shadow does Loch Ness monster improvisations on the sidewalk. Finally, in the distance I see it: The Wiccan Basket, the only store open on the block. Its window glows a bluish light. I aim myself toward this light, a driven moth in heels.

Up close The Wiccan Basket is old, worn, and warty. If it were a person, it would not have the stamina to stay up this late. The window is filled with exotic baubles—amulets, candles, crystals, little brown glass bottles with peeling labels—everything due for a dusting. Up front stands a bronze statuette of Barbie doll proportions, with accessories not available from Mattel: gray metallic snakes, one for each hand. Although this Barbie differs a great deal from the real Barb, it shares one major thing—its function: idolatry.

I open the door, prepared for it to moan out in creaking pain. Instead, it tinkles happily; teeny bells hang like a half-eaten bunch of grapes from the top of the door. I enter and am immediately greeted by a shrunken voodoo head hanging from the ceiling. Attached is a sign:

SHOPLIFTERS
WILL BE PROSECUTED TO THE FULLEST EXTENT.
HAVE A NICE DAY!

The second thing I see is a woman sitting by the cash register reading a book: *The Modern Woman's Guide to Demonology.* She's not a particularly attractive woman. Her facial features are size thirteen, stuck on a size four face. Her eyes are smothered in black liner. Her hair's a bleached blond shade I recognize as "Viv, January 1987."

"Uh . . . Hello," I say.

Her eyes remain focused on her book, as if weighted downward by the gobs of black liner and mascara.

"Looking for anything in particular?" she asks without glancing up. I note she's underlined phrases in red: "how to recognize psychic attack" and "the lemon uncrossing ritual."

"Love spells," I say. "I'm looking for love spells."

She turns the page, underlines some more: "practical uses of astral projection."

"I specialize in apartments and jobs," she says. "Love is not my area. That's Scotty's specialty. You'll find him in back."

There's a choice of two aisles to walk down, each with category signs, like in a supermarket, except instead of "Beverages" and "Canned Goods" I have my pick of "Egyptian Sex UFO" and "Feminist Native American." It takes me a second to realize these are combined headings.

I head down the "Egyptian Sex UFO" aisle. The air is musty.

The lighting is dark. Incense is burning somewhere. I pass a shelf filled with little bronze pots, with a sign that reads:

CAULDRONS:
AUTHENTIC CENTURIES-OLD DESIGN,
A VALUABLE WITCH'S TOOL,
OR A HANDSOME OBJECT FOR YOUR COFFEE TABLE

Beside them hang hooded robes:

HAND SEWN BY OUR SEAMSTRESS, DARLENE,
FINE QUALITY 100% COTTON, W/ FULL HOOD

For those with musical interests there are "spirit trumpets":

THE BEST INSTRUMENT
FOR COMMUNICATION W/ DEPARTED
LOVED ONES

They even have voodoo dolls:

CAN BE USED FOR EITHER SEX,
COMPLETE W/ PINS AND SPELLS
FOR 13 POPULAR OBJECTIVES—EVERYTHING FROM
CROSSING AN ENEMY TO WINNING A COURT CASE

To the right of the voodoo dolls are candles (Mogen David of all kinds, the brand my mother uses for our Hanukkah menorah!) available in almost as many colors as Chromostix.

Finally, I reach the back of the store, which is one huge counter filled with bottles and jars labeled with things like "Controlling Powder," "Graveyard Dirt," "Love and Success," and just "Success." Though I don't know why one would buy plain old "Success," when for the same price you could get "Love" thrown in. Or maybe one costs more. I wonder which is the most expensive magic powder. "Love"? "Happiness"? "Health"? I must get some prices.

"Hello," says a man's voice behind me.

I turn around. I gather this is the Love Specialist. Though he looks more like the guy nobody would go with to the prom—or on any date, even a Tuesday nighter. He's tall and bony with a mouth of teeth, and long straight black hair that falls limply to his tiny, narrow shoulders. He's wearing a loose-fitting T-shirt that reads:

Fight your Battles & Dare the Odds!
Drink Some Mead & Praise Our Gods!

"Looking for something in particular?" he asks.

I'm embarrassed to tell him I want love spells. It sounds so female. It's like asking a man for tampons.

" ....
....
.... I'm looking for love spells," I say.

"To find a lover, or have someone be in love with you?"

Perhaps this guy *is* a love specialist. He's hit upon an important distinction, one I usually don't stumble upon until I'm cobwebbed to the phone, willing it to ring.

"Well, I'd like to lure someone to be in love with me," I say. "But while I'm here, I'll also take one of those voodoo dolls and a box of very sharp pins to punish an ex-boyfriend, who foolishly isn't in love with me anymore." I laugh—a lonely laugh. "Just kidding," I quickly add.

"Do what ye will an' it harm none," he says. "You have to take responsibility for your actions. What good you do returns to you threefold. What harm also returns threefold."

"But what if the guy's a real jerk and deserves to suffer—like, a lot?"

He looks at me like I'm out of my mind. Great, a warlock who works in a witchcraft store with a shrunken voodoo head hanging in the entryway is looking at *me* like *I'm* weird.

"If someone is presently doing you harm," he says, "I recommend a brown Return to Sender candle. I'll inscribe on it 'Return to Sender,' and whatever pain this person's causing you will go back to him. But basically, I'm against manipulation magic."

"Isn't all magic manipulation?"

"Not if you're willing positive energy to nonspecific people. But if you have a specific person in mind, you're playing with that person's will. *That's* manipulation. And you'll find if you mess with a man's will, once you get him, you'll never get rid of him."

"Sounds good to me."

"Not if you later change your mind, Look, if you want, I can give you something to help lessen your love."

"Like Valium?"

"Balm." He walks behind the counter with all the bottles. He steps to the right of them, allowing me a complete view. Some are filled with ashy gunk. Some chunky. Some twiglike. He brings over a container filled with brown leafy particles.

"This is balm. Now's a good time to drink balm, while the moon's waning. It's a time for lessening a feeling, eliminating a person from one's life. It's also the perfect time to lose weight."

"Is that a hint?"

"I was just saying—"

"Just kidding, don't worry."

He obviously isn't going to.

"What's in those little brown bottles?" I ask.

"Love potions."

"What do they taste like?"

"You don't drink them. You wear them."

He removes a bottle from the bottom shelf, unscrews the lid, waves it under my nose. I'm expecting something musky, but it's flowery, light, delicate. I dab some on my wrist.

"It's our top seller for attracting love," he says. "It's called Mystery."

"How appropriate. A good love repellent would most likely be 'Mystery Revealed.' "

"We have everything here—the most complete supply in the city. Success, family happiness, money . . ."

"Could I smell 'Money'?"

He plucks a bottle off the top shelf, hands it to me. It smells sweet, like freshly peeled cucumbers.

"Try some," he offers.

"Is it okay to wear both the money scent and the love attraction scent at the same time? Or will I become a prostitute?"

Again, he gives me a look that suggests even the UFO out-oftowners he's met have not been as alien as me. (Obviously, he's not a Kidder.)

"How much do these cost?" I ask.

"Twenty dollars a bottle."

I let out a low whistle.

"All purchases here are a tax write-off," he says, "as a religious expense. This is a registered Wiccan store. And Wiccan is an accepted American religion."

"Really?"

"Sure. In the American army there's a Jewish chaplain, a Christian chaplain, and now, for the first time, a Wiccan chaplain."

"What about a Charlie Chaplin?"

Just then, a woman appears behind me. I hear her before I see her. Her body jangles like a chandelier. She seems to have a thing for silver and amethyst jewelry.

"Cut those dreams out, will ya?" she says to my Love Specialist. On closer examination, I note that what I thought was an earring on her right earlobe is really a flower tattoo. She's very beautiful and she's got full welcoming lips and large green eyes that color-coordinate with the green in her earlobe tattoo.

My salesman smiles, all teeth and puppy dog innocence. "What are you talking about, Michele?"

Somehow I think he knows *exactly* what Michele's talking about.

She looks at me, then back to him, whispers: "Can I talk with you for a moment?"

"Excuse me," he says.

They walk to the cauldron section, leaving me to sort things out on my own. I wander behind the counter, to more closely inspect the merchandise. I'm sniffing at a bottle of "Good Health" when I hear a combination of giggling and jangling. The more the giggling, the more the jangling. I look up to see this beautiful woman embracing this dweeb of a guy on a large copper cauldron. What she sees in this bony creature is totally beyond me.

Then his title comes to mind: *The Love Specialist*. Maybe this guy knows his stuff after all.

I pile up my arms with red candles, assorted paraphernalia, and some interestingly titled books.

I'm a sucker for a good product demo.

According to the book I am reading I am ripe for voodoo tribal initiation. Page twenty-eight clearly states:

> *One should not participate in sexual intercourse*
> *for a month before the rites are performed.*

Some tribes suggest even longer restraint. They suggest castration. Though I can't imagine why anyone would want to belong to a club that would have him dismember—so to speak.

I underline passages with red Magic Marker. I just finished a section on wind patterns:

> *The wind represents the direction to which*
> *we can direct and redirect our personal energies.*

Or as Dylan said:

> *The answer is blowin' in the wind.*

The book has suggested I put a sock outside my window to see which way the breeze blows.

> *North winds are the time for ending or*
> *removing things;*
> *east winds, new beginnings;*
> *west winds represent gentleness and warmth;*
> *south winds are prime time to start love affairs.*

I double underline this south info, find a pair of old torn black lace stockings, and hang them out my window. To my delight, they blow southward.

I am waiting till midnight—as the book suggests—to perform my first mini witchcraft ceremony. The book has suggested doing it in a special room not used often. In New York, finding a square centimeter of unused living space requires a magic all its own.

Then it hits me: the kitchen. I'm rarely in my kitchen.

I create within my kitchen a circle of white candles, five feet in circumference. The book reminds its readers:

> The circle has been a respected icon since
> Stonehenge times.
> It symbolizes a place between worlds.
> To step out of a circle while in the middle of
> performing rites is the equivalent of stepping over a cliff.

There's photos of Cornish snake charmers who draw circles around themselves to hypnotize snakes. From the Valiumed expressions on these rope-limp snakes, it works.

Next the ceremony calls for water. "Not from the tap, but a stream." Having no babbling brook at my disposal, I improvise with the next best thing: Evian. I sprinkle in about a quarter teaspoon of salt ("Salt is Life"), and stir as advised with my right index finger. This is the most cooking my kitchen has witnessed in ages.

The ceremony now calls for music. To build my power, I'm supposed to:

> dance clockwise
> chanting to something with a strong drumbeat.
> Once your power is gathered,
> release it by getting a picture in your mind.
> Then focus, and shout a key word.

In my case the word is: *LOVE*! I have a choice of either writing my own chant or finding a song that represents my desires. The book suggests:

> phrases that are easy to remember,
> simple to say, full of feeling and rhythm.

185

Exactly my code for jingle writing. I peruse my record collection for possible inspiration, consider the Beatles' "Love, Love Me Do." Ultimately, I decide on Jody Watley's "I'm Looking for a New Love."

At last it's midnight. Time to begin. I strip off all my clothes, so as to be closer to the spirit world, throw them atop a pile in my bedroom, head back to the kitchen. I dip my finger in the salty water, hold it up, marking a Pentagram in the air and saying: *"Let this salt be pure and purifying as I use it in this rite."*

I light the candles and say: *"Gods and Goddesses, guard me and guide me to my goal. So mote it be."*

Together Jody Watley and I sing: *"I'm looking for a new love, baby, a new love!"* I dance naked in circles around my kitchen as I envision Mark. Mark coming toward me. Mark embracing me. I can clearly see us embracing. And unlike M&Ms, I am melting in Mark's hands.

"I'm looking for a new love, baby, a new love!" I sing out, somewhere between enthusiastically and ecclesiastically. Ah, the power of music. Plato feared it. He believed music made fools of men, got them clapping, leaping all over the place, getting into wild orgies. He had a point. All the ascetics were against music, against any form of excess. Except Aristotle. He allowed one excess: the excess in the pleasure of hearing. Aristotle believed music separated man from beast. Aristotle was half right. Sometimes music soothes savage beasts, and other times it creates them (e.g., now).

I dance faster, sing louder: *"I'm looking for a new love, baby, a new love!"* I envision Mark pulling me in for a kiss—a *real* kiss. I bite Mark's lower lip. Then kiss it. Bite. Kiss. Bite. Kiss. Mark laughs. He is so sweet, so gentle. *I'm looking for a new love, baby, a new—*

The phone rings. I trip. No time is a good time to set one's apartment on fire, but now in particular seems inopportune. I'd have a hard time explaining the circumstances to the fire department—or worse, my mother.

The phone rings its little throat hoarse. Could this be Mark? Having received my message telepathically, now reaching me telephonically? I take in a deep breath, try to relax. I'm still a little out of breath from running around in circles. My cheeks are hot and flushed. I pick up.

"Hello," I say with the calm of someone being interrupted reading *Walden Pond*, sipping a glass of red wine.

"I've been thinking about you all day, my sweetness," says my obscene caller.

Ah, loyalty, dependability, devotion, joy, comfort.

"I've been wishing I were licking you," he says, then slowly, confidently, begins to describe how he'd take the rose petals of my pussy into his mouth, how desperately he wants to taste the essence of me. I am seated on a kitchen stool. The candles are burning; wax drips down their sides in time to the slow rhythm of this guy's voice.

"My fingers search your moist peach, pussy, cunt, whatever. I want it."

"Oh, yeah," I say. "I want it, too." The candle flames pulsate wildly, casting shadowettes around the kitchen. It's a rather pretty effect. Except, what's this? Some brown glop on the counter—definitely not part of my black-and-gray color scheme. Sesame noodle sauce, is my guess. I roll off a piece of paper towel, scrub at this brown glop—dried on, yet pliant.

"My tongue on your nipples," says my caller, "licking, sucking, tugging . . ."

"Uh huh," I say, rolling off another piece of towel to scrub clean my apparently sticky cabinet door handles. Hey, I might as well use this time to clean the kitchen. This is one of the good things about phone sex: you can get a lot done while you're doing it.

"I wrap my legs over your shoulders," says my caller.

"Yes, yes . . ." I say, now wiping clean the greenish brown slime from the sink faucet handles.

"I watch my cock go in and out of you," says my caller.

"Ooooh, do it to me," I say, starting in on the dishes. They're piled high, a layer of dust gathered on top of the grime. I let the water get steaming hot, then scrape.

"Is that water I hear in the background?" my caller asks.

"I . . . I'm in the shower," I lie, "using the massage control on myself."

I hold the phone up to the sink, let the water spray down on a dirty dish.

"Ooooh," responds the caller. "Oooh, oooh."

Yes, words definitely have their powers. However, all the talk in the world couldn't awaken Snow White. True magic was sponsored by the kiss. Kiss power. An action, a kiss.

I await my Mark.

5.

DOTH ANY MAN DOUBT, THAT IF THERE WERE TAKEN OUT OF MEN'S MINDS VAIN OPINIONS, FLATTERING HOPES, FALSE VALUATIONS, IMAGINATIONS AS ONE WOULD, AND THE LIKE, BUT IT WOULD LEAVE THE MINDS OF A NUMBER OF MEN POOR SHRUNKEN THINGS, FULL OF MELANCHOLY AND INDISPOSITION, AND UNPLEASING TO THEMSELVES?

—BACON

I wake up to the song, even before I turn on the stereo. It's the music in my head again, playing clear as Nakamichi's finest:

I'm looking for a new love, baby, a new love . . .

I light a candle, put the real song on my stereo, stare at the flickering flame. I envision Mark sitting beside me on my sofa. He's wearing beat-up Levi's and a black T-shirt. I am wearing Bryce's sweater, a maroon Perry Ellis he left behind by mistake and I kept as a form of alimony. I enjoy the idea of Mark trying to feel me up in Bryce's sweater.

I'm looking for a new love, baby, a new love . . .

I'm not sure if it's due to my renewed hope that Mark will call, or the fact that my obscene caller did, but this morning I feel loved and alive. I feel pretty and witty—but not gay. I feel like someone named Heather. Which is odd, considering I just got my period. Usually the first sign of blood awakens the vampire within. I go for people's throats. But today I'm as playful and mirthful as the Pillsbury dough boy: tee hee, tee hee.

I'm looking for a new love, baby, a new love.

The candle burns. I sing. I dance. I gyrate. I glow. I rummage through my lingerie, find a vintage purple lace bustier from Harriet Love, slither into it, and let me tell you: I am no Pillsbury dough boy. I am a woman to be reckoned with. It's a shame to cover up this beautiful Maidenform body. So I sort of don't. I put on my miniest black mini skirt, and a dark gray pin-stripe blazer—sans shirt, so just a hint of purple lace peeks through, 'cause . . .

THE MAIDENFORM WOMAN

I'm looking for a new love, baby, a new love.

Outside, it looks like an ordinary day—though I know otherwise. I know today is different. I look around for some proof: a rainbow amidst the clouds, a rainbow in a puddle, a rainbow bumper sticker. Two men come toward me staring openly. Usually I would think they're staring because I have something in my teeth, but today I know better. I know it's because I am happening—and maybe thanks to an ignited candle or two.

"Wow, I wish she was my secretary," I overhear one say to the other as I pass by.

Whoaee! Don't you look hot today!"

It's Tony the Cro-Magnon. We're sharing an elevator up to The Miller Agency.

Tony takes my hand. "I've got an idea. If you're not married by the time you're thirty-five, you can marry me."

A marriage proposal before ten A.M.? Boy, this magic really works like magic!

"Thanks, Tony."

" 'Cause after thirty-five you'll only have so many good child-bearing years left."

I pull my hand away. "I'm not worried about the children aspect. I have an aunt who just gave birth. She's thirty-nine."

"Must be difficult for a woman to have a baby that late in life."

"Even more difficult for a thirty-nine-year-old man to give birth," I say.

"Even more difficult to give birth to a thirty-nine-year-old man. I'd like to see you give birth to a thirty-nine-year-old man. Actually, I'd like to see you breast-feed one."

"Tony . . ."

"Yes?"

Why bother?

The elevator doors to The Miller Agency unfold before us.

"Any phone calls?" I greet the receptionist.

"Nothing for you," she says.

"You're not doing your job," I tell her, feigning bosslike anger. "Next time, I want at least one message from a man waiting for me when I come in."

She stares at me, perplexed. I continue the charade, head stormily for my office, passing the two Jeffs, who are involved in an early morning game of Smurf basketball.

"Good morning," I greet them merrily.

"Morn," says JeffJeff.

"What's hap?" says MuttJeff.

"Morn." "What's hap." What is with this rampant usage of incomplete words? I guess here in the twentieth century we feel like there's so much filling our overstuffed days, we must cut down wherever we can. So we remove excess syllables. "Def!" and "S & L!" we now say. But the net effect is like that of the dieter who uses Sweet'n Low, then eats the cake.

It's now 10:10 (9:55). And though time, most of the time, seems lacking, it now feels overly abundant. I wish time would speed up a bit, so my day of work would be over and Mark would have called already. Then again, maybe I should want time to slow down. Maybe it's moving faster than Mark's fingers can dial. *Mark, call,* I think. *Call.* I close my eyes, envision Mark's face, the sweat clinging to his brow—how cute he looked sweating over his Szechuan. *Mark, call,* I think. *Call!*

Then the phone rings.

The plastic flower looks as excited as I feel. Could it be? I pick up.

"Hello. Sasha Schwartz, please," an unfamiliar male voice says.

"Speaking."

"I don't know if you remember me. We met at the health club? Mark Tivoli?"

"Mark? Hmmm . . ."

I pause a beat, not wanting Mark to know I know exactly who he is. It's a matter of good sales technique—and time enough to get my heart beating back on track.

"Mark? Oh yes, *Mark*," I say.

"I'm sorry I didn't call yesterday. But remember I told you about my mother?"

"Is she all right?"

"It's Chooch—her dog. Hit by the neighbor's car. Died. Mom was very upset so I left work early yesterday to be with her."

How sweet. Mark might just be the last eligible man in New York.

"How's your mom doing?" I ask. "She must be upset."

"She feels like my father's left her twice now, like she's mourning him twice."

Mark seems sincerely worried about his mom. And best of all, I sense underneath his sincerity is sincerity.

"And you?" I ask. "How are you doing?"

"Well, I never believed the dog was my father. I do know Edna Brown—our neighbor, the one who ran Chooch over—she and my father were rumored to have had an affair. The dog was sniffing around the rear of Edna's car when she backed up over him. Mom feels like Edna had gotten the better of her twice. She's definitely never going to speak to her again."

I pocket this information about Mark's father being the cheating type. This means Mark has latent cad genes.

"Is your mom going to get another dog?"

"I don't think so. Though she does feel very alone right now. I told her she should start dating . . . speaking of which . . . I had a terrific time with you the other night. I don't know if it's too late, but if you're not too busy, would you like to go out tonight?"

Incredible. In under twenty-four hours, my empathic sister goddesses have granted my request.

"Sorry, I am busy," I lie. (More good sales technique.) "But perhaps I can squeeze you in the following night," I say—careful not to say "Saturday" so as not to highlight the date-esque overtones of that night. I do, however, regret my choice of wording: "to squeeze one in" has a little too much sexual innuendo. I avoid that one around men—as well as "busy as a beaver." And "date." Men hate the word *date*. I once mistakenly used the word to describe an evening Bryce and I had shared.

"Must you call it a 'date'?" Bryce had asked, pronouncing the word painfully, as if it were the word *smegma* or something.

"You're right, we don't have 'dates,' " I acquiesced. "We have 'events.' "

"Tomorrow sounds great," says Mark. "What time?"

"How 'bout if we firm up then?"

"Firm up"? I must add this to my list of expressions to avoid around men.

"Great," says Mark—and I know he's really looking forward to it, 'cause he makes it a two-syllable "great," like Tony the Tiger.

I hang up the receiver, then pet it, showing my gratitude. It rings in response. (A phone orgasm?) I pick up.

"Oh, Sash. I'm so upset."

It's Frannie.

"What is it?" I ask softly, while my insides scream: "Mark called! Yahoo! Yippee!" It takes major discipline to hold this back, but I sense now's not the time.

"Arthur says he can't see me till his kid gets out of the hospital. Barbara—his wife—is too upset and needs him at home every night. Then—get this—to show how sensitive he is to my feelings, he asks me if I mind him calling her by her name, Barbara, or do I prefer he call her his 'wife.' I told him I prefer he call her his 'ex-wife.' "

"Good to see you haven't lost your humor."

"Just my mind." Frannie laughs, her laughter muffling into sobs. "Sasha, I have something horrible to admit. I've been hoping Arthur's child dies. It would be so easy for me if she did. I've been hoping she dies."

"Frannie, you've got to move on, find someone new. You deserve better."

"It's not a pretty picture out there being single. Look how bad you have it. I think about you out there, and it scares me. I really feel sorry for you. Both Viv and I have talked about how we really feel for you, Sash. Don't think we don't see the pain you're in. My heart goes out to you. Guys saying they'll call, then leaving you hanging. When I think about how bad you have it, it makes me want to make it work with Arthur."

Enough Ms. Nice Guy. I don't want to be an advertisement for having extramarital affairs. I don't want to be someone people pity—a beggar for love.

"Mark did call," I tell Frannie. "We have a date tomorrow night."

"Really?"

She sounds shocked and I am still a little, too. I have a date! A goddamn boy-meets-girl date! Or rather, an event! And from what Bob the psychic has predicted, what an event this will be! I can feel it. Love is in the air! Like Twinkies, Mark and I are meant to be packaged together. Love. Our raison d'être. The Holy Grail. A guaranteed Saturday night date. What people haven't done for love: swallowed poison, plundered cities, murdered, stolen, stayed on their diets—all in the name of love. I am entering a new era. I am entering the Mark Era.

Could all this be due to my candle ceremonies? To be on the safe side, I decide to light another candle before the date—a menorah of them! Maybe Frannie could benefit from a candle or two right now. Slowly, so as not to frighten, I tell Frannie about my dabbling with witchcraft.

"Are you for real?" Frannie laughs.

"Witchcraft isn't as freaky as you think. Witches were the doctors back in Greece. Even as late as the Middle Ages, sick people went to the local witch for herbs and potions."

"Yeah, very sick people."

"Look, we don't understand how all of our brain works. There are parts of it we might not be using, parts that witchcraft could be tapping into."

"I think right now there are parts you're definitely not using! I think you saw too many episodes of 'Bewitched' as a child. But thanks, anyway," Frannie says. "You've cheered me up immensely. You're a good friend."

J erry Jerry!" I say, barging into his office.

He lowers the paper he's reading, revealing today's choice of clothes: his PLEASE DON'T SQUEEZE THE SHA-MAN T-shirt.

"Yeah, babe? What's happening?"

"Mark from the health club called."

"Blessed be."

"I went to the Wiccan Basket last night, stocked up on candles and books and performed mini-candle ceremonies last night and this morning, and now Mark has called! I knew he was going to call. I could feel it when I woke up. I felt very positive."

"You have to feel like this more often, babe. This confident energy, that's what witchcraft is all about, channeling this natural positive energy."

"I feel so happy, I can't stand it. Shit, why do we have expressions like that about happiness? Stuff like 'it's too much' or 'I could die'? It's like our language suggests we shouldn't let ourselves be too happy too long. Weird, huh?"

"Well, your happiness won't last long."

"This from you? Mr. Positive Karma?"

"The Worm just called. He said he wants us in his office ASAP."

M ike's in his of-fice, seated be-hind his yacht of a desk, smoking a cigarette. Beside him sits Steiner, the account executive on Close-Up. An account exec is the middleman between creative and client. Muddleman is more like it. That's basically what an account exec does: muddle up the creative process.

"Let's see what you've got," says Steiner.

"Before we begin," I say, "could you repeat what you're looking for the spot to accomplish?"

This is a trick in presenting. The same way I keep in mind the consumer's needs when writing the ad, I keep in mind Steiner's and Mike's needs when selling the ad to them.

"I want a spot," says Steiner, "that clearly suggests Close-Up can help lead to love."

"Great," I say. "We're on the same wavelength. We've even named one spot 'Close-Up Leads to Love.' " (Up until a second ago, this was called our "Squeeze" storyboard.)

The next trick is to get their heads shaking yes, yes, yes, so as to give a subliminal feeling of connection.

"So, the client wants something straightforward, right?" I ask.

"Yes," says Steiner.

"Cheap?"

"Yes," says Mike.

"Easy to produce?"

"Sure," says Steiner.

"Yet breakthrough. Something that will break through the clutter."

"Right," says Mike.

"Great. Our spots do all this," I say. "But one warning. The first spot, 'Close-Up Leads to Love [a.k.a. "Squeeze"] is a really wild spot—you might be afraid of it."

Another trick. In the same fashion a movie described as "fabulous" has a hard time living up to its hyperbole, a spot labeled as "really, really wild" will seem a touch more tame once it's presented. Also, by saying "you'll be afraid" I'm playing on the fear of having fear. No one wants to be thought of as someone who's afraid.

The time is now ripe. First, Jerry takes Steiner and Mike through the storyboards. Then, he plays the drums while I sing the copy. It feels good singing, freeing and powerful. Music has always had this power for me. What I never realized before was that music's power was a form of witchcraft. A vibe/energy channeling thing.

As I present each storyboard, I feel my singing confidence build, my energy rise. I sing each board, no matter how hack, with passion and resonance, enunciating every word—watching out for that tricky word *love*, or "uh-lu-vuh," as it's known in the singer's world. We singers know to stress all three mouth motions for *love* to come out right. Like, in Sondheim's "Send in the Clowns," when you sing the line "Don't you love farce?" if you don't enunciate, it comes out "Don't you love arce?" Symbolic. Love: it's hard to say, hard to understand. Or was before for me. But no more. Now I have Mark. The thought of him makes me want to sing forever, never talk words again. Dylan was a believer in the power of singing over talking. Whenever he performed, he rarely spoke. He felt music said everything he needed to say. My man, Dylan.

"That's all," says Jerry when I'm done singing the tenth spot.

"This is an embarrassment of riches," says Steiner.

"Great. Usually it's just an embarrassment," I say.

"Your first spot is Genius," says Mike. "Love that 'squeeze' hook. It's not too wild at all. I was expecting you to present something a lot wilder."

"You've got a brilliant voice," says Steiner, "and great energy and presence."

"It's this lingerie I'm wearing," I say. "I put it on this morning. It's so lacy, so slinky, it just gets me going, you know?"

"It's working," says Mike.

"Yeah? Can I put in for it as a business expense?" I say.

"Just one simple fix," says Mike. "The client wants to sell Close-Up's plaque resistance. So blend that into your spots and we'll present them next week."

"Blend? Romance and plaque?" I say. "They're totally different strategies. I can't believe you're trying to pass it off as a simple fix. Why didn't you mention this before!"

This is just the kind of jerkaround that destroys an ad—and an ad copywriter. To understand the physics of why one strategy has more impact than a lot of strategies, take a sharpened pencil and pound it into your right palm. It will hurt. Repeat the procedure into your left palm with ten sharpened pencils. It will hurt a lot less, because ten points have a duller impact than one. Same goes with advertising. Too many strategies don't add, they dilute. Simple is

199

always better, just as herpes simplex is always better than herpes complex.

"Enough about Close-Up," says Mike. "What have you got on Mangia?"

"Mangia?" I say. "Well, uh . . . you said it wasn't due till Monday," I say.

"Well, since you did such a great job on Close-Up, I'll give you an extension till Monday," says Mike. "I want to see the Close-Up revisions and Mangia first thing Monday morning."

W orm," I mutter. "I can't believe we have to go back into all ten spots and weave in plaque! I hate advertising. I should have been a teen rock star idol."

"You were great presenting. You know you were right about your lingerie giving you power. Witches are very into lingerie—particularly the garter. It's a badge of rank. You're supposed to wear one above the left knee."

"If I'd known, I'd have worn one. Maybe we could have avoided this stupid plaque thing."

"You know, a lot of things you do wear have witchcraft power. Like your nail polish. The color pink you wear is known for attracting romance. And the makeup you wear was first created for magical purposes. Eyeliner was to protect folks from the evil eye, lipstick to keep the soul from disappearing through the breath. And our date nights—Friday and Saturday—evolved into date nights from an old-time superstition that these nights have romantic power. It's good you're getting together with Mark on a Saturday night."

"Really? So . . . uh . . . do you have any helpful spiritual hints from Heloise to offer me for my date tomorrow—you know, to help things along?"

"Maybe a rose petal love bath."

"A what?"

Jerry races out of my office into his. I hear a drawer open, then close. He returns with a thick red book in hand.

"This should answer any of your questions." He hands me *The Modern Witches' Guide to Love*.

"You can read it while I'm at the rolfer's," says Jerry. "I have a one o'clock appointment."

I open the book to page one: "How did simple little Susan get the local millionaire to propose marriage?" it begins.

I don't notice when Jerry leaves the room.

*S*ince the beginning of time, guys and gals have searched for love. Ancient Greeks worked love magic with brains of calves, bones of snakes, and dead bits of humans—these bits were especially potent if they came from someone who died a violent death. Many of these ancient philters themselves led to death. But folks risked it all for almighty love.

In the fourteenth century in Ireland, philters were made from spiders, the flesh of adders, and the brains of unbaptized babies. In France, mercury, dried toads, lizards, marjoram, and mint. In England, a popular ingredient was the left index finger of a hanged man—best taken while the body was warm and swinging aloft.

A hundred years later, European witches upgraded to hemlock, the venom of toads, the flesh of a brigand's parboiled limbs, the skin of green frogs, the blood of infants, dust from a grave.

In the next century, more advances were made, love potions now including dead men's clothes, a swallow's heart, the penis of a horse, and the ropes with which a man had been hanged.

Apalache tribes use human excrement. The Navajos, cow dung. Medieval German girls rolled naked in wheat before the grain was ground. From this, they baked bread they then fed to their men. In Bali, they believe in the power of twin coconuts, snake saliva, and children's tears. In many cultures, a macho animal's penis and its accoutrement are eaten, for obvious associative benefits. Penis substitutes are also potent, including such phallic-shaped foods as asparagus, carrots, cucumbers, and bananas. Seafood as well is supposed to inspire desire, since sea energy is deep and soft, while at the same time strong and changeable—kinda like love.

I am contemplating cooking up a feast for Mark, a seafood-asparagus-carrot stew, when the phone rings.

"So, did the big penis call?"

It's Viv.

"I have a date with him tomorrow night," I say proudly.

"Really?"

She, like Frannie, sounds shocked. Even more so when I'm done describing my experiments with witchcraft.

"Sasha, do you hear yourself? Witchcraft? You've totally lost it."

"There's really nothing paranormal about it—"

"No, just *ab*normal."

"Witchcraft just channels our natural energy—natural energy that's all around us. Look how in moments of crisis people can suddenly lift a heavy car off a loved one, or run superfast away from a murderer. Witchcraft is about getting in touch with those untapped powers. It's about controlling our lives, creating our own future."

"Oh, Sash. Why can't you just join est, like other disillusioned New Yorkers?"

"But it's working."

"I'm worried about you, Sash."

"But I've never been better. Really."

"I'm almost afraid to tell you about the latest Natasha report on Bryce."

"Bryce who?"

"Wow. Maybe this witchcraft stuff is good for you after all.

Maybe you won't mind hearing this. Bryce is sick. He asked Natasha to come over, cook and clean for him. She told me she found some things that will be of interest to you. She couldn't say what—she didn't want Bryce to hear her on the phone—but she sounded weirded out. She's going to drop a package by your office later today."

"I hope she comes soon. I want to get out early, do some supermarket shopping. I might cook for Mark."

"Now you're really shocking me. Cook! You?"

"The way to a man's heart is through his stomach."

"Try a little lower down."

"His feet?"

"No, his *penis*," says Viv.

"And oh, what a penis it promises to be!"

"You still believe that psychic, huh?"

"Let's just say I'm curious to get a peek at Mark. Geez, I hope I can resist sex when I do. At least for a while. It's rare relationships work out when you sleep with someone too soon. Though some say if it doesn't, it never would have worked out. You just find out sooner. But I disagree. When you speed up the process, it's like microwaving something. It comes out different in a microwave than in a conventional oven. Though I could use some sex right now." I sigh in memory of my last encounter with Bryce. "Viv?"

"Yes, Sasha?"

"If I make love with Mark and I don't love him, does that mean I've 'made like' to him?"

"No, Sash, that means you've fucked him."

I f I'm going to be cooking, I'm going to need cash for groceries. I head out to the cash machine. On the way, I pass the homeless man who insulted my hair.

"Hey, honey!" he yells at me.

I speed my pace.

"Hey, honey! Can you spare a date?"

Yes, this witchcraft stuff is incredible. I don't know why witches have the reputation for being such hags. L'Oreal should throw a little graveyard dirt into their Burnished Bronze blush.

I arrive at the bank to discover the cash machine broken, meaning I have to bank the old-fashioned way: make human contact. A ridiculously long line of humans is queued up inside. I head for the line, as does a man behind me. I pick up speed. But his strategy is to limbo under the rope, so he arrives in line first. I shoot him a laser-sharp glare.

"Fine, you go first. *I'll* be the man," I say.

"You got a pen?" he asks.

The nerve. Then he smiles at me, a big, wide, sexy smile. He's a handsome man, older, maybe even forty, but a well-maintained forty. He looks like the type who uses Clinique moisturizer for men.

I reach into my purse to find a pen. "If you like, you can borrow this," I offer Clinique.

"Thanks."

He smiles even wider—an it-all-starts-with-a-squeeze smile. I feel a sexual tension vibrate between us. Or maybe it's the tension from the people behind us cursing because we haven't moved up, though the line has. A huge humanless gap looms before us.

"Hey, one of you go!" advises a tall, burly woman who has the look of having at one time been a man.

"Sorry," I say to the crowd amassed behind me, then stroll ahead of Clinique. As I do, I get a good whiff of him. He's not wearing cologne exactly, but something clean and expensive, like patchouli soap mixed with new car.

"What are you doing?" Clinique laughs.

"My pushy broad imitation," I say. "I believe I should be going before you, so I am."

Clinique laughs. Then the weirdest thing happens. I feel like I'm cheating on Mark. I'm so certain it's gonna work with Mark, I feel it's wrong to be flirting with another man. I unhook my eyes from Clinique's Velcro gaze and force myself to stare ahead, at the guy in front's bald spot. It's a test. The fates are testing me for my loyalty to Mark, seeing how appreciative I am to have found a Good

Man. I said I wanted to meet one Good Man. I found him. I shouldn't be greedy.

Then I turn around to get another look at the man I shouldn't be looking at. He's balancing his checkbook—literally—on his knee. I peek. Over three hundred thousand bucks in his checking account. That much in a checking account? He's rich. It makes sense. Where else would I meet a man with money but in a bank? This is definitely a test.

Again, I concentrate on the bald spot of the guy in front. Actually, he's so bald it's more like a hair spot. I quickly finish my transaction, race for the door, eager to get out of this den of temptation.

Then I see him. Clinique is racing toward the door with me like he did for the line. He is laughing. This is our shared joke. Already Clinique and I have a shared joke. I get to the door first, push it open. At least I try. I push, and push, and push. The door doesn't budge.

Clinique leans in, *pulls* the door open.

"Sometimes pushy broads have to know when to pull," he says, and asks for my phone number.

I can't believe it! This very handsome, very rich man is asking for my phone number. A wave of guilt splashes up on the shore of my emotions. *Mark*, I tell myself. *I have Mark.* Mark's great. He's sweet. He cares for his mother. Always a good sign as to how a man will treat a woman.

"I don't think my boyfriend would like it if I gave you my number," I say. "*Our* number," I add, to seal the deal.

When I return to my office, I find Jerry sitting on one chair, a package on my other. *Natasha's package.* I study it: plain white, generic in size, shape, weight, leaving me no hint as to what's inside.

"You can open that now, if you want," says Jerry. "I don't mind watching."

But no, I will wait, prove to myself I'm no longer obsessed by Bryce. I have my life back.

"That's okay," I say proudly. "We've got work to do."

"Cool. So, let's talk plaque. Listen, I was thinking *plaque* rhymes with *attract*, right? We could write about attracting the right thing—meaning *love*, not *plaque*. Even make it rhyme. What do you think?"

I am thinking: I hope there's nothing AIDS-representative inside that box, now that I have something to live for, someone to live for, now that I have Mark. I can't wait to kiss Mark—really kiss him. I want this even more than I want the act of sex. What I really want, with all my skin, is to sleep beside Mark, feel his body beside me, our bodies curled together, shifting and turning throughout the night, mysteriously in sync, as if we are one living, breathing organism; as if we are attached by Velcro. We play a silent game. One of our body parts must touch at all times. My ankle to Mark's calf. Mark's wrist to my thigh. My big toe to Mark's big toe. In the morning, Mark and I will kiss even before brushing, a sticky-mouthed kiss. But who cares? Let our tongues stick forever together, fine by me. Then we will shower, lathering each other up with soap. Or better yet, Mark and I *won't* shower, so we can smell each other, our scent of love, throughout the day.

"Yo, babe."

"What? Oh, sorry, Jer."

"You seem distracted."

"No, no. Let's work."

"Would you rather work Sunday?"

I raise my hand to slap him five. "Jer, you're a better psychic than Bob."

I head home with Natasha's box under my arm, proud that I didn't tear it open in front of Jerry. Proof I'm over Bryce. I have Mark, the anti-Bryce, the antidote

"*I'm looking for a new love, baby, a new love,*" I whistle. People look at me with asymmetric eyebrows. Nobody whistles anymore. Nobody even hums. Forget about gathering 'round the ol' piano to share in a medley. No, now we silently gather around MTV. Maybe I'll write to MTV, suggest they offer follow-the-bouncing-ball lyrics so everyone can join together in singing once again.

Yes, I am feeling buoyantly happy—*boy*-antly happy. I'm confident things are going to work with Mark. Well, not so confident I'd go witchcraft-free. I stop into a Korean store, pick up some roses for my rose petal love bath.

The rose, so I've now read, is a powerful tool in love. Red roses attract lust; yellow, tenderness; and pink, the purity of love. I can't decide which color is my priority. Lust? Tenderness? Purity? I want them all! I buy a half dozen of each color, seeking the perfect blend of loves. Then, to be on the safe side, I buy another half dozen. Admittedly, I am a woman of excess. I hold true to the belief that the only thing in moderation should be moderation.

"Excuse me. Have you ever been on 'Soul Train'?"

A very bald man stands before me. To make up for his lack of hair he's wearing extra cologne. In fact, it's more than a cologne, it's a room deodorizer: Lysol Pour Homme.

"You look like a woman I once saw dancing on 'Soul Train.' My name's Ralph." He pulls from his striped blazer a postcard of himself dressed in a police uniform—but with clown's makeup and a large neon-yellow flyswatter. "Perhaps you've seen me on TV. I have a cable show called 'The Swat Team.' It's on at midnight. I give pointers on getting the bugs out of the system. Mind if I walk with you?"

"I . . . uh . . . I think my boyfriend would," I say.

The guy scribbles something on the postcard, gives it to me: "You've got the goods, Ralph, tele.: 874-3298."

H

i, Mark, I'm home!" I yell out into my apartment.

I like the sound of it. Yes, I could get used to it. I push my way past the bags of trash and laundry into the bathroom, start running the bath. I head over to my stereo, peruse my tapes, find a homemade oldies one, plunk it in and out blasts: *"I used to love her, but it's all over now!"*

Natasha's box stares up at me like a challenge. I sing along with the music, pump myself up, so I'll be ready for anything the fates might sling at me: *"Yeah, I used to love him, but it's all over now!"*

The box lid lifts up easily, revealing pretty pink paper, light as gossamer. I pull apart the paper gently, as if spreading open the petals on a rose. I'm greeted by a flash of red: lacy royal-red lingerie, a very feminine design, with spagetti straps, a wire underpin bra, and a matching royal-red garter belt.

Could this be Bryce's new nightwear? Is Natasha suggesting Bryce wears women's lingerie?

Then I find a card:

You're beautiful.
Believe it.
Be it.
So be it.
Love,
Jerry

I guess I was mistaken. This is not Natasha's package but Jerriatrics's. No wonder he wanted me to open it at the office. Upon closer inspection I see Jerry's given me a size C bustier.

Size C?

To hell with rubber duckies. The true secret of bathtub ecstasy is soaking with roses—minus thorny stems, of course. Little petals float around me like tea leaves. Perhaps when I'm done with the bath I'll read them, see what shape they make around the bottom of my tub: a slain dragon, a man, a wedding ring.

The twenty-four decapitated rose stems lay stacked on the toilet seat. I feel a little guilty about destroying their beauty, but they gave their lives for a good cause: a loveless woman finding love. But enough. I must concentrate on feeling positive. In the spirit of positive thinking, I shave my armpits. I had let them grow unruly: two forests memorializing Bryce's departure.

Jerry's book listed innumerable bathing spells, explaining how our bodies are mostly water—how all life emerged from the sea— and how bathing reunites us with our watery past. Witchcraft isn't the only religion to value water's power. Roman Catholics sprinkle Holy Water in mass. Christians are big on baptism. Muslims wash themselves each time they pray—which can be up to five times a day, and in India, the Mother Ganges exists as one humongous bathing ritual.

Lying here in the tub, water wafting around me, rose petals sailing by, I understand what the hydro-hype is all about. I feel relaxed, at peace. I am soaking in the essence of love. I am making love gravy. I'm part of a delicious, delicate stew. I wonder what this broth I'm creating would bring to the drinker. The roses with their seasonings of various romantic flavors, and me, my body, my being, would add a touch of fear and longing.

I'm reminded of a story. Two cannibals are talking and one says to the other:

"You know, I don't know how to tell you this, but I can't stand your mother-in-law."

The other one says: "So, just eat the mashed potatoes."

My windows aren't energy efficient. Some leakage somewhere is breathing onto the two dozen red candles lined up along every room's sills, causing their flamey heads to sway side to side, like rock 'n roll fans. I have stripped down buck naked, so as to be closer to the spirit world, and I am doing a major cleaning job, hoping Mark will agree to my plan to come over for home-cooked aphrodisiacs.

Witches, it turns out, are notoriously clean. They believe that like attracts like. A dirty house brings negative energy—and negative comments from Jewish mothers. My mom's always bugging me to clean. She's teased me: "You can eat off the floor in your apartment. Not that it's clean. There's food down there."

My mother would be overjoyed I'm cleaning, though underjoyed that it's part of a witchcraft ritual. What would my mother say, a nice Jewish girl getting into witchcraft? I guess if I'm Jewish, and a witch, that makes me a "Jewitch."

"I'm looking for a new love, a new love, baby!" I sing as I vacuum under the sofa.

The candle flames seem to be swaying and saying *"Yeah, yeah, yeah!"*

I envision Mark as I vacuum: Mark sitting on this very sofa tomorrow night, me nestled beside him, wearing Bryce's maroon sweater. Mark's hand sneaks up under Bryce's sweater. It feels cold and hard like metal. Slowly it warms, merging with my body temperature, my pulse. Mark's forehead is sweating, just like when he was eating Szechuan.

"I'm looking for a new love, a new love, baby!" I sing as I fantasize Mark's hand shyly lingering on my belly. I am nervous about him going further—nervous he won't. I breathe into his ear, tickle his ear with my tongue, give his thigh a squeeze. One of Mark's fingers stirs. Then another. Slowly, his fingers surge to life.

Soon his entire hand is moving—it's moving toward my breasts. It's alive! I've done it! Eureka! I've created a man!

Soon those Y chromosomes are kicking in. Mark's clutching at my breast with one hand, grabbing my face with the other. He's like a little boy the way he reaches for my breasts, in shy awe, as if he's never touched a breast before.

Then the phone rings.

Darn, just when things were getting good. I turn off the vacuum and pick up.

"So what was in the package?"

It's Viv.

"What package?" I ask. "Oh that? Jerriatrics's lingerie."

"Jerriatrics wears lingerie?"

"No, no. A gift from Jerriatrics. I got the wrong package. I'm going to the office Sunday. I'll get Natasha's package then."

"Sasha?"

"Yes, Viv?"

"Sasha?"

"Yes, Viv?"

"Sasha . . . I'm pregnant."

"I know, Viv."

"In real life."

"What?"

"In real life, I'm pregnant. I guess I'm some amazing actress. I'm so good at playing a pregnant woman, I've convinced my body into becoming pregnant. Talk about mind and body being one— though as bloated as I feel now, my mind and body feel like two or three."

"I don't believe it—you're pregnant now—in real life."

"I tried denying it myself. I made all these deals with God not to make me pregnant—deals in which God was to benefit greatly, while I sacrificed all. I even started wearing white pants—with no tampon—hoping to appeal to the sadist in God, since the saint in Him didn't seem to be responding. And I say 'He' now in terms of God for good reason. Being pregnant like this, I am convinced, no way is God a woman. Only a man would set up a woman like this." She sighs deeply.

"Are you okay, Viv?"

"Oh, damn him!" Viv shouts.

I wonder if the "him" she's referring to is God or Keith.

"Viv?"

But there's this gaping silence.

"Viv, are you okay? Do you want to talk? Have you talked to Keith?"

"These damn raging hormones. I feel like shit. Look, I'm sorry to dump this on you."

"Dump? We're friends, Viv. You're always there for me. It's about time I could be there for you."

"I think I'll order a pizza."

"Viv, what did Keith say?"

"Or maybe sushi. I know a sushi place around the corner that delivers."

"Viv—"

"Look, let's just drop it, okay? I'm sorry I even brought it up."

"Viv, don't be crazy. You're upset. We should—"

Then Viv's call-waiting clicks in.

"Be right back," says Viv.

I can't believe how Viv's denying her feelings. It's up to me as a friend to help her out. It's up to me as a friend to help her get in touch with all those horrible, nauseating, depressing, devastatingly ugly emotions.

"Hi!" says Viv, clicking back onto the line. "It's Gary. I'm going to take the call."

"Are you okay, Viv?"

"Fabulous. Don't worry. Gotta go, girl."

And I can't believe how perky she sounds. Too perky. She clicks off. I try to go back to my vacuuming and witchcraft.

"I'm looking for a new love, baby," I sing. But my energy is sapped by my friend's misfortune. It's hard for me to put my full spirit back into my spell. Funny. I'm more upset about Viv's problem than Viv is about Viv's problem. If I know Viv, I'm sure she wouldn't want me to be upset about her. Geez, if she's able to deny her feelings, I should be able to.

"I'm looking for a new love, baby," I sing.

I close my eyes. I try to envision Mark . . . Mark's hands shyly searching under Bryce's sweater, slowly slipping it up and off me, revealing my black tattered lingerie beneath. He releases a low, soft sigh. Then I smell popcorn.

Popcorn?

I look around my apartment. Where is that popcorn smell coming from? I resume vacuuming. What's this? Now I hear popcorn popping. I stop vacuuming. The popcorn stops popping. I vacuum again. The popping starts up.

Finally I figure it out. Last week I ate popcorn on my sofa. Some unpopped kernels rolled beneath, and are now being popped from the heat of the vacuum. Calmed by the knowledge I'm not going insane, I go back to my witchcraft ceremony.

"I'm looking for a new love, baby, a new love!"

Then the phone rings. Damn these interruptions. I pick up.

"I can't get your breasts off my mind," says my obscene caller.

"Poor darling," I say, sprawling back on my carpet, a freshly vacuumed section. "Must be hard to find hats." I twist the vacuum cleaner cord around my right index finger.

He laughs. "Yeah, I wear two yarmulkes."

I sit up. "What?"

"A yarmulke is a Jewish head covering."

"You're Jewish?"

"Circumcised and everything. I hope you've been envisioning a circumcised penis doing all this to you."

I laugh. A Jewish obscene caller? Bizarre.

"Are you Jewish, too?" he asks.

"Yes, but not practicing. I haven't been to temple in a year or two."

"Me either. The last place of worship I was at was the Limelight. You know that place?" he asks.

"The church they turned into a disco?"

"Exactly. You know, I was joking with a friend about turning a synagogue into a disco. I've got the whole thing planned. We call it the Synagogo. We charge fifteen bucks admission—but then let our patrons bargain us down to a wholesale price of, say, seven seventy-five. The bouncers at the door would make our patrons feel guilty if they didn't come regularly. 'What's the matter?' they'd say. 'I

213

didn't see you here last weekend. I was worried.' And of course the establishment's house drink would be Manischewitz. What do you think?"

He's a Kidder, is what I think. My obscene caller is a Jewish Kidder. I wonder who my mother would prefer I spend time with: an obscene caller who's Jewish or an institutional broker who's not? I choose the latter. Then I realize I should choose.

"I met someone," I tell my caller. "I feel it's wrong to continue these calls. We're going to have to stop."

"What? Why? You're not doing anything unfaithful—just talking about it."

My caller's right. These are words, not bodily fluids, we're sharing. What could be so wrong?

"It's weird," I say. "I still feel like talking is cheating. It wouldn't be right."

"Is he good in bed?" my caller asks, his voice now an octave softer.

"We haven't slept together yet."

"So, what's the problem?"

"He's shy. I don't think he's impotent or anything."

"Not *his* problem—*your* problem. If you're not sleeping with the guy, how can you be cheating on him? Listen, I've got to admit something. Lately, I've been fantasizing about taking you to dinner."

"How kinky."

"I'm serious. I want to meet you. I can't stop thinking about you. There's something about you. I want to find out what you're really like."

"It probably would be a big disappointment. I probably make a better fantasy person than a real person."

"I'm willing to prove you wrong. I know we met in an unusual way, but I'm a nice, normal guy. I'm a sound engineer at a recording studio."

"Do I know you?"

"Would you like to? Would you like to meet me tonight?"

I single out one of the red candles on the windowsill, stare into its flickering flame. My obscene caller has helped me through some lonely nights. But he's getting a bit obsessive. All this fantasizing isn't healthy. Besides, now I've got someone real, someone tangible to make love to me. I've got Mark.

"No, no, I can't," I say.

"We could meet at a public place, if you're afraid I'm some perverted serial killer, which I'm not. I'm just a nice Jewish guy from Great Neck."

"It's not that. I'm sure you're really a nice guy. It's just I'm starting to see someone."

I'm proud of my honesty. I'm sure Mark would be proud of me too. Faithfulness is an important ingredient in a healthy relationship.

My caller breathes deeply on the other end, regular breathing, not the sexual kind. "Fine, I won't call anymore. But at least take my number in case you change your mind."

In the tradition of our calls, I don't write down his number, merely pretend to.

T he candles on the sill have melted down to crayon height. Although shorter, they burn just as brightly. *Mark, love me, want me,* I chant, staring into a particularly torchlike flame. *Mark, love me, want me.* The flame wiggles wildly, as if reacting to the intensity of my wanting.

I envision Mark. Me, subtly slipping off Mark's right shoe, left shoe, right sock, left sock, his briefs. Soon it's a frantic pulling off of clothes, underwear dangling from ankles. I become nothing but skin. Even my hair becomes skin. My body becomes parts, not a whole. Warring parts.

"Touch me!" cries my right breast.

"No, me!" cries the left.

Is that my leg, or Mark's? Well it's *ours* now.

Tongues like snakes in the Garden of Eden, weakening the flesh, the will. His tongue—Mark's tongue—ever so easily finding my G-spot, my H-spot, my I, J, K, L, M, N, O, P, Q, R, S, T, U, V, W, X, Y, and Z spots. See Spot. See Dick. See Dick find Spot. Go Dick, go! *Mark, want me! I want you, Mark! I want you in me! I want to lose myself in you!*

6.

HOW MUCH
TRUTH DOES A
SPIRIT ENDURE,
HOW MUCH
TRUTH DOES
IT DARE?
—NIETZSCHE

**Dilute before using.
Contents may be too strong
for most purposes when
applied full strength.
—Ms Kleen**

Frst thing in the morning, I call Viv. There's no answer. I'm certain Viv's home, screening my call—all calls. I envision her lying immobile in bed, her long legs splayed every which way, her huge feet hanging limply off the bed's sides, empty Chinese food cartons and bonbon wrappers scattered about her. Poor Viv. I really feel for her.

When the phone rings, I think it's her. But it's Mark!

Of course it's Mark.

"I'm looking forward to tonight," he says.

Of course he is.

"What do you want to do?" Mark asks.

Heh, heh, heh, I think.

"I thought I'd make dinner," I say—though "make aphrodisiacs" would be more like it.

"You don't have to go to all that trouble," says Mark.

"No trouble. You like seafood?"

"Love it."

"Great, I'll fix us some bouillabaisse. If you want, you can bring a video."

This is part of my seduction plan. The video date being the nineties equivalent of the drive-in movie.

"Any video you want to see?" Mark asks.

"Your pick."

I'm eager to see Mark's personal taste in movies.

"So how's your mom doing?" I ask.

"Better, thanks. I saw her again yesterday. While I was over, she bugged me to cut my hair."

Yes, Mark and I have so much in common.

"So, I let her," says Mark.

Oh, no! It wasn't like Mark had the follicles to spare. "How short did she cut it?" I ask.

"Remember the movie *An Officer and a Gentleman*?"

"Please tell me it's Debra Winger's length."

"Sorry."

I hope this doesn't ruin everything. Love is such a frail thing, something like this could blow it all off course.

Time is one strange dude. Last week I was too depressed to meet Frannie for our Saturday manicure. Today—a mere seven days later—I'm practically tap-dancing down the street. The sands of time cannot hold water.

As instructed on a taped-up sign on the nail salon's door, I PLEASE PRESS BUZZER. One of the sweet Korean girls sees me through the glass, presses a button hidden beneath her workstation. With a loud click, the door unlocks.

It's crowded as usual, with a sampling of females so disparate in appearance it's hard to believe we're all the same sex.

Seated up front is an obese redhead in a turquoise smock dress and black sneakers, a woman who has totally overlooked her general appearance, yet has decided to spend the afternoon caring for her fingertips. The expression "forest for the trees" comes to mind.

Next to her sits a girl in her late teens, with dyed black hair (a "black head") garbed to the max in black leather. Her nail color of choice has been thematically chosen: black.

Across from her sits a well-kempt older woman—obviously wealthy. I can tell by her eyes. The skin around them is pulled tight as a tambourine: a definite mass surgery vibe. Although the wrinkles have been removed, there's years of pain and worry in her eyes just the same.

Then there's Frannie, her straight black hair hanging loosely over a big gray sweatshirt hanging loosely over loose baggy jeans.

"Hey, dudette!" I greet her.

"You're late," she says.

My regular manicurist, an especially petite Korean waif of a girl, motions me to sit in the empty workstation beside Frannie.

"How are you today?" I ask my manicurist.

She smiles, but doesn't answer. She grabs my hands, immediately starts filing and snipping. Each time I come in, I try talking to these manicurists, but none of them speak English. They barely speak anything, really. They're always so silent. At first, this "Englishlessness" made me uncomfortable. Then Frannie explained that's what's so appealing about the place. She never has to talk to anybody. She can get her nails done in peace. And if she and I want, we can talk fluently to each other without worrying about being eavesdropped on.

"So, how you doing, Frannie?" I ask.

"I'm bitter."

"Oh, don't be."

"Don't be better?"

"Didn't you say 'bitter'?"

" 'Better.' I said 'better.' "

There is silence, except for the soft *shoosh* of nails being filed. My manicurist yells something in Korean to another manicurist across the room. They both release a series of little high-pitched giggles. When I first started coming here, I was convinced whenever the manicurists laughed like this it was about my stubby nails. Now I trust them. The women working here seem like nice gals.

"Have you ever thought about making it with a woman?" Frannie asks.

"I've thought about dressing up in women's clothes," I say.

"I've had it with men," says Frannie. "I think I'm ready to check out being with women."

I laugh. As usual, my manicurist doesn't react. She's busy filing what little nails of mine remain. She takes the towel from beneath my hands and is about to throw it out.

"Excuse me," I say. "Can I keep that?"

I point to the towel. She stares at it—and me—suspiciously.

Slowly I remove it from her delicate grip, carefully fold it in half, put it in my pocketbook. I plan to use these fingernail scraps in an aphrodisiac recipe. I'm ready for Frannie to ask me to explain my need for nail clippings. But she's staring off, lost deep in thought.

"I had a dream last night I made love to a woman," Frannie says, "and you know what? It was incredible."

Frannie describes to me her dream in 4-D detail while my manicurist punches at my hand, shiatsu of the palm.

". . . and than I licked the woman's nipples," says Frannie.

I can tell the dream excited her, because her right hand waves furiously through the air as she talks, like an unattached electrical wire—which annoys her manicurist, who's trying diligently to paint these nails. For me, this is definitive proof the manicurists here don't understand a word of English—if impatience is their only reaction to the kinky, graphic details Frannie is supplying. Frankly, the dream makes me very uncomfortable—especially the part about Frannie and the woman eating the cucumber "afterwards."

"Weird," is all I can manage to say.

"Want to know what's really weird? The woman in my dream was you, Sasha."

Frannie dreamed she made love to me? This *is* weird. Then I remember: last night I did my rose petal love bath and lit all those red candles—two dozen of them.

"I'm telling you, Sash," says Frannie, "this dream was a turn-on. You're very good in bed."

I don't know what to say. Thank you? I am thinking maybe I overdid the number of candles I lit. Maybe you're not supposed to exceed a dozen in a twenty-four-hour period.

"The dream has gotten me thinking," continues Frannie. "Maybe bisexuality isn't unnatural. Maybe it's a very natural thing that Bryce could be bisexual."

"What?"

"I mean, if someone's attractive, why shouldn't both sexes pick up on it? Why is that so odd? You're attractive, Sasha. You're putting it out there. Isn't it natural I might respond to your attractiveness? It just shows a heightened sense of sexuality."

Frannie stares at me with eyes so wide and penetrating I worry she'll give me an acne flare-up.

"Lesbianism makes sense," says Frannie. "I mean, who understands a woman's mind better than a woman? And who understands a woman's body better than a woman?"

I seek the serene wilderness of my manicurist's eyes, but she's lost in Cuticle Land.

"Yeah . . . uh huh . . ." I say.

"Look," Frannie says, "I don't mean to make you feel awkward. But you know me, I have to say how I feel. And . . . well, I mean, you know I love you."

"I love you, too."

"No, I mean I think I *love* you."

I'm definitely gonna have to cut back on the candles.

"Frannie, I don't think this is what you want. You don't sound . . . of sound mind."

"Why? At least I'm not going for someone who's married, right? I know you're uninvolved right now, right? You see, I'm learning from my mistakes." Frannie smiles flirtatiously.

"I . . . uh . . . Frannie."

"In so many ways I feel closer to you than I ever did when I was with Arthur . . . or even with Paul. Oh, come on, Sash. You know you get along better with me than you ever did with Bryce. I understand you. And more importantly, I'm *communicative* with you."

Communicative being another word in the euphemistic series for "confrontational."

In the four years Bryce and I were together we never had a big knock-me-down-drag-ya-through-the-muck-and-mire fight, like I have with Frannie on a regular basis. I had at one time seen this as proof of a good relationship—until Frannie explained otherwise. She taught me that the dishonesty in polite compatibility can be a dangerous form of distancing; and anger, blessed in-your-face anger, can be a powerful form of intimacy.

Bryce never shared with me this intimacy.

There were only two times I remember Bryce getting upset. Once, when I bought generic toilet paper.

"You spend two hundred bucks on shoes!" he screamed. "Then go to save ten cents on toilet paper?"

The other time was any time Bryce was watching basketball on TV. The emotions he could work up, the passion, the energy he'd give to this inanimate object, this box of chips and cables, while I sat with my pumping heart and pulsating brain alone, on the bed beside them.

I wonder: if Bryce were a woman, would I want him as my friend? He's so lacking in communication and emotional exchange, the crux of friendship.

"Aren't you curious about being with a woman?" Frannie asks.

I think how great it would be if I were a lesbian. I know so many gorgeous, smart single women. I'd have a much perkier social life. But I'm not.

No questions asked: I'm not.

Viv says one of the reasons she has trouble being in relationships with men is because her female relationships spoil her. It's hard for Viv to duplicate the intensity of communication she has with a woman with a man. And hard to settle for anything less. Hence, Viv's often breaking up with men who on the surface seem swell. Viv never would have settled for Bryce's coldness. Me, I always felt Bryce kept those defenses up to protect himself, and that with a little love and tenderness on my part he could be very warm. I saw him as a tortured soul. So tortured . . . Oh no. Perhaps his sexuality was what was torturing him. Perhaps I should have seen this as a sign. After all, if he wasn't able to communicate clearly his preference for a toilet paper brand, how could I ever expect him to express his preference for one sex over another?

If all this is true, I'm not angry at Bryce for lying about his sexuality. He was probably lying to himself. To admit it to me would be to admit it to himself. Yes, he must have been tortured. I'm actually complimented. I had the power to break through—our love had the power.

And Frannie . . . Now I wonder: were there ever clues as to Frannie having a latent alternate sexuality? Her wardrobe, maybe. She dresses like a lesbian, with all those asexual baggy clothes. Though Viv's theory has always been that Frannie hides herself in her clothing as a means of distancing happiness. *And,* I suppose, *that's* what Frannie's making a pass at me is about.

"Frannie," I say, "I don't think you really want me like . . . *that.* I think this is yet another one of your subconscious strategies of going for someone you can't have, because you're afraid of commitment."

Frannie's mouth opens, then shuts. Then her mouth opens and shuts again, like a ventriloquist doll without the voice projection.

"You may be right," she says quietly.

"You're angry at Arthur right now, so you think it's men you hate."

"Men are pigs."

"Oh, come on. No, they're not."

"You're right. Men are worse than pigs. At least a pig has a heart."

We both laugh heartily.

"Oh, Sasha," Frannie says. "You know, in so many ways, you *are* my dream man."

For the rest of the manicure Frannie sits as quietly as a Korean manicurist.

I am holding two zucchinis side by side, trying to establish which is the longer. I've decided to definitely cut back on the candles, rely more on my cooking. This way I can be sure to lure in the right admirer. So far I've filled my cart with the longest asparagus, the longest carrots, the longest bananas.

"Pardon me, you look familiar." It's a guy with long black stringy hair wearing a rumpled T-shirt that reads:

Nothing says lovin'
Like something
from the coven

It's the Love Specialist from the Wiccan Basket.

"How do I know you?" he asks.

225

"It's not a past life, it's this one," I say. "So don't go thinking it was Vienna 1938. It was only Thursday, in your store."

"It's not my store. I just work there part-time."

How defensive. Maybe he's not a witch but an out-of-work actor who got bored with waiting tables. Maybe he doesn't believe in anything he sold me.

"What do you do when you're not working there?" I ask.

"I'm a medium."

Not as sizable as my Mark. I glance down at his basket, which is filled with about a dozen cans of pitted olives. I wonder what the deal is with olives, if I should buy some?

"How did it go with your love spells?" the Love Specialist asks.

I tell him about meeting Mark, and my plans for keeping him. I hold up a zucchini: Exhibit A.

"If you want a really good love potion," says the Love Specialist, "try wine. It's the best love potion going. It was the undoing of Tristam and Yseult. Wine with herbs, that is. Oh, and even more potent is wine mixed with blood."

"Blood?" I repeat.

"*Your own* blood," says the Love Specialist.

This quells my interest. I've never been good around my own blood. I even get squeamish changing tampons. Then I get an idea. Hmmm, what a perfect time to have one's period.

"What's the recipe?" I ask.

Sticks of jasmine incense are burning in every room of my apartment, jutting out from available orifices: my toothbrush holder, a half-empty Diet Pespi can, the broken eye socket of an old teddy bear. I am again naked to be closer to the spirit world.

"Gods and Goddesses up above, do what ye can to help me find love," I say as I stir my stew of oysters, clams, and shrimps. I sprinkle my fingernail clippings, stir some more.

In a big bowl behind me marinates my Miracle Love Potion: two bottles of Cabernet Sauvignon, one quickly dipped tampon, and a teaspoon of finely diced pubic hairs. I've taste-tested the recipe, and it's not as disgusting as one might fear. It's got a nice spicy kick to it. A little more full-bodied than your typical Cabernet.

I've surrounded the bowl with a circle of red candles, and have already spoken to the Gods and Goddesses about my love for Mark, and thanked them in advance for any help they might offer.

The entire apartment is sparkling clean. Rose petals are scattered on the windowsills, vanilla extract lines the doorway to my bedroom. I am dressed, as I've fantasized, in Bryce's maroon sweater. I am looking forward to this evening, to all the evenings that lie ahead. I've decided I won't have sex with Mark. Sex so soon is no good. Sex messes up everything—your hair, the sheets, the potential for a future. Women are more in control before sex, men afterward. There's something about a woman's legs opening that makes a man's heart close a bit. Many women think sex is the way to hook a man, but they are looking for love in the wrong place. It's not in the uterus. If it were, then the uterus, not the heart, would be seen on Valentine's Day cards. Little uteruses. And we'd give uterus-shaped boxes of candy.

The only problem is: I am curious to see Mark's penis. Maybe I'll sleep naked beside him—but no matter how tempted, I will remain in control of the situation.

To hell with doing Mark. I want to "I do" him—to wed him, not bed him. My mother will be pleased with her son-in-law—even if he isn't Jewish—once she sees how happy Mark makes me.

"I've never seen Sasha glow like this before," she'll tell Mark over brunch at her place. Mark will be wearing one of the textured antique blazers I bought him. His blond hair will be grown in long, a little below his shoulders. On his right earlobe will sparkle a teeny diamond stud, my first-month anniversary gift to him.

"Thanks, Mrs. Schwartz. I love making your daughter happy. She means the world to me. Oh, and great sushi."

"It's lox," my mother will politely correct him—then ask me in private what sushi is.

When our children are born. Mark will insist we raise them, as tradition suggests, according to the mother's religion. We will have one boy, one girl. The boy will be very protective of his sister. The both of them adoring of the both of us.

"Mommy, Mommy, tell us once again how you and Daddy met!" they will ask.

"Well, kids, I had just about given up on the male species."

"Yeah, yeah . . ."

"In my loneliness I headed to the gym. Your father—so young and handsome at the time—was standing in front of me in line at a Nautilus machine, and, oh well, kids, you know the rest."

Yes, we will be happy, Mark and me.

Why is it I'm either remembering having loved, or looking forward to loving, but rarely ever presently loving? For me, love comes in its verb form: blurlike, hard to grasp. I want to get my hands on some of that noun *love* stuff, as in to have and to hold love—as in to have and to hold Mark.

At 8:16 (8:01), the door buzzer buzzes. For extra good luck, I run to the kitchen, dab vanilla extract behind each ear. Mark buzzes again.

Let the game of the sexes begin.

The Visitors begin with a twenty-point penalty. Mark's hair is indeed short. I didn't notice last time how much he looks like Spock from "Star Trek."

"Let me take your coat, come in, sorry the place is a mess, come on in," I say.

"Thanks. You look very beautiful tonight."

I trip over my coffee table.

"Are you all right? I'm sorry," Mark says.

"No, it's me. Listen, next time you compliment me, make sure I'm sitting down. And whatever you do, don't compliment me while I'm walking down steps."

"You're limping."

"It's just a flesh wound. Not to worry. So how about some wine?" I offer, waving an unopened bottle (a decoy), then go into the kitchen, fill two glasses with my Miracle Love Potion.

When I return, Mark is sitting on my sofa. How sweet. If I were at his place, I'd be circling around Sherlock Holmes style, picking up objects, searching for photos of girlfriends past. I give Mark his wine. I don't know if I'm imagining it, but I think Mark's hair has gotten shorter since he arrived. I head to the stereo, plunk in a mood-inducing CD: Cowboy Junkies.

When I turn around, Mark is sitting on my sofa just like I've fantasized—except something is wrong. I can't place it, but there's something wrong about Mark's presence. He clashes with my decor. He looks like something temporary—like an ironing board that's out for a few hours but will eventually have to be put away. Quickly, I join him on the sofa, hoping closer up Mark will feel right. A myopia utopia.

"Cheers!" I say, landing on the sofa with a bounce, merrily clinking my glass to his.

"Cheers!" he says.

I watch Mark drink his Miracle Love Potion, studying him for some change in attitude toward me. So far nothing. He doesn't seem to mind the taste. He drinks it down enthusiastically, as if it were a tequila shot.

"More wine?" I ask, and pour.

"Thanks. I went to the health club today, benchpressed two-fifty. I've never done that much before."

"Perhaps it's my influence."

"I think it's carbohydrates. I had pasta for lunch."

"What kind of pasta?"

"Regular spaghetti."

"Imagine what you could have done with fettuccine."

Silence. A silence that is not golden but leaden. Shit. What is wrong? I am too eager, that's my problem. I must cool out, give things time. The best thing to do is not think so much. The way Bryce doesn't think so he doesn't have to feel, I won't think, so I can let myself feel.

"Good wine," says Mark.

"Have more," I offer.

I pour more into his glass. Our fingers touch. I frisk my heart for my emotions, but come up empty. I have no urge to throw Mark bodily to the floor as I've fantasized, run my fingers through his hair (hair nubs). *Relax,* I tell myself. *Drink, don't think.*

"Oh, by the way," Mark says. "Here's the video. I hope you haven't seen it."

"I'm sure whatever you got—"

He hands me the box: *Under the Volcano.* Bryce's and my old drinking film. Just looking at the box is enough to drive me to drinking again.

"You've seen it?" Mark asks.

"Sort of. How about if we start on dinner?" I say. "I made bouillabaisse. We'll eat in the kitchen."

Mark follows me. I am reminded of how I disliked his walk. I motion him to sit at my small table, which I've set with my best black paper plates and two jumbo red candles.

"I see you have a juicer," Mark says.

"What?"

"Over there—a juicer."

Minus twenty points. Mark's pointing to my cappuccino machine.

"That's my cappuccino machine."

"Oh, right. Wow, you have one of those."

I want to like Mark. I really do. I'm rooting for Mark all the way, convincing myself his naivete is refreshing, his sincerity a relief, that hair eventually does grow back.

"Our appetizer," I say, placing a plate of the longest asparagus the world has ever grown in front of Mark.

"Looks great," he says.

I light the candles, say a silent prayer to the Gods and Goddesses.

"I told Mom I met the girl who wrote the Bully commercial," says Mark, cutting his asparagus into bite-size pieces. "She was impressed. Your job sounds like so much fun."

"It's a lot of work," I say, biting the treetop tip off an asparagus. "Sometimes I have to write over a hundred storyboards before we narrow it down to the one we test—which then dies in testing. It can get depressing. With the same time and effort my agency has me slaving over one silly jingle, I could compose an entire album of rock songs. Sometimes I think I should have pursued being in a rock band. It might have been less stressful."

"I doubt that."

"I'm joking," I say, sipping my wine. The taste is growing on me. I kind of like that tampon tang. This is good wine. At least, this *was* good wine. I pour myself another glass.

"So, you play any musical instruments?" asks Mark.

"Just my stereo."

"What?"

"Another joke."

I am worried. I can't be serious with a man with whom I can't be humorous. So far, I haven't witnessed any magical effects from my Miracle Love Potion—except for the alcoholic kind. I'm personally feeling a bit dizzy. Now, there's not only blood in my wine, the wine is at one with my blood. It's a nice give-and-take thing.

"I have this friend, Rick," says Mark, cutting his last remaining tiny chunk of asparagus into two even tinier pieces. "I know him from high school. He's got long hair, down to his waist. He's a bass player. Just made it big. Plays bass for Mick Jagger. It can't get much better than that. Bass player for Mick."

"Except to be Mick."

"What?"

"It would be even better to be Mick Jagger." I clear away our empty plates, bring out the bouillabaisse. "That's what I would go for."

"Yeah, right." Mark laughs. "You're joking again. You are funny."

"I'm serious," I say, generously scooping bouillabaisse into two bowls, stirring first to make sure no nail clippings are overtly showing. "That's what I would have wanted to be. A star—not some backup vocalist, but the lead singer."

"Do you know how impossible it is to make it as a star in the music industry?"

"One can always fantasize. I often fantasize about it, the filled stadiums, the dry ice smoke effects, the screaming fans, the David Letterman interviews. Right now, rather than tearing my hair out over ads, they'd be selling it in rest rooms—along with my personalized satin tour jacket, stolen from my tour bus when I was inside Annie Leibovitz's apartment posing for photos for *Rolling Stone*. Yeah, it would be fun to be immortal, even if it were only for a few years."

"It's not good to fantasize like that. It only leads to disappointment with your own life to fantasize that big."

"What? I should fantasize smaller? It's enough we compromise in real life, but to compromise a fantasy? That's the whole point of a fantasy, to be fantastic—*fantasy-iacal!*"

Mark stares at me. I have this feeling of impending doom—like Goofy on skis.

"I don't need the fantastic to be happy," says Mark. "I have simple needs. Basically, I'm a simple guy."

"You say that so proudly, like that's something great. I think it sounds bland to be simple."

"Simple things don't break."

Then the phone rings. I wonder if it's my caller, and if so, if I should answer. I might have a friskier time with him. Or maybe I should let Mark get it. It might put him in the mood. Finally I opt for the answering machine getting the phone, and me changing the topic with Mark.

"Let's talk about something else," I say.

"Sure, what do you want to talk about?"

"Sex."

Mark coughs.

"How old were you when you first learned about sex?" I say.

He thinks. "Hmmm, I first learned about sex, I guess, when Mom told me not to throw girls into the swimming pool because they might have their periods." Ironically Mark sips his wine right after the mention of the word *period*. "How about you? When did you first learn?"

"I learned about sex from my father—not that I had sex with

my father." I laugh heartily. Mark looks perplexed. I pour him more wine. "My father told me babies come from Milwaukee," I say.

"Milwaukee?"

"My dad was joking," I explain. "My dad had this warped sense of humor. He was always giving me wacked-out information. Like, he taught me the word *M-I-S-L-E-D* was pronounced with a long *i*. 'Mi-sled.' As a kid he had first seen this word in books, and thought this was how it was pronounced. So he decided to pass this mistake down the family tree to me."

"That's horrible," says Mark.

"No, it's not. It's funny."

"Uh . . . where's your rest room?"

"I hope you're not asking as a result of my cooking." I giggle.

"What?"

"You know, my cooking didn't make you sick, I hope. I mean, it's a joke—I hope."

"Dinner was delicious," Mark says very seriously.

I stand to show Mark where the bathroom is. That's when I become aware of just how much the wine has gotten to me. The room feels like one of those spinnaker lounges. I hear the bathroom door click shut, then the toilet seat lid smack against the porcelain base. I think about how shiny and clean and deodorized every crevice of my bathroom is, and I can't help but think: I scrubbed the bathtub for this? What is going on here? Or rather: What is not going on here? I remember how Bryce would suddenly burst out with: *Something is happening here, and you don't know what it is, do you, Ms. Jones?* I must forget about Bryce, concentrate on my future, on Mark. I realize things aren't going too swimmingly, but the night is young—and I'm an elderly twenty-nine and single. I must keep trying.

I totter over to my stereo, put on *Highway 61 Revisited*, sit on my sofa, drinking my Miracle Love Potion, listening to the lyrics of "Ballad of a Thin Man":

> *You raise up your head, and you ask:*
> *"Is this where it is?"*
> *and somebody points to you and says:*
> *"It's his"*

I sit thinking: It's got to work out with Mark. I've had such hopes for me and Mark. I can't give up yet. I already promised our children it all worked out.

Which reminds me, where is Mark? He's been in the bathroom a while. Then I remember my moody doorjamb, known to trap occasional visitors. It's interesting watching the various reactions, discovering who the claustrophobics are amongst my friends.

I tiptoe over to the bathroom, hear Mark jiggling the doorknob, muttering. He is indeed stuck.

"Sasha? Sasha?"

"Mark, are you okay?" I ask innocently.

"I . . . uh. I . . . I'm a little stuck," he says.

I open the door. Mark comes spilling out. I suppress an urge to laugh hysterically. I don't want to offend him. I want things to work.

"You look like you could use some wine." I hand him his glass.

"Thanks." He swallows some quickly. "Mmmm, this really is unusually good wine. Oh, and good music. Who is this?"

"Dylan."

"Oh, yeah? I love Dylan Thomas."

"Bob Dylan."

"Oh, right. I have one of his albums. *Live at Budokan*. It's got all his greatest hits."

This and *Self-Portrait* are Dylan's worst albums of all time. I pour us each a full glass of wine. I'm not about to give up yet.

"If you want," I say warmly, "I can recommend better albums. In my opinion, Dylan sang like a bad Catskill performer at that Budokan concert. All words, no soul."

Mark and I sit next to each other on my sofa, staring straight ahead at my Man Ray print.

"I think this song is on my Budokan album," Mark finally says.

"Can you hear the difference? How he sings the song on my album, with an added intensity, a spirit that's way more powerful?"

"I don't hear anything different," says Mark. "I guess you have a real ear for music, a natural ear."

"I guess. Actually, I believe each of us has a dominant sense. Which do you think yours is, Mark? Sight, sound—touch?"

"Yours must be your ears."

"Not necessarily. I've been to a lot of clubs. You can go deaf like that."

"But you know what to listen for in music."

I look down at our glasses: both are very half empty. I fill them twice as full.

"If you really want to listen to music . . ." I say, sipping my wine. "You know how a blind person hears better, or a deaf person sees better? The trick is to get rid of the clutter of your other senses. Let me turn out the lights. You'll see how you're forced to listen more closely to the music."

I turn off the lights. Perfect. I can't see Mark's haircut this way.

"You hear that?" I ask. "That guitar . . ."

"Yeah. I think so. Oooops."

"What was that?"

"I spilled my wine," says Mark.

"Let me—"

"Hey—"

Then we kiss. A real kiss. The first thing I notice: Mark's mouth tastes wrong. Sweet and minty, with a splash of Cabernet. None of that sooty cigarette feel I'd grown accustomed to from Bryce. It's as if the taste buds have been sandpapered off his tongue. We kiss some more, but it's more motion than emotion.

I feel like an alcoholic with a bottle of Moussy beer.

7.

WHERE AM I? WHO AM I? HOW DID I COME TO BE HERE? WHAT IS THIS THING CALLED THE WORLD? AND IF I AM COMPELLED TO TAKE PART IN IT, WHERE IS THE DIRECTOR? I WANT TO SEE THE DIRECTOR.
—KIERKEGAARD

B

ob the psychic is a fraud.

I am sitting in the Acropolis Coffee Shop in a booth for four, alone, not even a twosome, and the way I am feeling, barely even a one.

"What's the matter, Chicken Lady?" the waiter says. "You seem so sad."

Amazing, this stranger, a man who knows nothing about me— except that I require Sweet'n Low for my coffee—this man, somehow *he* knows. He's a better psychic than Bob.

It took zero willpower to resist sex with Mark. There was no chemistry, and no tempting carrot on a stick. Mark was far from ample. "Teeny wienie" is the appropriate description. I couldn't even find it at first. I worried he was a eunuch. And Mark wasn't even circumcised, which meant he had an extra couple centimeters going for him. It was all so awkward. Not so unusual for the first time. But with Mark nothing in particular made it awkward. Literally, and clitorally. It was nothing, hence it was awkward. We fooled around a bit, then fell asleep—or at least Mark did. Me, I stayed awake thinking psychic thoughts, like: *Leave! Mark, leave!*

At 9 A.M. I took his watch from the nightstand, turned it forward two hours, then turned up my alarm clock to match. I pretended to pop up from bed startled.

"Wow, is it eleven o'clock already? Mark! Mark!" I shook him. "I told my boss that I'd meet him at eleven to go over a few things. I'm late!"

We got dressed fast. I walked him to the subway, then rushed over to the Acropolis, where I called Viv. Finally, she picked up the phone. I told her to meet me here. I figured we could both use the company right now. Thank goodness for Female Support Systems.

After all, it's difficult for a gal to slash her wrists with a plastic Flicker.

The waiter, seeing my empty cup, runs over with a fresh pot.

"Coffee, yes?" he asks.

Before I answer, he pours. He remains standing over me, staring. Doesn't he have tapioca pudding somewhere that requires stirring?

"Such a pretty girl. How come you not smile?" he persists.

I am thinking: Because this pretty girl, amazing as it is, cannot find a man, that's why, buddy; now buzz off.

I say nothing.

I smile for him.

Where the fuck is Viv?

The couple at the next table giggles in lovers' delight. In a fit of self-destruction, I dump a whole Sweet'n Low into my coffee. Usually I use only half a packet. But the way I'm feeling, I think— what the hell, I'll use the whole toxic pack. I tap diligently at its little pink corner, releasing every last rat-killing particle.

"Sasha!"

It's Viv, at last. She is wearing a lime-green minidress and a Carmen Miranda hat—an L.A. version, decorated mainly with plastic kiwi. She gives me a big kiss and is blending me in when the waiter arrives, coffeepot in hand.

"Coffee, yes?" the waiter asks.

"Yes," says Viv. "Well, sort of. I'll have half decaf, half caf. I'm trying to cut down on caffeine."

The waiter hurries off. Viv yells to him across the room for all to hear: "Oh—you know what? Make it three-quarters caf, to start, then the rest decaf, but after this, the next cup, make it half decaf, half caf. You got that?"

Everyone stares. Viv doesn't just want service, she wants attention.

"You wanna split a Farmer's Omelette?" Viv asks me.

"I'm not hungry."

"Oh come on. A Farmer's Omelette . . . *gooey melted cheese*."

"I'm not hungry."

The waiter returns with Viv's special-edition coffee.

"You know what, we'll have one Farmer's Omelette, too," she tells him. "Now, what's the matter, girl?"

"Oh, I don't know. I'm just fed up!"

"That's interesting."

I look at her quizzically. The phrase "That's interesting!" is Viv's verbal tofu. Taken by themselves the words are plain. But Viv seasons them with all sorts of meanings, so "That's interesting!" can mean everything from "That's ugly!" to "That's gorgeous!" to "That's amazing!" to "That's typical!" and only rarely ever "That's interesting!"

"You said you're fed up," says Viv, "and you say you can't eat. You can't eat because you're fed up."

Sometimes the girl really makes sense.

"So what's the matter?" she asks.

"I had my date with Mark last night and it was horrible. He's nothing like I thought—or the psychic thought. Turns out Mark's the equivalent of a woman's 28-AAA. And he wasn't even circumcised."

"Really? I've never seen one of those. What's it look like? Does it look like a corndog? I heard they look like corndogs."

"It was more like a miniature pig in a blanket. Plus, it didn't help that Mark could barely get an erection."

"That means he really likes you."

"Would you stop with that, Viv! There was no chemistry. Nada! I don't like Mark, and I'm very disappointed about it. I was really hoping I was gonna fall in love with the guy. I want so badly to be in love."

I am thinking: *Déjà ecout.* I've heard this before.

Viv's omelette arrives. She shakes a bottle of catsup at it that defies all laws of gravity. Finally she knifes the bottle.

"You know," says Viv, "you weren't being fair to Mark. You were using him for love the way a man might use a woman for sex, looking for a quick-and-easy love, not caring who the recipient is— desperate for someone, anyone, you can molest with your emotions. You were being an emotional slut."

Somewhere along the way I *did* stop caring who Mark was and began projecting onto him qualities that weren't there. A hologram of love. A hollow gram of love. The lies I told myself, the pleasure so clearly imagined, as clearly as my obscene caller imagined me: *lick, love, throbbing, fuck, love, love, love.* At least the good thing about phone sex is you have a phone in your hand to signal a fantasy is going on.

Viv shovels a stringy cheesy omelette bite into her mouth. "I think you're like this because of the media. You're looking for the ad fantasy images you and everyone else in your industry has created."

"Oh, come on, Viv. I write the stuff. I know the behind-the-scenes manipulation."

"I know, it's as ridiculous as me looking for soap opera passion, but sometimes I do. I get confused. It's hard to resist these beautiful fantasy images. Especially advertising's, 'cause we're so bombarded. I read in the *Wall Street Journal* that in 1990, American corporations spent a hundred and thirty billion dollars on ads. That's about six bucks a week per person—fifty percent more money than any other nation's ad budget. Supposedly, by the time we're forty, we'll all have seen over a million ads. That's a lot of images to try resisting the power of."

"Yeah, and not only do I have those million to deal with, I have the hundreds of ads my mom clips from magazines and mails me as haircut and fashion suggestions."

"That's exactly what I'm talking about here, Sasha; the way people think they should strive to emulate ads. Plus, it doesn't help you're *always* working on some love strategy. You even used one for that soft drink, where you sold it as a love potion, used that 'Love Potion Number 9' song. That's ridiculous."

"Hey, love is a top seller. But I've used other stuff, like health and wealth and good family relations. For Chromostix my strategy is 'fun.' But that's kid's advertising. Kids basically only have one strategy: 'fun.' "

"Kids have their priorities straight."

Viv smiles up at me, proud of how she's managed to synthesize her philosophy minor into major philosophies. Her upper lip has a smudge of red. I can't tell if it's catsup or lipstick. Other than that one smudge, her lipstick has remained miraculously plastered to her lips. Viv sure has it all together. She can eat an omelette without smudging her lipstick, and keep a man desperately in love with her.

I bet Keith offered to marry her when she told him about the baby. I wonder . . .

"So did you tell Keith about . . . you know?" I ask.

"Did I tell you I convinced Gary to have my character go to Paris to get that new abortion pill, the RU 486? Don't you just love that name, like in a restaurant you 'eighty-six' something." She laughs.

"Forget about your soap life. Tell me about your real life."

"I am. Gary agreed shooting in Paris would be great for ratings. So on the show I go to Paris to get the pill. While we're shooting, I'm really going to get the abortion pill. Gary and I might smuggle some into the States. The pills sound great. There's no side effects — and best of all, no anesthesia. Too bad our government isn't keen on developing them. They're worried about the costs of liability. You know the U.S. spends less on contraceptive research in a single year than the Defense Department spends in fifteen minutes? It's a joke!"

"Gary agreed to help you bootleg abortion pills? I thought he was anti-abortion."

"He's a lot more open-minded than I thought. And a lot sexier."

"Viv, why are you smirking?"

"Why am I smirking?"

"Viv . . ."

"Sasha . . ."

"Viv . . ."

"Sasha . . ."

"*Viv!*"

"Okay, okay! Gary and I have sort of been fooling around."

"What?"

"We've had the most incredibly sensuous weekend."

"You've been cheating on Keith?"

"Relax, I didn't have sex with Gary, so I didn't totally cheat. Eating isn't cheating. Though this weekend was tempting."

To think I'd been thinking Viv was busy crying in bed all weekend, when in reality she'd been *crying out* in bed. To Gary. Wow. Incredible. The girl really knows how to turn things around to her advantage. No wonder she leads such a charmed life. It's because she puts the verb *lead* into "leading a life."

"So, are you going to see Gary now?" I ask.

"Maybe. Yeah, sure. Gary's great. Yeah, I'll probably break up with Keith. I don't know. I'll see how things go."

Geez, Viv sure has no problem finding men to fall in love with her. That's because she doesn't need men. She offers herself at emotional prices that say: "I'm difficult to attain." Men all come flocking.

Keith will be devastated if Viv leaves him. He's paid a high price all along to be with her, and hasn't stopped paying. Viv's constantly making him earn the right to her company. Yes, Viv understands good positioning in the love marketplace.

"So," I say, "what did Keith say when you told him you were pregnant?"

"He doesn't know."

"What?"

"I didn't want to hurt him. Knowing Keith, he'd want to talk about getting married, having the baby."

"But shouldn't Keith know the truth?"

"You know, Sash, sometimes the truth is not the best thing."

I shoot Viv a stern stare, but I've lost her attention. The waiter is parading by with two plates of thick, plump french toast.

"Mmm, take a look at that," says Viv. "Doesn't that look great? I should have gotten the french toast." Viv laughs. "Oh, Sash, how am I supposed to decide on the man I'm to spend my life with, when I can't even decide what to order in restaurants?"

When I arrive at my office, I find Jerriatrics already seated in my guest chair, a bag of popcorn in hand.

"Are you sick?" he asks. "Your aura is totally wrinkled."

I grab the popcorn from him. "Nothing contagious. Just from drinking too much last night. Not that drinking too much isn't contagious. It can be, if you're around someone who's drinking too much. Then it can be very contagious."

"How was your date?"

"You don't want to know. Oh, by the way, thanks for the lingerie. It was a nice gesture. But size C? Really, Jerry!"

He grabs the popcorn. "That's the way I envision you."

"Well, a definite thanks then."

I reach for the popcorn again, but this time Jerriatrics holds it just beyond reach. "No popcorn till you tell me the scoop on your date." He shovels a handful of kernels into his mouth. "Mmmm," he says. "This is really delicious popcorn. Mmmmm." He smiles. I sigh.

"Okay. You want to know about my date? It was depressing. It was a case of opposites repelling."

"So you and Mark are already broken up?"

"Yeah." I snatch back the bag. Not many kernels remain. Just a few sneaky unpopped ones.

"Sasha, do you ever think that maybe, possibly, sometime in the not-too-distant future you could maybe feel something for me that might sort of resemble love? You know, sometimes I feel that maybe I can sometime, in the future, feel something for you that is in the love family. Sometimes I even feel like I don't have to wait till the not-too-distant future, and sometimes I even feel it's not just something that only sort of resembles love. Do you know what I'm getting at, Sasha?"

"Jerry, I'm touched . . . but . . ."

"Sasha, I want to make love with you."

"Jerry!"

"Okay. Could we just go out for a beer together sometime?"

"Jerry, please. You don't know what you're saying. You don't know me. You gave me C-cup lingerie."

"We're a good team, Sash. We'd be a good team in love, too."

But I feel Jerry doesn't know what he's saying. It's this love magic I've been messing with. First my obscene caller gets confused into thinking he wants me. Then Frannie. Now Jerry. It seems the only person my love magic didn't work on was Mark—but that's because I was depending too much on my cooking. I should have known better than to depend on my cooking. Now what do I do? I

245

must cut back on the candles. Or stop using jumbo ones. But first I've got to talk some sense into Jerry.

"Jerry, we've got to talk. . . . I'm worried . . . this is important. I . . . I'm worried . . . about all the work we have ahead of us today—a Mangia spot we haven't even started and ten Close-Up love songs we've got to blend plaque resistance into. I was thinking, maybe we could convince Mike not to mess with our TV spots, and do a separate print campaign for the plaque strategy. Print is a better medium for serious information anyway. People see long body copy—they don't even have to read it—and they usually don't—but a plaque print campaign will make Close-Up look very informed about plaque."

I am talking, talking, talking, using these words to avoid using other words. These are swap 'em, trade 'em, collect 'em words. Conversational helper. Emotional helper. I don't want to deal with what I'm truly feeling—whatever that is.

Jerriatrics removes his sunglasses so I can see his eyes. They are small and deeply set. I'm always surprised whenever Jerry removes his shades, because his eyes are not as I envision them to be: long-lashed and penetrating. No, out of all the features his face has to offer, his eyes are the weakest. Perhaps this is why Jerry wears the shades. Men can't wear mascara and eyeliner, so Jerry wears Ray-Bans to add drama. A drama that his being rightfully deserves. He is special, my Jerry. And sweet, understanding, looks good on his motorcycle. I'm sure many a woman has flipped for him. Enza, the psychic, I bet, saw a great future with him. So what's my problem? What does lead to love? The smell? The mind? The body? The spirit? What mysterious vapor is missing that I'm not madly in love with Jerry?

"You know what the worst feeling for a drummer is?" Jerry says. "When you've got a great sense of time, and no one else in the band does."

Jerry is right. Timing *is* everything. Now, thanks to my new procrastinatory need (dealing with Jerry's love declaration), I'm able to let go of my usual procrastinatory need (writing ads) and actually get some work done.

Print headlines for Close-Up plaque strategy:

HOW CAN YOU MAKE SOMETHING YOU CANNOT SEE DISAPPEAR?*
(meaning invisible plaque presence)

HOW CAN YOU TAKE AWAY SOMETHING AND BE LEFT WITH MORE?*
(meaning the benefits of removing plaque from teeth)

WHAT'S RIGHT UNDER YOUR NOSE YET IMPOSSIBLE TO REACH?*
(meaning the plaque found in one's mouth)

Mangia spokesperson spot
:30 TV

THE VISUAL:
A Woody Allenesque man as spokesperson, standing behind a counter with two dishes of food in front of him; behind all this is a white seamless backdrop.

THE COPY:
What is reality?
How can any of us be sure of anything when there's a frozen dinner that tastes just like fresh?

Mangia. Their frozen Chicken Parmigiana tastes just like fresh Chicken Parmigiana. Frozen broccoli, fresh broccoli. Frozen rice, fresh rice. If I can't tell frozen from fresh, how can I be sure my mother is my real mother? And did she really love me?

THE TAGLINE:

MANGIA. THE FROZEN MEAL THAT TASTES REAL.

Well, we did it," I say.

Outwardly, I am referring to having solved both creative assignments.

Inwardly, I am referring to avoiding talking about the potential of an Us, or rather, the nonpotential.

"I hope Mike goes for the separate Close-Up print campaign concept," I say. "I dread messing with the music on that 'Squeeze' spot. It's such a sexy, hypnotic beat you created. You really did a great job with that music."

"You know, Sash, on the surface it might be a jingle about toothpaste, but I created that music with you in mind. Spiritually it's not about toothpaste, it's about you. I think I'm in love with you, Sash."

Darn. I was hoping Jerry would forget he was in love with me. After all, it's happened with men in the past.

"Sorry to interrupt." It's Joy, bearing a large manila envelope and an even larger impish grin, which makes me wonder how long she's been standing there.

"This was on the receptionist's desk for you, Sash." She hands me the envelope. The word *pirsonnal* is scribbled across the front.

April 19, 1986
Dearest Bryce,
I hated seeing you leave.
I loved seeing you come.
. . . and I do mean love.
Glen

August 18, 1987
Bryce,
Hope your OK with the little lady, and she didn't catch on. Do you
think we could arrange a weekend sometime?
Love,
Glen

June, 1989
Bryce,
You asked me if you should tell her. Of course I think so. Of
course, I have my own selfish reasons. But I also want what's best
for you. I feel good knowing I've helped you realize you've been
needing things she can't give. I feel good about opening you up to
another way of life.
Love,
Glen

May 19.1989
Bryce,
Had a wonderful night.
Wanna fuck Wednesday?
Love,
Glen

November 3, 1989
Blood, sweat, and tears. We had them all last night, didn't we?
Didn't you feel uncomfortable lying? I don't know how long you
can continue to live this double life. At least I don't know how long
I can.
Love,
Glen

Mozart's "Eine
Kleine Nacht-
Musik" is blasting on my stereo. I've
turned up the volume as loud as it goes.

The candle flames on my bedroom windowsill vibrate in rhythm to the music's punctuation. I am lying naked on my bed, drinking wine, the sans-blood vintage.

Nausea . . . weight loss . . . insomnia . . . it all adds up.

And what's this? A bluish mark on my calf. How long has that been there? How long am I to be here?

After all, Bryce is presently sick. Who knows with what or for how long?

The envelope included over a dozen love letters written across the span of the last four years—our *entire* relationship. (Plus, there was a receipt for Natasha's Kinko costs: $2.25.) My only comfort was that Glen spelled *your* wrong in one of his letters. It should have been "you're." The idiot!

I swig more wine.

I suppose I could get tested. But that's a worse proposition than a commercial being tested. I'd rather not know. Though I feel I do know. In my head I am already a dead person. In my head I am a skull.

Does this mean meeting Bryce was in actuality one of the unluckiest things to ever happen to me? That every one of those shared moments of joy was tragedy in a disguise?

No, I don't regret anything. I'd take Bryce back, even now, even with the threat of AIDS. I'd die with him, for him, as Romeo did for Juliet. AIDS: the Romeo/Juliet poison of the nineties. Those kids Romeo and Juliet had the right idea about relationships. They killed themselves off before problems arose. Jealousy, boredom, fighting over the *New York Times* Arts and Leisure section. They understood true romantic love, in all its illusory glory. *Illusory love.* I guess that's all I had with Bryce. I guess I never knew him completely. He gave me a bunch of dots without the numbers. I connected them into the picture I wanted to see. So much of my love life now seems but a mere fantasy—which is but a euphemism for "a lie." Not just my love life—most people's love lives are whitewashed with white lies.

Keith believing in his version of Viv. Frannie in her version of Arthur—and me. Jerriatrics, too, believing in a me he wants to see. The lie begins within ourselves, the who we say we are to the outside world. It's like that Fitzgerald quote from one of his novels: "He allowed her to be who she pretended to be." That's what love is.

It's in our nature to seek out these fantasy lies. We do it every night in the form of dreams, lying to ourselves for eight hours straight by telling ourselves these fake events are real. There's nothing moral stopping us from dreaming. We even enjoy it, like we enjoy fairy tales, which are a form of lies. As are novels, films, paintings. All art is a kind of lie—to say nothing of advertising, which is the art of the lie.

Advertising is the lie we say we hate, but secretly root for being told. We all want to believe there is something we can do to be more beautiful, more loved, stop our aging process. We all want to believe it's as easy as buying a product, and all shall be fixed— none shall die.

No, in theory and practice we don't mind lies. If they're upheld, we're happy to have them on hand. It's only when we're forced to face a lie's unpleasant consequence that we get miffed. My job in advertising is to make sure nobody ever sees behind the lies, pulls back the curtain to reveal the balding twirp of reality. And, who knows, if I do my job right, perhaps I can even help people, by giving them the power of positive thinking. In the same way Jerry urges me to create positive pictures in my mind, TV spots are filmed versions of these visualizations. There's not much difference between toothpaste companies, cosmetic companies, and perfume companies having us believe in the love power of their products, and Jerry having me believe in the love power of a candle.

Then I think about it. The Wiccan Basket had jars filled with powders labeled "Health," "Love," "Money," and "Family Happiness." These are all advertising strategies. Witchcraft uses music. Advertising uses jingles. Witchcraft uses chants. Advertising uses taglines. Witchcraft uses symbols. Advertising uses logos. Witchcraft uses colors as power. Advertising recognizes the power of specific colors for packaging. Witchcraft hypes the circle. Advertising incorporates the circle into many product logos, like the image found on Schlitz beer cans—even this wine label.

My ad craft and witchcraft are not so different.

I guzzle more wine.

No wonder Jerry doesn't mind being in advertising. It's the natural career choice for a witch. There's magic in the fantasies advertising creates—magic in all fantasies, really.

My obscene-phone caller was plenty happy with his fantasies. For the time I was fantasizing about Mark, I too was happy. Sometimes fantasy alone suffices, without ever going for the reality angle. Like, for me, I'm happy just sitting around listening to music and fantasizing about being a rock star, without ever having to go out and do it. Just listening to music alone is enough to make me happy. Like this Mozart music surrounding me now; there's magic in this. All great art has a magic about it. And the experience of all great art is really about living in the present moment, or "being" as Jerry calls it. So living in the present holds magical powers.

The "present," as in a gift.

The music pounds through me like a second heartbeat, overtaking my heartbeat, what little remains of my heartbeat. No question. I'm definitely experiencing major insomnia tonight. I can't imagine falling asleep ever again. But if I'm going to die, I'm going to spend an eternity lying around in darkness anyway. Why waste time doing that now? I'm lucky to have insomnia, to be awake, to experience every tick-tocking moment of life.

8.

X

WE MUST ALL DIE; WE ARE LIKE WATER SPILT ON THE GROUND, WHICH CANNOT BE GATHERED UP AGAIN.
—SAMUEL 14:14

Absorbs fast when you need it most.
—Bounty Towels

I awake to find a huge pimple on my face. At least I hope it's a pimple and not a pubescent lesion. Whatever it is, I feel it's some sort of sign, marking me as a pariah. I go through the motions of washing, brushing, dressing, not fully aware of what I'm doing, what I'm feeling.

I head outside, aiming myself bodily toward The Miller Agency. Although it's my usual route, things look different. For instance, I just now notice the fire hydrant on the corner is painted blue. The public telephone on University is missing its receiver. Don's Shoe Store is going out of business. Under the sign announcing 50% OFF is printed in large type: GOING OUT OF BUSINESS. I didn't notice that the other day. A huge truck is double-parked outside. Men in bright orange jumpsuits are hurriedly stacking boxes of shoes into the back of this truck. I watch them move, the boxes piling up in their arms, then dissolving into the truck's inner darkness. For some reason I think of coffins, that these shoeboxes are like mini coffins.

Sasha! Where have you been? It's noon," says Jerry. "Look, I'm sorry if I made you feel awkward yesterday, but please don't avoid me."

"I'm not, it's just that I . . . I . . . I . . ."

"What's that on your face?"

My hand reaches up to touch my lesion. "Is it that noticeable?"

"Let's just say I've been with women who have breasts that are smaller."

"Thanks."

"Just trying to give you a dose of that humor you love so much. Are you okay?"

"It's . . . I . . . it's . . . I . . . it's . . ."

I reach into my pocketbook, pull out Glen's love letters, now stained with red wine. Jerry reads them silently. I gnaw at my right index finger. In the last twenty-four hours I've managed to nibble off all ten of my new fake fingertips, and am now onto my "au naturel" tips. They say fingernails continue growing when you die. If so, I might soon have naturally long fingernails. Something to look forward to in death.

Jerry reaches up, pulls my hand away from my mouth, holds it, squeezing gently.

"Are you going to get tested?" he asks. "What are you going to do?"

"I already did, do it. I . . . I . . . I told Mike I needed a few days off to relax. He refused. Next thing I know I was screaming at him, telling him what I really thought about how he runs this agency, insisting he present our Close-Up TV spots as we wrote them. I totally tore him into him."

"Oh no . . . Don't tell me. Did he fire you?"

"I got a raise."

"You got a raise?"

"And you one, too. It was weird. I felt so bold, so powerful. I figured, what's the worst that could happen? Death. And it might have happened anyway. I have nothing to risk, except not getting the most out of my life, which I don't think I have been. I'm living in the past and the future. I need to get in on some present action. I feel so strong. Not to sound corny, but it's like the fear of death has made me less fearful of life."

"It's like windsurfing."

"What?"

"This death thing is like windsurfing."

"Death is like windsurfing. Thanks, Jer. Now I know what to expect. A shining light, then a surf."

"The first thing you learn when windsurfing is not how to wind-surf. You learn how to fall. The wind can blow you all different ways. You can land on your stomach, your left side, your right side. First they teach you how to fall in different positions, so you won't get hurt. Then you learn how to windsurf. This way, when you finally get up on the board, you're not afraid of falling. You feel like you can take more risks, because no matter how you fall, you'll know how to land. You now feel like you can fall without getting hurt."

"I know I never would have had the guts to demand the things I did from Mike it weren't for Glen's letters."

"Let's go celebrate," says Jerry.

"Celebrate? But I'm dying, Jer."

I like my wine red and my margaritas blue," I say to Jerry. I'm on my third blue margarita—"Tidy Bowls" they're called here at Tortilla Flats. I'm feeling a little dizzy, a lot confused. Am I supposed to be happy or miserable?

"What's the difference between a tostado and a burrito?" Jerry asks.

"Fifty cents?"

"I guess when it comes down to it, it's all the same ingredients anyway: cheese, beans, meat, lettuce, hot sauce. They're just piled differently on the plate. Just a different layout."

"More ad hype," I say.

"Can't escape it."

"Though I almost did. You should have seen Mike's face when I told him off." I laugh. "It felt good. My friend Frannie's gonna be proud of me for being so upfront. Oh, and Viv, too, for showing some of that old-fashioned integrity stuff."

"I'd like to make a toast to you," says Jerry, raising his glass. "To windsurfing."

"I think I'd rather we make a toast to my health, Jer."

"Oh, you're not going to die. I didn't read it in your aura."

"Forget reading my aura. Read Glen's love letters. Bryce is bisexual, and has been for who knows how long. It does not look good for me, Jer."

"You're not dying."

"Oh, God!"

"What? You see God? So soon? Funny, you looked like you had at least a few good months left."

"Speaking of the devil."

"Now you see the devil? No more margaritas, Sash."

"There's Bryce."

"Where?"

"You see the tall leggy woman with the long blond hair and short red skirt?"

"That's Bryce? No wonder you questioned his sexuality."

"Bryce is next to her. And to his other side is a man in black leather pants."

"Is that Glen?"

"No. I've never seen this guy before. Maybe Bryce is seeing another guy behind Glen's back. Maybe Bryce is a gay sleep-around—which only speeds up my odds of dying."

"He's attractive," says Jerriatrics.

Bryce or his lover? I wonder. Bryce looks healthy, thank goodness. But now that I look him over anew, he does seem gay. There's something about him, his haircut, his Hawaiian print necktie, who knows. But it's obvious: Bryce is not entirely straight. What a fool I was not to see it all along.

Both he and this man are laughing. This makes me tingle with jealousy. Laughter. The sharing of a joke, the shared pleasure exchanged. I might as well have overheard Bryce moaning in sexual ecstasy. The leather-panted guy puts his arm around Bryce. They look so happy. Poor Bryce, so tortured by his attraction to men. No, I shouldn't be angry. I should pity him. I just don't want Bryce to pity me, seeing me here, all alone.

But I'm not alone.

"Jerry, hold my hand," I say. "There will be something in it for you later."

Jerry understands the role he is to play immediately, and decides for an Academy Award. He pulls me in for a kiss. His tongue entwines mine, then hides behind a bicuspid, shy, but wanting, the puppet of his emotions. What am I feeling? I wonder. I feel someone tap my shoulder, that I now know I feel. Oh, no. It's Bryce. What do I say? How do I act? At least he's seeing me kissing Jerry. Then I realize Jerry's solid grayish-white hair makes him look like a ninety-year-old man. Bryce probably thinks I'm making out with a senior citizen. I compose myself. After all, I know how to windsurf on the wave of life.

"Yes?" I ask.

"Margaritas?" asks the waiter.

This windsurfer is now riding a wave of relief. "We didn't order those," I say,

"They're from me," says Bryce's voice.

I look behind the waiter and see him: the love of my life, the love of my death, my killer, my murderer, my Bryce.

"You look great," Bryce says. "You get your hair cut?"

"No, why?"

"There's something different about you, the way you look."

"Same with you," I say.

"I'm Jerry," says Jerry, disattaching his arm from my shoulder, raising it up to Bryce for a handshake.

"Oh, sorry," says Bryce. "I'm Bryce, and these are my friends."

"I'm Todd," says the guy.

"And I'm Glen," says the woman.

Glen is a woman? This woman is Glen? *The* Glen? Bryce is heterosexual and this is the Glen he's been fucking behind my back? I examine her up and down. She's tall, like a model, only without the face. She's got small, beady eyes that look like if you shook her up and down, they'd shake around in her head. Her arms have cat scratches all over them. Good, Bryce's cat makes life tough for her, too.

"Well, we've got to get going," says Bryce. "Enjoy your meal."

"We will," says Jerry, squeezing my hand tight.

I watch Bryce walk away with this Glen. What does this woman—a woman who doesn't know her "your" from her "you're"—have that I don't—besides Bryce? She's as tall as Bryce. Her thing is obviously her legs. They're very long, very lean.

"Are you okay?" asks Jerriatrics. "You look a little pale. What are you feeling? Shortness of breath?"

"No, just shortness. Look at those legs."

"I feel sorry for her," says Jerry.

"You crazy? She got Bryce. He was supposed to be mine."

"You obviously have a guardian angel. The guy's a creep. He was sleeping with this woman the whole time he was involved with you. It's this lying creep who left you—not the man you've been fantasizing about in your mind—which means it's less of a loss. Rather than being jealous of Glen, you should pity her. The man she's got is a mega creep."

This does change everything. Bryce wasn't wrestling with bisexuality; he was wrestling with a long-legged blond woman—and telling me the whole time "I love you." This is love? I wonder. It's certainly not my definition. This must be some other esoteric SAT definition nobody taught me about. Boy do I hate words. You can tell someone "I love you," then shoot them. A lot of meaning these words have if you're lying in a pool of blood. And what's the difference if you describe that blood as crimson or ruby or sepia if you're lying there with the word *love* said or not said, the word *crimson* said or not said, dying just the same? Death. There aren't any substitute words for that. No synonyms, no double meanings. Just "death." If only all words were as definitive as that. Death.

"It's funny," I say, "but I always thought the worst thing I could find out was Bryce was in love with another woman. But compared to death, it doesn't seem so bad. At least I'm not going to die. Well, I am. But the betting odds of it being sooner not later have gone down drastically. I can't believe I was ever willing to die for that scumbucket."

"You should always live your life as if it's your own," says Jerry.

I laugh. Jerry reaches over to brush the hair away from my face, I suppose in an attempt to read in my eyes how I'm handling all this.

"You're still not sure about me, are you?" asks Jerry.

"Jerry, look, I do care about you—as a friend. We should keep it at that. We have too good a friendship to risk ruining it."

"Oh, come on, Sasha—our friendship isn't *that* good. Let's go ahead, risk ruining it." He laughs. "Just joking, don't worry. Look, the last thing I want is you to convince yourself into wanting me."

"And the last thing I want is to hurt you, Jer."

"Sasha, relax, I'll land okay."

I chuckle appreciatively. I really do admire Jerry, his attitude toward life.

"Do you think maybe I'm afraid of intimacy?" I ask.

"There's nothing wrong with how you feel. Nor how I feel. We shouldn't deny our emotions. All this is part of being alive. That's why you should feel sorry for Bryce, and whoever winds up with him. He's so closed off to his emotions. At least we can feel. Sure, it means sometimes we feel like shit, but at least we feel."

"You know I love you in my own way."

"I know. That helps make it easier for me. That, and knowing that right now in another dimension we are making mad passionate love."

And Jerry flashes me his best Close-Up smile.

My mother has ordered her favorite: a cup of boiled water—available free of charge here at the Acropolis. From her purse she pulls a plastic bag filled with chamomile tea bags. She removes one, dips the bag up and down like a yo-yo into her steaming cup.

"So, what's the occasion?" she asks. "You never find time to see me. Do you have something important to tell me? Are you getting engaged?"

"Mom, please," I say. "I just wanted to see you, that's all. No big deal. We haven't seen each other in a while."

Actually, since my near-death experience, I'd been doing a lot of thinking about people I needed to see more of. People like my mom—and Dr. Yaffe, my favorite general practitioner and AIDS adviser. I visited Dr. Yaffe's office last week. He poked, stabbed, prodded me, then charged me a hundred bucks to let him perform these perpetrations. But I'd have been happy to pay him ten times that to hear what he eventually told me. Yes, my man Dr. Yaffe told me those three little words I've been longing for: "You're HIV negative."

Today I've arranged time for my mom to do her version of a complete checkup on me. I was due. Six months had passed since we'd gotten together. I decided to find out just what I've been missing, not sitting across from her, face to face.

"So, what are you doing to take care of your skin?" my mother asks.

"What?"

"What products do you use to wash and moisturize? I think I have something in my pocketbook you could have if you want—"

"Pleeeeeasssse," I hiss. "If you're talking about this pimple, it's a rare thing. My skin isn't usually broken out."

"Don't get so huffy, Sasha. I'm not talking about that big pimple. You're always so defensive with me."

"Sorry."

"I'm talking about your wrinkles."

"Mom."

"I only say this because I care about you. I want the best for you."

"Mo-o-om."

"I want for you to be happy, for you to find what you want in life. I want for you what you want for yourself."

"Thanks, Mom. You wish me lots of cocaine and wild sexual orgies."

"I want you to want to go out with Aunt Rosalie's friend's son, is what I want."

"Mo-oo-oo-om."

"I want you to have love in your life."

"I do. I have you, and my friends, Jerry, Viv, Frannie. And I have my love for writing. My love for music. I have lots of things that bring me joy. I don't have to have a man to have love in my life."

"I gave Aunt Rosalie's friend's son your number."

"What?"

"You want some tapioca? You always loved tapioca."

"You gave Aunt Rosalie's friend's son my number?"

"Why not. He sounds wonderful. His name is Mark, so you'll know when he calls."

"Mark?" I laugh.

"Mark Goldfine."

I laugh heartily. A Mark? Maybe this is *the* Mark? Maybe I was with the wrong Mark? Maybe I won't regret this after all.

"I guess one date couldn't kill me," I say—then laugh again, this phrase taking on new meaning.

"It's good to hear you laugh," says my mother. "I've hardly heard you laugh lately. You used to laugh all the time. You were such a happy child. I remember when you first learned to walk."

"I know, Mom. I've heard this story a million times."

"You'd fall down and laugh, fall down—"

"Fall down and laugh. I know, Mom, I know."

Then Jerry's windsurfing thing comes to mind, and I think: wow, it's in me, a primal, instinctual part of me knows: *fall and laugh, let all falls strengthen me, not weaken me.* It *is* in me.

It's in Viv, too. She has a way of transforming her problems into something positive. Frannie, however, I worry about. She's always so hostile. I hope this Arthur disaster hasn't permanently turned her off to all men.

I'm reminded of this brunch date I had with Frannie. It was daylight savings time. By mistake, I moved my clock up instead of back. I thought it was noon, when it was only ten. Frannie answered the door, tired and irritable.

"Sasha, didn't anybody ever teach you? Fall back, spring forward? In the fall you turn the clock back, in the spring you move it forward."

"Yeah, Frannie, I know, only I got confused. I remembered it fall forward, spring back."

"That doesn't make any sense."

"Sure it does. You can fall forward, you know, trip, maybe hurt yourself a little, then spring back up, like be okay."

Frannie rolled her brown eyes upward. "Fall forward, spring back! Only you could make sense of that, Sasha."